PRAISE FOR *FLIGHT RISK*

"The characters and emotions portrayed make this well worth reading."
—*Booklist*

"Joy Castro's writing is like watching an Acapulco cliff diver. It takes my breath away every time."
—Sandra Cisneros, author of *The House on Mango Street*

"Funny, sexy, and transfixing, Joy Castro's *Flight Risk* is a meditation on love, marriage, art, family, womanhood—and therefore, life itself. Castro skillfully builds tension, and the slow intensity with which the plot's arc forms gives the novel its exquisite and powerful impact."
—Chigozie Obioma, author of the Booker-short-listed novel *An Orchestra of Minorities*

"Completely captivating. Part Patricia Highsmith, part *Mexican Gothic*, part Daphne du Maurier, Joy Castro's *Flight Risk* is my favorite kind of story: one in which an outsider, dodging and weaving among insiders, stirs up tension, intrigue, and suspicion. With raw energy and sharp storytelling, *Flight Risk* is a novel about light and shadow, and I found myself craving its every twist."
—Timothy Schaffert, author of *The Perfume Thief*

"From the stunning opening lines of Joy Castro's *Flight Risk*, we know we're in the hands of a master storyteller, and it held me captive until the final page. With writing so evocative I could taste her words, Castro has wrought a sharply observed love story with a social conscience—an investigation of class, family, and the many ways we get each other wrong."
—Jennifer Steil, author of *Exile Music*

T0021829

"*Flight Risk* is a compelling, gritty portrait of class in America. Joy Castro traffics the rural-urban divide with complexity and compassion. The protagonist, Isabel Morales, an outsider turned artist, guides the reader through poverty, wealth, and the beating heart of our political divide as she reclaims her roots in coal-country West Virginia while reconciling the privileged life she's built in Chicago. This is outlaw fiction at its best."

—Melissa Scholes Young, author of *The Hive*

"A deftly intelligent literary thriller, *Flight Risk* is that rarest of beasts— beautifully written yet a real page-turner, too. Wonderful."

—S. J. Watson, author of the international bestseller
Before I Go to Sleep

"Joy Castro writes with a balanced urgency—elegant sentences tempered with grace and intelligence, clear and gripping character arcs and story lines—and with a depth and dimension that leans into the transformative. Another strong book."

—Chris Abani, author of *The Secret History of Las Vegas* and
Song for Night

ONE

>>> <<<

BRILLIANT

>>> <<<

FLAME

ONE
BRILLIANT
FLAME

A NOVEL

JOY CASTRO

LAKE UNION
PUBLISHING

Text copyright © 2023 by Joy Castro
All rights reserved.

Published by Lake Union Publishing, Seattle

www.apub.com

Amazon, the Amazon logo, and Lake Union Publishing are trademarks of Amazon.com, Inc., or its affiliates.

ISBN-13: 9781542038041 (paperback)
ISBN-13: 9781542038058 (digital)

Cover design by Kimberly Glyder
Chapter icon design by Olivia Benson
Cover image: ©Pump Park Vintage Photography / Alamy Stock Photo / Alamy; ©AZ / Shutterstock; ©Roy Bishop / ArcAngel; ©ONYXprj / Getty; ©Alicia Sandlin / EyeEm / Getty
Interior image: ©ASolo / Shutterstock

Printed in the United States of America

For those who burn

To Leticia Amapola Castro,
Lourdes Caridad Castro, and
Linda Lucilla Castro,
my beautiful Key West aunts

He was on familiar terms with everyone with whom he drank champagne, and he drank champagne with everyone.

—Leo Tolstoy, *Anna Karenina*

"You are not in your right mind."
"That is quite possible; but let me continue."

—Leopold von Sacher-Masoch, *Venus in Furs*

1898

PROLOGUE

ZENAIDA

Just after dusk on the evening of Friday, August 12, when the heat of the day had passed—the bank's mercury thermometer read only eighty-two degrees—my mother and I, both freshly scrubbed, perfumed, and dressed in our finest clothes after the long workday, entered the San Carlos Institute to play bolita.

It was a very ordinary Key West night. A soft salt-scented wind blew through the open windows, stirring the cloth of our skirts against our calves and sifting the tendrils that escaped down the backs of our necks. The men wore their best dark trousers and white guayaberas, their thin pleats crisply pressed. The women were sheathed in bright sleek dresses that bared their collarbones and more—unless they were quite old, in which case they wore sober black and pursed their mouths at the rest of us. Little clusters—couples, families, friends arm in arm—promenaded from room to room, pausing, chatting, moving on, as waiters whisked through, offering small glasses of sherry and thimble-sized cups of cafecito from round trays. Children raced about, laughing, playing tag or hide-and-seek. Gauzy blue veils of cigar smoke wreathed the air.

Strains of music wafted from the ballroom, where couples whirled in each other's arms, oblivious to the rest of us.

The San Carlos Institute, though already eight years old and quite plain—since all our funds went to support the fighters in Cuba—was still new enough to inspire admiration. As we strolled through its various rooms, we stoked with conversation our visions of a more beautiful future. We waxed rhapsodic (as Cubans do) about the sweeping staircase of white marble we'd import one day from the Isle of Pines, and the Moorish arches we'd have—as high as those of any palace in Havana!—and how the walls would shimmer with hand-painted tiles in shades of turquoise and teal that would put peacocks to shame. How our ballroom would glitter with real chandeliers.

Key West's Cuban community had long outgrown the original San Carlos, the little wooden one on Anne Street founded by the first wave of ragged refugees, and after the second San Carlos around the corner on Fleming Street—the one I'd known best—had burned to the ground in the Great Fire of 1886, we'd saved and donated and debated architectural sketches for four long years. Arguing was, after baseball, our second favorite sport.

Finally, though, we had agreed. This new San Carlos was a beginning, and it belonged to us all.

From its lending library, we borrowed books. In its lounges, we met to sip coffee. The gallery of portraits showed off our heroes: Carlos Manuel de Céspedes, José Martí, Simón Bolívar, and a stern array of generals and guerrilla fighters. Upstairs were the schoolrooms where I gave lessons in Spanish and English to children of all shades.

In the mahogany-paneled conference room, the Cuban leaders of the town—men and women, Black and brown and as white as the North Americans—argued and planned and collected funds for the passion that united us all: Cuba's fight for independence.

My mother and I drifted slowly toward the theater, where the winning bolita ball would be drawn. Her ticket, I knew, was safely folded in her reticule. Each week she invested a nickel of her profits from the boardinghouse, hoping for the eighty-to-one payoff that could turn five cents into four dollars, as much as she earned from a cigar-factory worker for a whole week's room and board.

Across the wide and crowded hallway, a man yelled something about Spain—"those gutless bastards"—and gave someone a shove. His companions merely burst into raucous laughter, lifting their drained sherry glasses, and nodded, clapping him on the shoulder. Frustrated, he stormed away, weaving a little as he exited.

His agitation was understandable. We were all on edge. The United States had joined our war against Spain in June. Each day, reports came on the telegraph cable from Havana, and we all held our breath, hoping that President McKinley and his generals really could wrest our homeland, the Pearl of the Caribbean, from the grip of Spain's imperial lion—if only to grip her in their own paws, some of us feared. There were many ways to own another nation, and the United States seemed good at all of them.

The North Americans had been fighting for two months, but we Cubans had been at war with Spain for three decades—our whole lives, in some cases—ever since the Cry of Yara in 1868, when Carlos Manuel de Céspedes had freed the slaves on his sugar plantation and taken up arms.

Since then, Key West, our tiny coral island at the tip of the United States, had become not only a prosperous and bustling village, thanks to the booming cigar industry, but a tinderbox of Cuban revolution, a rebel base for the insurgency, a safe place for wounded guerrilla soldiers to recuperate, only ninety miles from Cuban soil. In Key West, we gathered funds for weapons and ships to send them back across the sea to fight.

All of us had lost men. My mother had worn widow's black when I was a child.

Over the last few decades, too, Key West had seen more than its share of riots and strikes. Because disgruntled cigar workers could catch a steamer to Tampa or New York or even back to Havana any week of the year, factory owners had to cave to their demands. And because the lectors—hired by the cigar rollers themselves—read aloud in the factories not only three newspapers a day but the work of radicals like Marx, novels by Hugo and Tolstoy, and political tracts by anarchists like Enrique Roig de San Martín, the workers had restless minds as well. During strikes, we supported our own. We had our own grocers and bakers and teachers. Half the population of Key West was Cuban.

But no one liked not working. When strikes occurred, there weren't enough dominoes in the world to fill the time, which hung heavy in the hands of men and women accustomed to rolling a hundred cigars a day.

Yes, we were all on edge.

The hard wooden chairs of our bare-staged theater could seat three hundred and fifty souls, and they were filling up fast. My mother and I settled ourselves in a row near the front, and she drew her folded bolita ticket from her reticule, rubbing it with her thumbs for luck. I dreamed of the red velvet chairs our theater would have one day, soft and comfortable, and the sweeping balcony with the curving lines of Art Nouveau.

People streamed in, milling about in the aisles, chatting. At nine o'clock precisely, eight men would ascend the stage and toss the bolita bag to each other until the hundred numbered ivory balls were thoroughly mixed. Then the town's young beauty du jour would climb the steps, grip one ball, hold it tight while it was cut free from the bag with scissors, and cry out the winning number. People climbed over one another to find a spot to sit.

"Telegram!" The shout erupted at the back of the theater, and my mother and I twisted in our seats, craning to see. A lone hand shot above the crowd, clutching and waving a scrap of yellow paper. "Telegram from Washington! They've signed the protocol!"

All around us, the crowd exploded in deafening cheers. My mother gripped my arm, her dark eyes wide, as we stumbled to our feet. People grabbed and kissed each other.

I felt dizzy and dazed, a little unsteady. It all seemed too startling, too abrupt, too good to be true—the miracle we'd worked for all our lives, suddenly real: Spain and the United States had signed a preliminary peace agreement, ending the fighting. At long last, Spain would withdraw from Cuba.

As the cheering went on and on, men lifted the telegraph-office boy onto their shoulders and paraded him down the center aisle. The bolita bag lay forgotten on the stage.

My eyes landed on Señor and Señora Roméo, standing several rows behind us. I remembered when he had been just Líbano, the mysterious boy who lived at my mother's boardinghouse—long before he'd been Señor anything, much less the proprietor of the city's most prosperous coffee roastery, and long before I'd become girls' headmistress at the San Carlos.

Our eyes locked. I knew he was remembering that night of flames a dozen years ago. I didn't move, didn't change my expression, didn't lean even slightly in his direction. His wife clung to his arm, and her elderly mother, ravaged by illness, gazed about in confusion, as if she had not grasped the import of the moment.

That night a dozen years ago, we'd thought Maceo would change everything for us. We'd believed with all our hearts the tide of war would turn. We had believed in Maceo. We had equipped him. He could do it. We waited, hoping for victory while we rebuilt our town from the ashes.

But no victory came, and we heard no word from him.

Maceo, who never came back.

"My daughter." My mother squeezed my arm. Like so many, she was weeping openly with joy. "My daughter. My dear daughter. Can it be true?"

The ruckus took time to die down. But eventually—when we'd been kissed and embraced six dozen times, when celebratory sherry had been poured and drunk and poured and drunk again, when the lectors and their acolytes had opined loudly about how it would still be months before any treaty could be signed (the conference wouldn't even begin until October, in Paris, they said)—I took my mother's arm.

"Mamá, I feel tired."

If I'd simply suggested that we leave the festivities, she'd have resisted with every stubborn fiber of her body.

But she'd always had a weakness for my feelings—since I expressed, I suppose, so few.

"Yes, let's go, then, my daughter." She patted my hand, and we made our way through the happy throngs.

The night was dark and soft. Clouds covered the moon as we made our way back to the boardinghouse.

"This will change things," my mother said, glancing up at me. "Maybe it will be safe for you to go to Cuba now."

We walked between the palm trees and shuttered houses.

"And maybe people will come back here," she continued, "now that the fighting's done. Old friends, maybe."

"Mamá." I shook my head. "Enough. I'm middle-aged."

"You're twenty-seven."

"As I said." I laughed. "Twenty-seven and a schoolmistress and a spinster."

"Prettiest schoolmistress on the island."

"Mamá, I'm not looking for a husband."

Her smile was sly. "Did I say anything about a husband?"

We walked on through the quiet streets.

In the shadowed front room of the boardinghouse stood a vast mahogany china cabinet, my mother's pride and showcase, a far cry from the raw wooden shelves that had held tin plates in my childhood. I wanted to be alone, but she lit a lamp and stood near me, watching, as I reached into my small handbag, snapped open the tiny coin purse, and withdrew its sole contents, a brass key, from where it lay nestled in the satin folds. I turned it in the lock and pulled open the china cabinet's center drawer, the one my mother had given me as a place to store my teaching certificates and important papers.

I drew out the old Las Flores Cubanas cigar box, adorned with its two bare-breasted beauties—mirror images of each other: one light, one dark—floating on clouds of roses, with a misted green view of Cuba behind them.

I turned and set the box on the dining table. I sat down, trying to ward off the strange sensation in my knees, as if they had begun to liquefy. My mother pulled out the chair next to mine. We had chairs now, upholstered with needlepoint cushions, not the rough benches of my childhood. Her boardinghouse had flourished, but it was my schoolteacher's wages that had finally bought the things for which my mother—raised in slavery, married to a penniless journalist, and widowed young—had always dreamed.

"Ay," said my mother, reaching out to draw a finger across the long black braids of the dark beauty. "Ay, to be young again."

I would not regret my choice. I had promised myself never to regret my choice.

A tremor ran through my hands as I opened the box.

Inside: a small white shell, pearlescent. I set it on the table. A single brown tobacco leaf, so brittle with age that, though I drew it out carefully, fragments broke away, crumbling at my fingertips' gentlest touch. Below lay stiff sheets of paper, thrice folded to fit: broadsides, printed with poems. I didn't need to open them to hear the lines echo in my mind. I lifted them out and set them aside.

And there they lay: ghost faces. From the bottom of the box gazed a cast of characters from a dozen years ago. A shudder of pain ran through me.

"Ay, how beautiful," my mother said. "So young and beautiful."

I lifted out the photograph, taken before I knew I'd never see most of them again.

We girls stood in a row, formally arranged for the pageant—I remembered holding my smile until my cheeks ached. The young men hovered at the periphery.

"Look at you all," she said. "All of you. So young, so innocent."

I swung my eyes to her.

March 30, 1886. That night of terror, the air was black and windy—flames leapt from house to house. Our little island's only firefighting steam engine had been hauled north to New York for repairs, so we had to hurl by hand each precious drop of water we'd collected in cisterns as the military firemen used hand pumpers—to no avail. Choking clouds of black smoke billowed. The air rippled with unbearable heat. Each face wore a mask of rigid desperation lit by flames as we worked with buckets to save what we could—which was, finally, so little. Scraps. Frantic, we watched in speechless horror as our small city, the center of our world, roared up in flames that seemed unstoppable.

More than six hundred homes were swallowed by the fire that night: six hundred families without shelter. Eighteen of the cigar factories that furnished the livelihoods, directly or indirectly, of everyone we knew, burned to the ground. Churches. Warehouses. City hall. The San Carlos itself, the center of our social world. Grown men sobbed in the streets.

Was it accident or arson? The authorities investigated, but they could never prove a thing.

We only knew it turned our lives to ash.

The next day, bleak crowds lined the docks, gripping their valises, shuffling numbly onto the steamship that waited—too conveniently?—to take them to Havana, or to Tampa, where the owners of newly built cigar factories needed their nimble fingers but would not tolerate the labor strikes that happened in Key West. I imagined the stoicism in the émigrés' eyes: that beaten expression that says, *Again, my life collapses. Again, with nearly nothing, I cross the water to a strange and unknown land—to who knows what fate?* I clung to my mother as our neighbors disappeared.

My friends and I were all so young, except Feliciano, and even he was only twenty-four, not the thirty years he claimed—Feliciano, the dashing Galician lector with his fiery speeches about anarchism and liberty. All so young. Yet we thought we were grown up: wealthy Sofia fluttering her lace fans, flaunting her status as the daughter of a factory owner; Líbano, the poor young cafetero, kind and silent, his hesitating eyes unsure; Maceo, dark like me, the brave and handsome soldier who

11

fought a brutal undertow. And Chaveta, the girl named for a knife, my companion, my comrade, my conspirator—gone now, all these years, scattered to the winds by that night of flames.

And I, Zenaida—reluctant beauty-pageant queen, daughter of a slain Havana printer and the freed slave woman who ran Key West's cleanest boardinghouse—I brimmed with secrets of my own.

I looked down at our tiny faces. It was true that we were all so young then, so fresh and full of hope and desire: desire for freedom, desire for work and a future in which we could believe. For each other.

Young: yes. And fresh, and eager.

But not innocent.

"No," I said to my mother. "Not so innocent, I think."

1886

ZENAIDA

"But where is she?" Sofia's porcelain cup rattled against her saucer. "Insufferable girl."

I sipped my tea. "You know Chaveta's late sometimes," I said. "It's not her fault. Her parents make her help with the little ones."

"But it's Sunday." Sofia's lips pursed. "Surely she can break away."

I made no reply. Sofia was used to servants. She had no siblings, and certainly no chores.

Her table was laid with a perfect tea, and a fresh sea breeze blew through the veranda, which faced Duval Street. Gem-bright majolica tiles, painted with tiny peacocks, lined the floor and the little half walls that rose around us. The white wicker chairs in which we sat were plushly cushioned, and the teacups and silver shone. On the street, couples and families promenaded past, dressed in their Sunday best. Sitting on Sofia's veranda was, I imagined, what it must be like to have a private balcony at the opera, or to be tucked inside a jewel box with a view.

"The tea's going cold." Sofia shuffled the stack of valentines she'd received and tossed them down on the table with disgust. "Why can no man on this island write a verse worth reading?" She rolled her eyes. "Do they really think we don't know what color roses are?"

I smiled. "Well, it's a girlish custom. Men aren't made for such things."

The laborers who lived at my mother's boardinghouse would never have dreamed of spending their hard-earned wages on something as frivolous as store-bought cards, much less have attempted to compose flowery sentiments. Sofia moved in a different world.

Peacocks waded through the Robleses' garden like majestic ships, their massive tail-fans swaying, and there was a little gazebo, where we sometimes had tea. It was surrounded by trees, hidden from the street and from the main house. Green with shade and luxuriously appointed with little wicker sofas, it made you feel as if you were in a palace underwater, like some fairy-tale mermaid.

And there was a little guesthouse there, too, fully furnished. I'd only looked through the windows, but it seemed very nice: a plush bed, sofas, and so on. When important businessmen visited, they sometimes stayed there.

Another building, closer to the main house, held the kitchen, which was separate from the living quarters for fear of fire—a grander version of my mother's old cook-shed (though my mother mostly cooked indoors now, despite the risk, due simply to the time-consuming difficulty of carting everything back and forth). The Robleses had a cook, who slept in the kitchen shed, and two lady's maids, who also waited at table and greeted visitors at the door, and there was another woman who cleaned everything and then a laundress, too. All of them were darker-skinned than me or even my mother. It was very like what I'd heard the plantations and city mansions were like back in Cuba. The Robleses had two vast sugar mills in Matanzas—one inherited from Sofia's mother's family, one from her father's—in addition to the cigar factory here, but Sofia might sell the plantations one day, she said. She wanted to be a real North American: A businesswoman. Efficient. Enterprising.

"Where's Chaveta?" she grumbled. She rang for the maid, who appeared almost instantly. "More pastries."

The girl nodded and disappeared.

"Come," I said. "Let us distract ourselves. Tell me, of all the many adventures in Mr. Hugo's novel, which was the finest, in your opinion?"

Sofia smiled. She liked this kind of game. Asking her to choose or judge something was how I always diverted her when she became impatient. She liked to exercise her taste.

"When Cosette finally weds Marius, I suppose," she said. "Yes, certainly. A well-earned triumph, after all she'd suffered. Poverty! The convent. To find true love at last—and then have her guardian thwart it, again and again! Yes, their wedding, most surely, is the novel's finest moment." She poured us both more tea. "Would you not agree?"

I took a drink and set my cup down. Sofia had her own copy of *Les Miserables* to read at home, whereas I'd had to stand outside her father's *fábrica*, leaning close to the open window, to hear the lector read aloud. There were days I'd been unable to finish all the housework with my mother, so there were scenes I'd missed.

"I think my favorite was probably—"

"Chaveta! Have you gone quite mad at last?" Sofia shook her head as our friend came strolling up the street. "Really. Have you lost what wits you ever had?"

Chaveta, hands in pockets, leapt up the tiled steps. It was the pockets that provoked Sofia, because they were angled into the hips of trousers, men's trousers, cinched with a brown leather belt.

Chaveta stretched her arms wide and spun slowly on one heel. "Don't be jealous." She flung herself into one of the Robleses' overstuffed wicker chairs and crossed her legs like a man, ankle to bent knee.

Her old scuffed boots looked strangely elegant jutting from the cuffs of trousers. She pulled a cigar from the breast pocket of her shirt.

"Don't you dare," said Sofia. "If you smoke that thing on my veranda, I'll kill you." Her glance darted up and down Duval Street. "Why can't you behave?"

Chaveta laughed and tucked the cigar back in her pocket, her dark eyes dancing. I knew she'd taken it out just to bait Sofia, which was almost too easily done.

"So pour me some tea, Lady Macbeth," Chaveta said. I didn't see what Shakespeare had to do with it, but Sofia, grumbling, shook her pretty head and poured tea into a porcelain cup so fragile you could read a headline through its pure white walls. She held it out on its softly curved saucer to Chaveta, who took only the cup.

She drained it in three gulps. "It's lukewarm," she said. "Am I late?"

"Only by half an hour," said Sofia, her mouth twisting in a cool little smile. "Here." With silver tongs, she gripped small oblong pastries and lowered them onto Chaveta's plate. Pale cream erupted from their edges. The Robleses' chef was French.

At home, in my mother's boardinghouse, we cooked for the appetites of working men who cleaned their plates twice but wiped their mouths only once, at the end, with the clean rags she provided—or their sleeves, if they forgot. Though my own tongue preferred my mother's creamy flan or empanadas filled with sugar-sweetened yams, I was far too eager to taste the world to decline any offer of Sofia's.

The breeze blew across the veranda, and the sugar lay sweet on my tongue. I watched how Sofia patted her lips—softly, lightly—with her linen napkin after each bite. Unobtrusively, I followed suit.

"There you are," said Sofia when the maid appeared. The girl laid more pastries on the silver tray.

"Hey, Julieta," said Chaveta.

The maid froze.

"Your mother says hello," Chaveta said. "She says to tell you—"

"Oh, do stop," Sofia broke in. "Let her do her work, for heaven's sake." The maid melted away. She was a little older than we were but small and shy, a shadow. I always felt sorry for her. Sofia, difficult enough as a friend, could not have been an easy mistress.

The three of us had been friends for some time, though only Chaveta and I had played together as little girls. Our parents had all come to the island from Cuba in 1868 or '69, during the early days of the Ten Years' War. My own mother labored to birth me during the Great Hurricane of 1870, on the top floor of our wooden boardinghouse that swayed and shuddered in the gales, she said. Half of Key West flooded, and the colonial Spaniards across the sea in Havana gleefully believed that our little island and its rebel base were done for.

But such was hardly the case. My father kept printing his newspaper, calling for revolution; Chaveta's parents had five more children; and the Flores Cubanas cigar factory flourished so well that Sofia's father built a new and bigger building—along with the Robles mansion, with space for all the elegant furniture and rugs he brought back from his trips to Havana and New Orleans and New York. Sofia had been to New York only once but spoke as if it were her destiny, though her mother wanted her to marry a member of the Andalusian aristocracy and move to Seville, land of lacquered fans and Moorish arches and flamenco. Sofia affected fans by the dozen, though she was, as she often claimed, "an American at heart."

"Good heavens," she said. "Would you stop wolfing that down? You eat like a boy."

"I work like a boy," said Chaveta matter-of-factly, licking whipped cream off her thumb. "I'm hungry like a boy."

"Be that as it may," said Sofia. "With those abysmal manners, you'll never catch a man."

"Who wants a man," said Chaveta, giving me a sly wink, "that can be caught?"

The veranda felt suddenly warm. I pulled out my own fan and turned away.

"Oh, Zenaida," said Sofia, "what a very lovely fan." It was just unbleached linen stretched across wood slats; Sofia liked to compliment my plainest things. A long green iguana, bright as a jewel, stalked slowly across the Robleses' front lawn, its legs bending like machinery.

"Now, since Chaveta has joined us at last," she said, "let's exchange our valentines." She handed each of us a pretty envelope with a thin red ribbon tied around it. Chaveta rolled her eyes and ripped it open.

"Nice," she said, scanning whatever Sofia had written. "I didn't bring any cards. You want a cigar?"

"No, thank you." Sofia's smile was thin.

I handed Sofia the valentine I'd made—just a sheet of folded fools-cap with a little inked illustration of a frangipani flower. I'd written a couple of lines inside that exaggerated my affection for her.

She read it and laid her hand on my arm.

"You are most dear, Zenaida." She leaned back. "But what's sad, girls, is that none of us has valentines from a suitor." She prodded the thick stack of cards at her elbow with a disdainful finger. "At least, none worth reading."

Chaveta tucked the card from Sofia back in its envelope and tossed it on the table. "Who's got time to read love poems?"

Flushing, I looked away. I had time—Petrarch, at the moment.

"However, our luck may be about to turn," Sofia said, ignoring Chaveta and refilling our cups. "A new lector has arrived in town."

We looked up with sudden interest. Lectors, who read to the cigar-factory workers, were our heroes, our stars, our professors, our bards. Each large fábrica had one, and even if we didn't work in the factories ourselves, the lectors brought us literature, because in the afternoons, after chores were done, housewives and single girls would gather in clusters outside the open windows of the factories, clutching our parasols against the subtropical sun and listening to the great novels: Cervantes,

Dickens, Galdós, Dumas . . . At night, the lectors who still had voice enough to speak would gather in cafés or at the San Carlos to debate the news and great ideas of the day. The lectors, the most educated men in town, knew more about politics than even the white North American lawyers, and all the fathers respected their opinions. Crowds would gather around their table, listening, watching avidly as the lectors drank their rum or sherry or coffee and puffed their cigars. The next day, even the butcher's boy would drop the phrases the lectors used, waving his hands the same way.

Most lectors were older, fathers or even grandfathers, with great drooping mustaches and the thick, heavy bellies that came from the good food their wages let them afford. They lived in style. Some were good patresfamilias, supporting their families in comfort, while others preferred what my mother called "the free life," spending their nights with paid company in the bordellos by the harbor or catching a steamship to Havana or New Orleans for a little variety on the weekends. Not even the most moral Catholic on Key West batted an eye. We worshipped our lectors. They did as they pleased.

Birds squawked in the palms overhead. February's thin sun glazed the world.

SOFIA

Both girls' eyes were upon me, dark and eager.

"Yes, a new lector," I repeated. "And he has rather an interesting story." I paused to restock each of their plates with more of Gastón's napoleons, and then I raised the little bell and rang. The maid appeared. I frowned at her severely. "The tea's gone cold." She whisked away with the pot.

I turned back to my friends, whose eyes were still locked on me. "Now let's see," I said. "What was I saying?"

Chaveta nodded, impatient as always. "The new lector?"

"Oh yes. Just so. Well, they say he comes from Spain—I'm not sure where. Madrid, perhaps." My mind darted to my mother's gilt-framed intaglio prints of palaces in Andalusia, her own mother's homeland: the high arches, lush gardens, orange trees dripping with fruit, the fountains, the slender aqueducts carrying streams of pure water . . . These prints hung over the grand piano like a promised future. "If you marry an aristocrat from Seville, I can die happy," my mother liked to say, crossing herself—and I'd certainly have settled for that, on both counts—but I longed to marry a Cuban as rich as Croesus who'd take me to New York. I wanted a beautiful apartment with silk drapes and a terrace overlooking Central Park.

"A Spaniard?" Chaveta scowled.

"Yes, but he was raised in Havana by his wealthy godfather, who sent him to Rome to be educated by Jesuits. He returned to Havana afterward and was writing for the free press—rather fiery things, I understand, in praise of Carlos Manuel de Céspedes and so on—but when his godfather suddenly died, he had no protection and had to flee the Spaniards." The maid came out with the freshly filled teapot and disappeared back into the house's dark interior. "He's been in Tampa these last few months, reading in a new factory there, but he heard the life was better here in Key West." I helped myself to another napoleon. "I can't think why." Out of the corner of my eye, I saw Chaveta bridle, and I laughed. Her pride in Key West was legendary. "Anyway, Señor Pedroso's ill at home this week—as you well know, Chaveta." She'd worked in my father's factory for years. "So this new gentleman offered to take his place while he recovers."

"I hope he can read worth a damn."

"Apparently, his elocution is paradise. Or so Pura says; he's staying with the Salazars. But perhaps the most interesting thing of all . . ." I gave a little sigh and ate the last bite of my napoleon. It wouldn't do to grow plump—but then, there were corsets for that. "Delicious. Gastón has outdone himself."

"What?" asked Zenaida. "The most interesting thing is what?"

"Yeah. Spill it."

I dabbed my lips. "He's young. Not yet thirty, they say. Young," I repeated, my voice low with thrill. "And single. And very, very handsome."

"When will he start?" asked Zenaida. Not that she stands a chance. I leaned toward my friends. "Tomorrow."

3

ZENAIDA

Chaveta walked part of the way home with me, whistling, her long braid swinging, her hands tucked in the pockets of her trousers. Winter is the cool, dry season in Key West, but the breeze had ceased, and the air felt hot and still and heavy in the late afternoon.

"Ay, Chaveta," called Old Man López from his rattling junk cart as he passed. His mule twitched its ears. "You wearing men's clothes now? The Devil got you, sure."

"I've got the Devil by the tail," she shot back. He drove off chuckling. We walked on.

Housewives clucked at her as we passed their porches, frowning at her attire, but she just cocked an eyebrow at them.

"I'll miss *Les Miserables*," I said. "I'm glad Señor Pedroso chose it." We walked along Duval, Chaveta's shoulder occasionally brushing mine. "What was your favorite scene?"

She didn't hesitate. "When Jean Valjean lifted the wagon."

"Really? Even though he knew it might expose him?"

"Of course," she said. "What good is strength without guts?" She turned to me. "What was yours?"

"I guess I liked the part when the monsignor lied to the police for Jean Valjean. When Jean Valjean had stolen almost all his silver."

"And he gave him the candlesticks, too?"

"Yes. I don't really know why I like that part so much." We walked along. "I guess because we're told to tell the truth, always. And to defend what's ours. But there are times when grace is more important, and generosity. More generosity than even seems reasonable. I'm not sure. It just struck me, somehow." Remembering tea, I laughed. "Sofia's favorite was when Cosette got married."

"Naturally." Chaveta grinned. We'd heard Sofia's elaborate plans for a grand wedding more than once.

At the corner of Duval and Petronia, we stopped. It was where I'd veer off.

Yet something held us there, lingering.

"So," Chaveta said. She pulled the cigar from her breast pocket and held a match to its tip, puffing until it lit. She held it away from her and inspected it, the way men did. "Are you going to come listen to this new guy tomorrow?"

Chores at the boardinghouse varied from day to day, and my workload fluctuated according to my mother's temper.

"If I can."

She nodded. Her eyes always seemed browner, larger, softer than other people's, her lashes longer and thicker and blacker. I wondered what it would feel like to slide off the leather thong that bound her braid and loosen her hair with my fingers until it swayed dark around her shoulders.

"Good."

She turned on her heel and strode off, trailing silver smoke.

I watched her go, but she didn't look back.

I walked the rest of the way alone in the late afternoon, still hearing her whistled tune in my head.

SOFIA

Each evening when my maid unpinned my hair, it fell thick and black and shining to my waist. She brushed it in long strokes while I inspected myself in the mirror: my skin like milk, my dark Spanish eyes men longed for, the small figure that made them feel deliciously big; I could sense their shuddering excitement when they hovered near me, eager to save me from something, anything, eager to fetch me something. They were such bores. These so-called gentlemen on this little spit of sand. Unrefined and coarse, always shouting about politics and weapons and raising funds for Cuba.

I very much wished to meet this lector. I wanted an elegant man who was at home in a drawing room and knew how to modulate his voice. A real gentleman—an aristocrat, even. *You have princess blood*, my mother used to croon when I was little, rocking me on her lap.

Oh, to see Spain, where my charms would have their proper chance! I longed to go to Venice, too, where canals were lined with palaces and the ladies dripped with jewels . . .

CHAVETA

Next morning, when the new lector entered, five hundred mouths hushed.

He crossed the long hall and climbed the wooden stairs of the tribuna. A king mounting steps to his throne.

Sofia was right. This new lector was a fine figure of a man. Lean but broad-shouldered, slim-waisted, with strong legs. His dark hair shone. Beneath his jacket and black tie, his white shirt glowed in the high-ceilinged gloom of the galley.

He stood, gazing at us all for a moment, his hands on the railing of the platform. The Pope in Rome. His dark eyes were large and serious, a child's. He did not smile.

"Good morning," he said. "I am Feliciano Galván, poet and journalist." He cleared his throat. "Anarchist." Some rollers gasped, and murmurs swept through the galera, but I grinned down at my pile of brown leaves. It was about time anarchy came to Key West. "It is my honor to read to you this week while your lector recovers from illness. May fine health return to him soon."

With that, he settled himself in the chair, shook open the day's *El Yara*, and began.

And never had the news been so spellbinding. It was his voice, his passion, his sincerity, as if everything he uttered mattered. Our fingers spun tobacco leaf into gold for hours as he read first the Spanish newspapers and then translated the English headlines from a three-day-old *New York Times*.

The cafetero, Líbano, made his way across the aisles, wearing his heavy urn, pouring each of us our coffee orders, which he knew by heart: cream or no cream, no sugar or a little or a lot.

People said Líbano was simple. Not all there, not quite right in the head. So quiet. But to remember all five hundred of our coffee orders here, and then to do two other factories—with workers leaving and new ones coming every day—

Not so simple, I'd say.

And not bad-looking, either, with that swoop of black hair that fell across his long-lashed eyes. But few girls looked his way, despite his strong body and good job. Something about the way he carried himself. Nervous, hunched in.

And of course he was poor, an orphan who came on his own from living on the streets of Havana. But most of us were poor. He lived in Zenaida's mother's boardinghouse—in the smallest, cheapest room: little more than a pantry with a bed. He kept it spotless and orderly, Zenaida said: everything in its place, clothes neatly folded, books neatly stacked. She knew; she had to clean the rooms. Most men weren't neat, she said.

He was kindhearted, too. Dogs followed him up and down the streets even when he was not carrying his little square of oilcloth filled with scraps for them. He often squatted to pet the cats that lingered on the steps of the dairy.

He poured my coffee black into my tin cup and met my eyes. A little twitch of his shoulder toward the tribuna and a quick lift of his brow: *What do you think of him?*

I widened my eyes and gave a nod.

He nodded back. *Thought so.*

That was Líbano. Good instincts, but he didn't trust himself.

He moved off down the aisle as the lector's voice rose and fell. It was like listening to an actor onstage. I drank my hot coffee. My hands moved on their own.

Choose a moist wrapper leaf, its stem already stripped away by the women and children who worked up on the top floor of the factory, and set it aside.

Select one leaf for strength. One for fragrance. One for combustion.

Roll each one into a tube, then roll all three of them together. Chop the ends with the knife I was named after. Wrap them in two binder leaves. Roll the whole thing into the moist wrapper leaf. Use tree resin from the little pot to smooth and seal the tube. Shape it, press it down. Use the side of the chaveta to roll it smooth. Pinch the tip. Trim, trim, trim, smooth. Done. Stack it.

Do it all again. And again. And again. Listening to the lector, my hands whirring, I fell into a trance.

When he folded the *Times* at last, he stood, sipped from his water, and held up a slim blue volume.

"Mikhail Bakunin," he said. "'Appeal to the Slavs.' After the failure of the revolution of 1848."

A few chavetas knocked against the workbenches in approval. Galván remained standing. He took a deep breath and gazed around, as if drawing strength from our eyes.

"'Brothers!'" he thundered, glancing down at the open book as he read. "'This is the hour of decision. It is for you to take a stand, openly either for the old world, in ruins, which you would prop up for yet another little while, or for the new world whose radiance has reached you and which belongs to the generations and centuries to come.'"

I rapped my chaveta hard on the table. Galván looked up. Our eyes locked. Almost instantly a dozen knives followed suit, knocking the wood, and then a hundred. A faint smile crossed his lips.

Then I understood: While seeming brave and bold, he had braced himself, hoping that we Key West Cubans were indeed the radicals of which he'd been told. Now he felt relieved and glad to be among us.

The old world, in ruins. Some of the men and women around me were thinking of Cuba and our long struggle to liberate her from the Spanish flag. Others were thinking of the gulf that lay between the wealthy and the workers. Still others recalled how recently they'd escaped the lash and hunger of Cuba's plantations, where slavery was still legal under the Spanish crown, though Céspedes had called for its abolition years ago, and even here in North America—so backward in many ways—it had been barred for decades. In Cuba, Céspedes had freed all the men, women, and children enslaved on his own sugar plantation, La Demajagua, on the same day he issued the Cry of Yara and began the Ten Years' War.

Céspedes was no mere mortal, said my father. He was a legend, a hero, the father of our country-yet-to-be.

But some men liked to dwell in their memories of legends.

I preferred action.

Whichever new world we dreamt of, this Galván had chosen his text well. The crowd was roused.

Graciela Saenz, who worked at my right, glanced over, her eyebrows raised. We all liked our usual lector just fine. Señor Pedroso was smart and read with flourishes.

But he was fifty-three, with pomposity to match his paunch and thinning hair.

This Feliciano Galván—he was something new.

Handsome and young, with eyes like fire.

6

ZENAIDA

Soft shafts of afternoon light fell across the galley, gilding the workers' black hair gold. Their hands worked swiftly, calmly, smoothly. Aside from the hour they took for lunch, the cigar workers had no regularly timed breaks from work; free agents, they came and went as they pleased: to the privy, for a smoke, or just to stretch their legs and crack their knuckles. Paid by the number of cigars they rolled each day, each roller had mastered the art of letting his mind rove abroad, carried by the lector's voice as it swelled or dropped, according to the drama of the book, while his hands kept steadily rolling tobacco.

Or hers.

After the dinner dishes were washed and wiped and neatly stacked away, I walked to the factory windows and waited for Chaveta to notice me, but her eyes stayed on the piles of brown leaves in front of her, which she deftly shaped and rolled as this new Señor Galván narrated the collapse of family harmony, reading from some new Russian novel in which a man had cheated on his wife—hardly the hair-raising adventures to which Señor Pedroso had accustomed this crowd, with *The Count of Monte Cristo* and *Les Miserables*.

I loved to watch Chaveta's slim hands move—light and brown and quick, like sparrows, the delicate lengths of her fingers put to such practical use. Her firm, sweet jaw, content in the knowledge of her competence.

Of course my reason for coming to the factory in the afternoons was to hear the lector read, but part of my pleasure had always been to see the play of his words upon the face of my friend: her stern frown, her furrowed brow, the sly smile that lit her lips, the quick, unhesitating rap of her chaveta when she approved.

In her efficiency, there was a grace. In her certainty, a kind of reassurance—like faith in God but located here on Earth, in her sure and supple hands that knew their work.

My own hands, in contrast, felt clumsy and unsure: strange, unwieldy beasts at the ends of my arms.

7

SOFIA

"Mamá," I began, my head bent over my embroidery (the usual: flowers and birds—yawn). "I hear the new young lector is quite the gentleman."

Her hands paused. "Oh, yes?"

I felt her face lift to study me. I kept demurely stitching.

"Very refined, everyone says." I'd found that if I added *everyone says* to my opinions, my mother was far more easily swayed. (My father, not at all. The ledger's bottom line was his only guide.) "Elegant. Well mannered." I didn't dare glance up. "And of course he is a man of information, educated by the Jesuits in Rome."

"Really?" My mother laid down her sewing and poured herself more tea. "And his family?"

"Now that," I said, "I do not know. Although I've heard he comes from Spain . . ."

"Ah!"

"But he lived with his patrón in Havana for some years. Until the wealthy old man passed."

"What region of Spain?"

"That I do not know, either. I confess it would be most interesting to find out."

"And this gentleman's name?"

"Galván. Feliciano Galván."

"Hmm." She sipped her tea. "There are some good Galváns. With whom is this Señor Galván staying?" This was my coup de grâce. "He resides with the Salazars." The Salazars owned the largest factory in town. My father's was merely second. Worse, the Salazar matriarch, Elvira, had real royal blood, not just third-rate aristocratic blood like my mother's. She was the niece of a princess back in Madrid; I couldn't recall the details, though my mother had talked of it until my eyes glazed. The lace at the Salazars' windows was no finer than the lace that hung in ours, but theirs had once hung in a palace, which, in my mother's view, made every difference. Whatever the Salazars had, my mother coveted—though never would she say so.

"He met the second son, Eduardo, in Tampa, where they struck up a friendship, and they came down on the ship together. He stays in their guest quarters." I drew my needle carefully through the cloth. "He dines at their table most nights, I hear."

"But perhaps he grows restless with the fare," my mother murmured. "Perhaps he would appreciate Gastón's."

I glanced up at her at last. Her eyes were distant, dreamy. I kept stitching.

"But if Papa were to invite him, would that not be seen as presumptuous?"

"Hmm? Oh, not at all. It would be most proper—and gracious, even. He's a stranger in our town. Surely he must want for society. Inviting him would be the hospitable, welcoming thing to do."

I'd finished a swathe of peacock green. I turned my embroidery hoop over and knotted the thread, clipping the ends with my small brass scissors. I looked up, caught her eye, and smiled.

"What a very kind idea, Mamá."

8

ZENAIDA

I was born in the year of the Great Flood, when the tempest came and nearly wiped our small town from the map. According to the Spanish loyalists in Havana, who longed to see our little city fail, the hurricane destroyed us, and they rejoiced. But prematurely—which was also how I came into this world . . .

In truth, we were not decimated, and we rebuilt quickly, though my mother mostly had to watch from the front porch of the little boardinghouse since she was busy tending me.

I'd only once seen Cuba, the land we all fought for, and then only for a day, and only in the city; I knew its countryside mostly from the pictures that filled the newspapers my father used to buy as if they were food itself. The wooden walls of the downstairs rooms were decorated with newsprint lithographs of Cuba's beautiful mountains (he assured me they were green as emeralds) and glorious beaches (he swore the sand was powdered gold, and the ocean sparkled sapphire), of the soaring buildings with their Moorish arches and all the grandeur of Spain (he promised they were nobler, though, despite Spain's heavy hand).

Because I loved my brave father, I loved Cuba, though it was only a legend to me, and I loved the work he did, writing and printing his rebel newspaper. Not everyone in Havana had been able to read and write, but my father had, and he'd apprenticed in a print shop as a boy, first sweeping floors and wiping the presses clean of ink for the next job. Eventually they let him set type, fitting all the tiny letters in upside down and backward, and then the large headlines, all capitals and sometimes inked in red. The announcements, advertisements, obituaries . . . He used to say a woman didn't lose her purse in Havana without his knowledge.

When he moved to Key West in 1869, fleeing the violence of the Ten Years' War and the brutal oppression by the Spanish armed forces, he brought with him only my mother, his savings, his small printing press, and enough paper for a month's worth of news. They bought the boardinghouse—already he knew her good cooking and clean ways would be a gold mine. He stored the paper up high in our little attic, wrapped in oilcloth. When the hurricane came the following year and my mother labored to give me birth, "Your father prayed more over that paper than he did about me," she used to say, laughing, back when he was alive.

"Why would I pray for a saint?" he'd reply, shrugging and looking heavenward. He'd wag his finger at me. "Take note, my daughter. The Virgin herself puts down her sewing when your mother speaks." When I was a child, it never struck me as strange that my father worshipped my mother, whose flesh was so much darker than his own. It seemed the natural order of things. Only later did the social oddity of their union begin to dawn on me.

My mother worshipped him as well, in her way. "Your father lives for Cuba," my mother used to say when I complained on the days when he spent too much time laboring over his articles and essays instead of playing with me. "You must not mock him."

And I never did.

At thirteen, I had just gotten my first blood, and my mother wanted to take me back to Havana, to Regla, for my blessing. I was very excited. The Iyalorisha—like a priest, my mother said, and a woman, but of Santería, the religion my mother secretly practiced—would tell me at last which orisha was mine and thus reveal to me my fate. I remember my parents arguing about the trip. My father said it was dangerous for us to go back to Cuba because of his reputation, but my mother promised that we would travel swiftly and unobtrusively—that we would draw no attention to ourselves, that we would go straight to Regla and back again, that we would travel under her maiden name and never mention him. Eventually, my mother won.

But the day before we were supposed to go, my father was shot in a duel on Elizabeth Street, killed like a dog because his newspaper called for a free Cuba: no ownership by Spain, no slavery in the fields. He died on his back, his red blood spreading in the dust. His murderer, a Spanish nationalist, fled that day on a steamship bound for Havana, where he was protected by the Spaniards for whose cause he'd killed.

Devastated, we forgot our trip to Regla.

I became water, limp and drifting, numb in my one black dress. Night after night, I washed it in the pail, hung it in the yard, and headed silently to bed, where I lay listening to my mother sob herself to sleep. During the days, I followed her around the boardinghouse, helping with chores, watching her face to learn how to understand this horrible new feeling, like being lost at the sea's dark bottom, every movement weighted and slow, every breath an effort and a confusion—but her face was a stone mask carved by grief. It taught me nothing.

I couldn't shake the image of my father on his back, eyes open to heaven, blood leaking from his mouth, his chest. My father, my sweet dear father, who'd carried me on his shoulders when I was little to watch the ships dock in the harbor, who'd taught me to read, to write, to draw, to fish, to dance by gliding me on the toes of his battered shoes. Now a silent body in the road. I heard the sound of sandals slapping and cries of "No, God! No, God!" as my mother came racing up the street. She collapsed upon him, weeping, as I stood immobile, useless, watching both of them there on the ground as the crowd gathered. My life as I'd known it was over. Around me, some men yelled of forming a band to chase the villain down, while others argued that, though the loss was great, the duel was fairly fought. The numbing whirl of voices rose until four men arrived with a stretcher and lifted my father's limp form. I fainted then.

When I woke, I was lying on a chaise on the wide veranda of the Robles mansion, confused by lace like the wings of a huge black butterfly fluttering in my face. A girl and her mother were anxiously fanning me. "Oh, she's awake! She's awake!" A maid brought cool mint tea. The rich girl, though only my own age, slipped her arm around my shoulder and kept patting my hand, saying, "There, there," as if she'd read in a novel that that's what gentlewomen did. "You poor child," Sofia's mother said. My mother had disappeared with the stretcher and my father's body, forgetting me in her grief.

After that day, I visited Sofia's house often, whenever my mother could spare me, sitting in my black dress that grew tighter and tighter at the chest and hips as the year went on and its hem crept up past my ankle bones, inching up my shins. The Robles house was a museum of wonders, so different from the stark austerity of home. We stayed quietly in Sofia's room with her china dolls or in her father's study, where she taught me to play chess and backgammon and how to open all the secret drawers of her father's desk with a little key that hung hidden behind an etching of a pelican. She spun his large globe and showed me where we were. I couldn't believe my whole world amounted to no more than a fleck of brown.

At home, I began to pester my mother for the trip to Regla. Chopping onions for the midday meal, she looked blankly at me, uncomprehending.

"I want my cleansing," I persisted. "I want to know which orisha is mine." My mother, a daughter of Yemayá, wore a blue-and-white headwrap always. I wanted to be one, too, and I wanted to know how to love, and who would love me. I admired the boys I saw, broad-shouldered and flat-bellied and bold, and I was in a hurry to grow up and get one.

"Orishas don't belong to you, girl." My mother shrugged. "You belong to them."

"Well, fine, then," I said, sighing. I was less interested in the theological specifics of Santería than in which spirit would guide me, which rituals I would perform, which colors I would wear. "But can we please go to Regla and find out which orisha I belong to?" Deprived of regular Christian churchgoing (for which my mother, like many Key West Cubans, had no patience), I wanted the benefits, at least, of the ancient religion her ancestors had brought with them from Africa. "I want to know my destiny."

She scraped the slivers of onion into a pot. "Your father ain't cold yet, girl, and you wanting to travel."

I turned away. It had been four months. I went to set the table for the boarders, who slid their hands up my sides when my mother wasn't looking.

At Sofia's, we traipsed up and down the attic in her grandmother's cast-off finery. Fur. Silk shawls and dresses, fine-heeled velvet boots sewn with tiny pearls. Steamer trunks big enough to climb into and close, squealing as if we were genuinely scared. Down in the drawing room, we took turns reading aloud from her mother's books: Cervantes, Shakespeare, Sor Juana Inés de la Cruz. One day a package arrived from Spain wrapped in thick brown paper and cardboard. Sofia's mother gasped with excitement and called the maid to bring a knife and open it.

"Just look," she said. "Just look at this." She lifted a dark-green leather volume from the packing. *Rimas*, said gold letters on its spine. *Bécquer*. "Gustavo Adolfo Bécquer," said Sofia's mother with a dreamy sigh. "Poems. I have been waiting a long time for this. He was a great Romantic." She turned to the maid. "Cut the pages."

The maid did, and Sofia's mother stood there in the foyer of their grand house, reading poem after poem aloud to us. We stood transfixed. The air in the room felt thick and cool, as if everything around us had frozen. I felt a kind of breathlessness, a kind of rapture. I forgot my mother, my father, my sadness, my longing to know to which orisha I'd belong, my longing for a boy.

Sofia's mother looked up from the book and smiled at us. I could tell she felt the rapture, too.

"That's pretty, Mamá," said Sofia, her face bland, and I looked at her in disbelief, wondering for the first time who she really was inside. Had she not heard what I'd heard? The poems were a kind of sorcery, a kind of spell that silenced all else. I stared out the open doorway into the green yard. *That was magic*, I thought.

And then, like heresy: *I could do that.*

9

SOFIA

At dusk, I sat sewing on the veranda. The sprawl of purple bougainvillea screened me from the street, and a small kerosene lamp lit my work. It was a decidedly romantic setting.

My mother was off visiting her pious Catholic friends, my father was dining at the Hotel Russell with business associates, and my grandmother was upstairs in bed, no doubt already half-intoxicated on her sherry and reading old Cuban romances. Even the maids had the evening off.

"Señorita." A young man mounted the steps. It was the cafetero, the one people called a fool. "I have a message for your father," he said. "From my boss at the coffee roastery."

No one else was about. I studied him in the lamplight. His eyes were dark and beautiful, his black hair thick. The muscles of his arms bulged nicely, threaded with thick veins.

"Come," I said. "Sit here." I patted the cushions next to me on the settee. He hesitated, twisting his cap in his hands.

"I couldn't, miss."

"No, really. Do," I said. "You must."

He sat. I could hear his breath. I embroidered, pulling turquoise floss through the damask again and again in precise and tiny stitches. There was no sound but his breathing and the sliding of the thread. He stared at the fabric, hooped taut, and at my hands—which did have a peculiarly beautiful waxen glow in the lamplight, very pale and very smooth. We both sat there watching my hands' serene and delicate movements, and I wondered if he could even think such words as *spellbinding* or *mesmerizing* or *exquisite*—if he even possessed such a vocabulary. He probably couldn't compliment me properly if he tried. He'd likely manage only *beautiful* or *pretty*. How dull it would be, such a courtship—which was why, I supposed, peasants simply didn't court ladies. Only knights—and even precious few of them—could make up sonnets on the spot.

The cafetero said nothing. Paucity of vocabulary aside, he should have at least tried. But he simply sat there. This irritated me. I saw, though, that his hand had dropped to the little expanse of green silk that stretched between our two laps and lay very near my thigh. But it didn't move closer. It didn't dare. He said nothing. I glanced up at his face. He was no longer staring at my exquisite hands, with their serene and waxen glow, but at my throat and décolletage, which was, if I remembered correctly, quite prettily arranged and edged with golden lace, though I'd been expecting no particular company. His dark eyes rose to mine, and they were sweet and hungry.

I looked down at that hand, brown and rough, against our green silk settee, and my needle moved through the air, quite slowly and deliberately. Its sharp steel tip came to rest lightly upon his flesh, and then pressed. It pushed in, just a little. The cafetero gasped. A red pearl of blood welled. I met his eyes, which were confused and pained and utterly humble, and a strange delicious heat tugged low in my belly. The air smelled different, an unexpected kind of hot burnt scent, like winter lightning. My legs shifted inside my skirt. I pulled away the needle. My eyes locked on his, and I lifted his great brown paw and leaned over it. My tongue lapped away the blood. He gasped again. Another, smaller pearl squeezed slowly out and sat there, red on his brown skin. I licked it off. He stared at me with his full lips parted, his eyes still hurt and wondering, as obedient as a hound's.

I set his hand on the place in his lap that had been stirring, and he groaned.

With men, the best way was to exit quickly and mysteriously, leaving them wanting and confused. So I did.

10

CHAVETA

At twelve, I got my first job stripping. But I'd already been stripping at home for years. It was easy. My father taught me. Grasp the stem between your fingers. Make a fist. Wrap the tobacco leaf around your fist, and twist. The stem and veins pulled away clean, and then you had something you could roll.

My father had been bringing loose leaves home, his weekly allotment from the Salazar factory, since before my memory started. I couldn't even read yet when he first showed me how to strip as if it were a game. A contest, a race. The goal was to strip as many as possible as fast as I could, without damaging the leaves. Even then, I loved a challenge. By the time I was twelve and the Flores Cubanas factory would hire me, I was already the fastest stripper on the bench. I worked for only a year on the top floor with the other children and some women (smaller hands) before they moved me down to the main floor. At thirteen, I became the youngest roller in a shop of five hundred souls.

Some workers grumbled, but skill was skill. The divisions of the larger world dropped away once we sat at our tables to work. Men worked alongside women, brown next to Black next to white. It was a microcosm of the Cuba we all dreamed of. We listened to the lector read all day from above us on his wooden platform. The hours flew. Our lector was a heavy old man with a booming baritone and a drooping mustache, and he made the stories come to life. When we liked a part of the story, we would rap our small knives on our wooden tables. Sometimes after a line of Marx or *Les Miserables*, the galley sounded like thunder.

Women came to the factories in the afternoons and clustered around the open windows, leaning to hear the latest. At night, around the dinner tables at home, the families of Key West would argue about what Jean Valjean should do next or how we could seize the means of production from the capitalists.

But we never argued about whether the Spanish rulers in Cuba should be overthrown. Violence, soldiers, horses, guns—We never argued, because everyone agreed.

Señor Pedroso, our lector for years, had gotten old. In the afternoons when it got hot, he would fan himself and pause, and you could see him sweat. Just when everyone was excited after lunch to hear the next chapter of *Great Expectations*, his voice would fade. We all loved and esteemed him, and we paid him from our pockets each week; the owners had nothing to do with that. The lectors were ours. We auditioned them. We hired them, and sometimes we fired them. We told them what to read, and our chavetas hitting the tables told them what we liked. Some of them wrote for the papers, too, so our passions shaped the arguments they sent to *El Pueblo* and *El Yara*.

This new guy, this substitute, this Galván: he lit us all aflame again.

Once a sad white man came from New York with a camera and took photographs. He arranged me and two other girls so that the props under our stools showed, to demonstrate how young we were. The idea, apparently, was to show how sad it was that children had to work.

Sad? I took home more money each week than some grown men. I paid the same dime each week toward the lector's salary as anyone, which meant I had an equal vote for hiring and firing him. No one except my parents even knew my real name anymore. Everyone called me Chaveta, after the sharp knife we all used to cut tobacco or rap loudly on the wooden tables when the lector read something we loved. Chaveta. It suited me, said my father. He said I'm like a little weapon, hardworking, dangerous, and easy to conceal, with a tongue sharp as a blade.

At noon we all left for lunch and a quick siesta. Sometimes I walked home and ate with my parents and brothers and sisters, but most days I walked to the boardinghouse Zenaida's mother ran. Señora Baliño's food was good and cheap, and I could talk to someone besides my family. "Call me Caridad," her mother always said, which seemed disrespectful, but I did.

On Tuesday at lunch, I sat at the long table, wolfing down her food.

"Sofía's right," said Zenaida, laughing. "You do eat like a boy."

"Like I said." I shrugged. "I work like a boy. I'm hungry like a boy. Why shouldn't I eat like one?"

A voice from the corner startled us.

"You don't twitch your skirts like no boy."

It was the cafetero, Líbano. He stared down at his plate, grinning. Zenaida lifted her eyebrows.

"The statue speaks," she murmured.

11

LÍBANO

For thousands of years, deep beneath the surface of the Caribbean Sea, the coral forests grew. Tiny living things clung to other tiny living things, silent beneath the rippling blue waves—whole cities of coral, teeming like Havana—and when they died, leaving only their limestone skeletons, new corals affixed themselves in a living layer to dead rock, and so on, year after year, century after century, stratum upon stratum, growing upward from the sandy ocean floor toward the sun. Generation after generation, they died and became stone, a vast and intricate mausoleum of a million-billion-trillion hardened corpses. Underwater currents deposited drifts of sand against the stone, and the sand piled up, too.

During the last ice age, the sea receded, baring the sand and coral to the open air, and a chain of tiny islands jutted above the waves.

Wind carried seeds there, and traveling birds left more seeds in their droppings when they stopped to rest. The seeds took root, and the land grew green and lush.

A thousand years ago, the Calusa people lived here. A shell people. Shells to scoop water; shells for dishes; crowns and necklaces made out of shells. They built their huts and hollowed out the long trunks of mahogany trees for canoes that bore them to Cuba, where they traded with the Tainos, the Guanahatabey, and the Ciboneys.

Back on their little coral island, the Calusa draped their dead with gold and silver ornaments and buried them in mounds of sand. At some point, they left the island for good. No one knows why. The sand blew away, leaving their treasure and skeletons exposed—so many skeletons, the Spaniards called it the Island of Bones. Cayo Hueso.

Key West, where I lived now.

At least, so I was told by the books that lined the library of the San Carlos Institute, which was where I went whenever I was not working at the coffee roastery or serving at the cigar factories or swimming in the sea or sleeping upstairs at the boardinghouse in a room so small that, lying on my bed, I could reach out and touch the opposite wall.

But at least it was a wall. At least above my head, there was a roof. At least the room was mine, with no one else inside it.

Once, I lived in Cuba, in a camp of tents in an alley with other orphans. We begged in the streets, sucked on rotten fruit to get drunk, and roasted rats for dinner.

In 1865—the year of my birth (or so I had estimated)—most of the world had not known of the existence of Key West. It was just a place where storm-wrecked ships washed ashore.

But before the Civil War, the United States imposed tariffs on imported Cuban cigars—though not on tobacco itself—so Cuban factory owners moved their operations here. Key West's damp, hot climate was good for rolling (far better than cold New York, where tobacco leaf quickly grew dry and brittle).

By 1875, this tiny island was producing twenty-five million cigars a year. Since then, manufacturing had only grown as other businessmen saw the wealth to be made.

Now Key West was the largest city in the state of Florida, with one of the most important ports in the United States. We had ninety cigar factories, some with five hundred laborers: men and women, Black and white and brown, all side by side, working. I'd been told this was unusual in the rest of North America.

Twice each day, I went from factory to factory with my urn and tray strapped around my neck: once for morning coffee, and once in the afternoon. I walked up and down the aisles of the galley, where the rollers worked, and then climbed up to the top floor, where the strippers twisted the stems away and stacked the leaves under damp cloths to stay humid until rolled. The top floor was the hottest. Heat rose. That was a principle of science. I learned it in a book.

I moved slowly up and down the rows. Part of my mind recalled each order (how many cubes of sugar, black or with cream) for every man, woman, and child who bought from me daily, so they did not need to speak, and the other part of my mind listened to the lector read from the high tribuna. In the morning, the lectors read the news: the rebel paper *El Yara* that José Poyo published and the Spanish newspapers that came from New York and Havana but took two or three days to arrive, so their news was old, but the opinions still burned hot.

Sometimes a lector would bring the local English papers—the *Democrat*, the *Key of the Gulf*—and translate the headlines for us so those who didn't speak English knew what the North Americans were saying. Sometimes a lector would translate a whole article for us, line by slow line, if it was especially important. But this work was very taxing, switching the words to Spanish in the mind while reading with expression, loud so everyone could hear.

After the news, the lectors read the latest political theory: calls for Cuban independence by José Martí, communist arguments by Friedrich Engels or Karl Marx, anarchism by Mikhail Bakunin or Pierre-Joseph Proudhon. Ways of living differently so that the poor did not suffer as much. The ideas were sometimes difficult for me to follow, going from one factory to another.

The workers were the ones who paid the lectors. Not the factory owners.

This caused problems.

Sometimes, having listened to Marx and Bakunin, the laborers went on strike. Sometimes their leaders disappeared. Sometimes lectors did. Later, bodies washed ashore.

Afternoon coffee was the best, when everyone came back sleepy from their lunch—a sandwich eaten outside as they leaned against the factory wall, or a hot dinner at home if they had someone to cook it for them. (I ate at Señora Baliño's boardinghouse. Meals were included in the cost.)

After lunch, I came with my urn of coffee to wake the workers back up, and the lectors read a novel to entertain them through the long hours of the afternoon, something dramatic from far away so they would be intrigued and inspired: *Don Quixote*, *Madame Bovary*.

My favorite was *The Count of Monte Cristo*. He was a daring fighter who knew how to escape. How to keep secrets. By contrast, my own life was very quiet.

Chaveta's voice tunneled through my thoughts. Bold Chaveta! She was the most exciting girl to watch, though I liked the others, too: the rich, eerie one with her fancy clothes and needle and her maid, and Señora Baliño's daughter, the tall, quiet one with her eyes full of dreams.

"I work like a boy," Chaveta was saying. "I'm hungry like a boy."

Half my gold tamal was still steaming on my plate. I smiled down at it.

"You don't twitch your skirts like no boy," I said.

12

CHAVETA

Wednesday at dawn. Behind the house, my mother retched in the dirt. I wiped vomit from her hair with a rag.

"Why don't you make Papi use what the sailors use with whores?"

"Ay, my daughter." She shook her head. "The godless mouth on you, these things you say." She pushed silt over the mess and rose groaning to her feet.

"Why not, though?"

"I am a married woman."

"You're a broodmare."

"Don't make me slap respect into your head."

But her voice was weary. She trudged back to the house, and I followed her up the steps. In the kitchen, over the bowl, she used soap to scrub her hands, her face. She rinsed her mouth and went to the back porch to spit. I watched her. She came back inside.

"What if I got you some?"

"Ay, my God, then what do I tell your father? Angelo, look, put this on, my love. Your daughter got it for us." She shook her head, her smile weak.

"Tell him nothing. Tell him when he bears the babies, he can complain."

"Then what do I tell God?"

I tore a hunk off yesterday's loaf and chewed. "Tell God the same. Or just quit talking to Him until He treats you better."

In Key West, some Cubans were Catholic, like my mother and Sofia's. Most weren't. They had left the Church behind when they left Cuba, or dropped it for good back in 1872, when Father La Roca betrayed the cause.

My father often told the story. It was October 10—the annual celebration of the Grito de Yara—and all the Cubans in Key West had gathered at the Catholic church at dawn for a ceremony to honor the slain rebel martyrs. As a symbol, they draped the flag of free Cuba over an empty coffin. But Father La Roca—who was supposed to talk forever, as was common in the Catholic Church—cut short the ceremony, capitulating to the bishopric of Havana, to the Spaniards, hand in glove with Rome, with gold.

A three-minute blessing? For all our noble dead?

That was it. Cubans turned on their heels and left the church.

Yes, October 10, 1872. I was barely three years old, yet my father would tell it fresh with outrage, as if it happened last week. "What has the Pope ever done for us? The bishops? Nothing. They love Spain. They love gold . . ."

Lectors described the Vatican's imperial wealth and read to us that religion was an opiate that kept the masses drugged.

I'd seen opium users drifting down the alleys by the whorehouses. Languid and soft, confused.

Like my mother.

"Well, I'll get you some," I told her, "and you can decide."

They didn't come cheap. I couldn't just walk into the pharmacy like a man and say, *Five rubbers, please.*

Black Marisel, Julieta's mother, who drank whiskey with me on the docks at night when business was slow—she sold me some, marked up.

"The rubber ones are best," she said. "The men don't like them, because they're thicker than the skins. But they protect you from babies and syphilis." Her eyes grew worried. "These aren't for Julieta, are they?"

"No."

"Good." She nodded. "I don't want her ending up here like me," she said. "Or you, either. Be careful, Chaveta."

"They're for my mother."

"Ay, I see." She smiled. "Yes, I see. You are a good daughter."

I shrugged.

It was a week's damn wages.

My mother's life was stupid. A waste. She was a milk cow in a barn—only she had to clean the barn herself. It was no life.

When I put them in the wooden crate where she kept her underwear, I stared down. Then I took one back and put it in my own pocket.

Because who knew.

13

ZENAIDA

Back in Havana, my mother went to church the same as anyone, but her real faith lay in Santería, in the orishas. In the bedroom we shared, there was an altar that honored Yemayá with candles, conch shells, and a little dish of rum. A stone Eleguá sat behind the door with his potato-shaped face and cowrie-shell eyes. Unnerving: the way he looked but didn't look. All-seeing. Unseeing.

When she finally took me to Havana, dressed in my best clothes, we slept all night on the ship, ate our packed breakfast by the docks, then went by ferry across to Regla, where we walked a long time down winding streets until we entered the courtyard of an Iyalorisha.

This Iyalorisha was darker than my mother and fat, and her red-veined eyes had a knowingness that spooked me. Dressed all in white, she sat on a little wall, and I stood before her as she gripped my hands hard. My body felt suddenly so slender and scared.

Chanting in a language I didn't know, she clenched her eyelids shut and rocked back and forth. Nervous, I glanced at my mother, who stood nearby. Her smile was calm, and she nodded encouragingly, as if nudging me forward toward the edge of something. The feeling in the air felt like when lightning strikes nearby, all hot-pink sizzle. The Iyalorisha, still clasping my hands, made a humming sound like the buzz of a hive of bees.

The woman's eyes flew open, and she spoke in Spanish. "You are a poet, child. You are a daughter of Ochún, orisha of rivers. Oh yes. Oh yes. You will sing on paper. Mm-hmm, mm-hmm."

She nodded. The whites of her eyes were yellow and thick, and small black-red veins twined through them. The center circles of her eyes were huge black disks, with only the thinnest rim of dark brown ringing them.

"But don't get confused, girl! The world may never know you. Fame may not be yours." Her voice rose. "I feel it, I know it. You are a river, child. Song will flow through you. It will not rest, and it will not cease. Let other people build cities. Let men erect statues. Cities rise, but cities fall. Kings rule, but kings are brought low. Rivers flow. Rivers bend. Rivers live. Rivers bring. They make no effort, but they travel far and bring life to many. Be river."

Then she sighed a little sigh, and her body rippled and relaxed. It was as if she were rejoining us.

"Get me yellow," she called to the empty air.

From within the dark and silent house, a small child in a ragged red dress shot out, clutching three stalks of gold gladioli. She gazed at me solemnly, handed the flowers to the woman, then skittered back into the house.

The Iyalorisha pulled me close to her and shook water from the stalks onto my dress. Grasping them firmly, she whacked my hips, my arms. I startled. She stroked the blossoms over my hair. She took the stems in both hands and broke them in half across my collarbones. I felt the impact in my throat.

Putting the broken stalks in my hands, she said, "Throw these into the sea." From a basket, she drew a bracelet of yellow twine and tiny yellow beads, and she tied it around my left wrist. "You are a daughter of Ochún now," she said. "Build her an altar. Pray to her every day. She will protect and guide you. You will lose love and find it again. You will die happy."

My mother paid the Iyalorisha from her reticule, and we walked the winding streets together back to the harbor. I felt dizzy. From the deck of the ferry, I threw the stalks into the water. My mother placed her hand on my shoulder, and her smile was proud.

But I felt disappointed. I'd never even seen a river in real life, just the endless flat ocean and the bright-blue salt ponds back in Key West.

I looked prettier in blue than yellow, too, I believed, so I'd wanted to be, like my mother, a daughter of Yemayá, orisha of the sea.

14

SOFIA

My father lacked nuance—also tact—which made him unusual among Cuban gentlemen of his class, most of whom were quite cultured. They read Locke, Rousseau, and Montesquieu (and liked to say so, I'd observed). They traveled widely and well, floating off to Europe or down to Brazil and Argentina without a second thought. They attended the opera and concerts where symphonies played classical music for hours.

My father, though, had become thoroughly North Americanized and seemed almost provincial at heart: a businessman, methodical. He liked his luncheon each day at noon precisely, pastries and coffee at three o'clock, and his dinner at eight on the dot. He never took siesta. After lunch, he went straight back to his office at the factory and dove into his ledgers. His only exercise came from walking back and forth, and he loved to chat in the streets with the white Americans: the shopkeepers, the industrialists, the ship captains—he didn't care. He was

North American in that way, too: a true egalitarian, a man of the people, jocular, rotund, and loud. A man with a hearty handshake.

Because he was wealthy and wore a fine suit, everyone in Key West treated him with respect.

But he was not the suave, elegant Cuban type who quoted Dante and graced the society pages of New York newspapers.

That was the sort I would marry.

15

CHAVETA

A wooden rectangle with five rectangles inside: that was our house in El Barrio de Gato, out on the far corner of Virginia and Duval, exactly like a thousand other workers' houses here.

If it were a cigar box and I opened the lid, you'd see the little parlor at the front with the woodstove we almost never needed to use (my mother was proud of the bright-flowered cotton curtains she'd sewn from sacks; they hung at all three windows).

Then you'd see the bedroom for the six of us kids, our straw-stuffed pallets side by side on the floor, the walls papered with pages we picked from old newspapers—neatly glued, some yellowing, the recent ones still white—and you'd smell the warm, comfortable, animal smell of us all nestled in our blankets.

In the evenings, sometimes I used those newspapers to teach the little ones to read, sounding out the words by lamplight.

Then my parents' bedroom, the only room with a door—so they could keep making more of us, Papi said—and then the kitchen with its cookstove, where a folding screen in the corner let us bathe with privacy, though no peace: one naked child after another ran through the house, wet and shrieking, as my mother grumbled after them with the towel. The long thin rectangle of the hallway ran along the south wall and ended at the back door, which led outside, where five wooden steps took us down to the water pump and the privy we shared with our neighbors.

Papi had added a front porch, a luxury, where we sat at night for the cool breezes.

All the cigar workers had these little wooden-box houses, slapped up fast as business boomed. Side by side, like tinder.

Back when he drank less and was fun, my father used to call me *my little Hatuey*. I'd climb up barefoot on the table and swing his chaveta like a sword. "Death to Spaniards!" I'd yell, leaping down. "Death to the lying dogs!"

My mother didn't care for my games or for the nickname my father gave me, the name of a warrior-chief who fought the conquistadors and was burned at a stake.

So that name died. Chaveta stuck.

My father said I had Taino in me, from his blood, and Arawak from my mother's—that while the Spaniards claimed they had expunged all indio blood from the island, that was a Spanish lie.

Arawaks were fiercer, my father said, which was why it was so hard for him, a peace-loving man, to wrangle my mother, like a wild horse that wouldn't be broken.

I laughed. "What do you know of horses?"

"Exactly nothing." He rolled his eyes. "Which is why it took so long to tame your mother."

No one would ever tame me. No one.

16

SOFIA

Knowledge, they said, was power, and understanding one's world was an obligation of all those who wished to be modern. Therefore, to better understand my father, I searched his desk routinely. It was by this means that I learned the details of his hereditary estate in Matanzas, with its two sugar plantations and cattle ranch. It had been his father's and his grandfather's and his great-grandfather's. Now it was his. One day, because he had no son, it would be mine. For this pragmatic reason, I was ambivalent regarding the institution of slavery—it was the only economically viable way of growing sugar, though of course I said nothing of the sort here in Key West, where everyone envisioned a free Cuba as a utopia for all.

Well.

Whatever happened, I would adjust and prosper. Slavery, however logical and beneficial it might have been, was a way of the past, and all things modern intrigued me. Perhaps there were ways to mechanize sugar and cattle production that my father had not considered. Machinery had reshaped industry in England, after all, and the eastern mill towns of North America, with their railroads and factories . . . Why not Cuba?

Well, we would see. My own utopia was whatever made me richer.

It was also by rifling my father's desk that I discovered my mother's old letters to him, full of sorrow. I felt guilty reading them but also obliged to learn what I could. One's parents never disclosed intimate matters directly, and yet their private affairs influenced every aspect of a household—the whole atmosphere in which their children must dwell, a mystery of silences and bitter glances shot across a room, tears for no reason, the slamming of doors, a father's abrupt departure from the dinner table after a mother's cryptic remarks, as if they spoke in code. As children, we had the right to know, just as citizens of a nation must learn the truth of their country's origin, however bloody, and live accordingly, rather than swallow the propaganda of the moment.

He had tucked them into the back corner of the lowest drawer, as if to bury his embarrassment.

> *Oh, my Husband, when was the last moment of desire or tenderness you felt for me? Can you even remember? Does it flicker at all in your recollections? You speak only of work or money, when you speak to me at all. Never love. Never the fond words of affection. You glance at me for my approval—which I give and give—as if you'd turned me into your second mother. (It's true I am a mother now, but hardly yours.)*
>
> *Oh, my Husband, do you not recall our courtship? Your sweet words, those soft caresses, the rapturous way you gazed at me? Do you not recall our wedding trip? Dawn in Venice breaking over the Grand Canal, the moment you suddenly waltzed me around the piazza?*
>
> *What has become of us, my Husband? I wanted a lover.*

But you wanted only a wife, dependable as furniture.
You've won. You have a wife. But where has my lover
gone? Have you given your heart to someone else? Can
you not turn back the clock, my Love, to the days when
you adored me?
In pain, but still devotedly,
Your Altagracia

The date: 1874. I was five years old then. My father already traveled often to Havana. My mother often wept in the gazebo. Sometimes she held me on her lap, clinging, in a way that felt nice at first and then horrible, as if I were a fly stuck to gluey paper. I would struggle out of her arms to go play, and she would gaze at me sadly.

This grew boring, so I learned to avoid her.

There were other things to occupy my attention.

17

CHAVETA

My mother was a tired rag, a hollow turtle shell. We six who slept side by side were the only six who had lived.

I didn't know what that did to a woman's soul: losing babies. I just heard her sobs through the walls. I just saw her, each dawn and dusk, drop a thin cushion from the sofa on the floor and kneel before the little picture of the Virgen de la Caridad del Cobre. The beads of the rosary clicked slowly through her fingers. Even her prayers were tired.

She had not been to the Catholic church since 1872, when my father had forbidden her. Few Cubans went. The lectors tried to outdo each other with their condemnations:

Priests are traitorous bastards, tools of Spain—parasites upon the people!

The sword and the Bible, the soldier and the priest: both oppress us equally.

My mother disagreed. "You can keep me from the Church, but not from my Creator," she told my father.

Not long ago, when he tried—frustrated again—to snatch the pillow from the floor, she pointed her finger at him. "God sees you! He sees! And He will judge." For once, my father fell silent. He dropped the cushion, backed out the door.

The next night, when I arrived home in the dark, the tip of his cigar glowed orange on the porch, a beacon.

"What's for dinner?" I asked, mounting the steps.

"You tell me."

"You haven't been in the house yet?"

"Never come between a woman and her God," he muttered.

I laughed and went inside.

18

SOFIA

What I really wanted was to move to New York, where we Cubans—the rich ones, that is—were viewed and treated as royalty, Old World ladies and gentlemen, exotic and rare. Not to suffocate here in this rough-hewn shanty town where we were forced—if we wanted any society at all—to mingle with common workers. Ugh.

I'd learned to make a delicate shudder, like letting a tremor run through me, so suitors could admire my fragility and refinement. I would conjure a feeling of coldness on the back of my neck, as if an evil demon were blowing his cold breath upon me, and then it was as if I truly felt it, and then the shudder happened.

It was not fake. It was real.

But I willed it. I commanded it.

And every true lady, my mother said, should be in perfect command of her bodily sensations, so I supposed that was proof that I was one.

My father lived in a world tailored to his wishes, swam in a universe my mother crafted for him, a world so fitted to his desires that he did not perceive that it wasn't the real world at all. She had trained the servants well, and if they were not there, she served him herself. He entered the house, and objects swirled effortlessly into his hands: his pipe, a glass of rum, the evening newspapers from Havana. She watched him, but he trundled on, the oblivious beast she'd created, without dropping so much as an affectionate glance or a word of thanks her way.

For sixteen years, I observed this nonsense, at first unthinkingly, uncritically, absorbing it as I absorbed my milk, my bread: *This is the way things are.* Or *This is what women do.* Or *This is what men get*—with the corollary, *what they deserve.* But when I turned eleven or so, the questions began to pour into my mind unbidden. *Why? How could she?* And *Why not do something else?* And they'd clamored in my brain ever since.

Not that my internal din changed one whit of my mother's behavior, my father's complacence. A cold, dull man, I would call him, though he was jovial enough with other men. A man's man, a company man, a boss. He could talk politics and baseball with other men for hours, puffing his fat cigars, with nary a glance at my mother—and why should he have noticed her? She was a fixture he'd bought and paid for long ago, a fine piece of furniture built so beautifully to fit him that he could not even feel her presence. Only her absence would have disturbed his world.

"Let's go to Spain," I'd said to her when we were alone. "Or to New York." My secret wish was that he'd feel the sting of our abandonment, or even just a sudden consciousness of himself, stripped of the cushion of her attentions.

But she could not imagine it, she'd said.

Not long ago, though, when my father had been in New Orleans or somewhere on business, and my grandmother was already asleep upstairs, my mother sat with me in the gold glow of the drawing room, pouring herself one snifter of brandy after another until her eyes grew glassy with tears, and she began—as never happens—to speak at length, and I sat quietly, making mental note of all I heard.

She said, "Love does not die easily or fast, my daughter. It dies a grueling, bitter death, like a young, strong man who will not give up even as an illness takes him.

"But then one day it is dead. You wake up, after long months or even years of trying, of crying, and what you feel inside is a perfect coldness. A perfect freedom. Who is that creature, you wonder, that lumpy body, those smells and horrible snoring, the slime and crunch of those chewing sounds? Like a cow or pig or goat, bestial. You will shake your head with wonder that you ever swooned at his attentions or wept when they disappeared. And you will be free then. Utterly free. Perfectly free. A freedom like Antarctica, white and cold and flat and endless, nothing but horizon and white ice.

"Your life becomes very simple then," she said. "He no longer loves or wants you; he no longer sees you at all, really. He no longer has to pursue you, so he is no longer curious about you: what you want, who you are. You're just a thing he can use when he wants it—and eventually he doesn't even want that anymore. Thank God. He'll find another way. Some men use the brothel or have a whole different family in a different town, or they set up a mistress who pretends to revere them and listens endlessly to the drivel they say, nodding and smiling the way they need. He might be cheating or he might not. You can't know, and you can't control it. Successful men are wily—or they wouldn't be successful— and rich men have the means to hide things from you.

"Whom can you control? Yourself, and yourself alone, so even if you think he's cheating, my daughter, you must act like a queen who could never imagine such disrespect. Treat him like a courtier who does not deserve you."

I thought of my mother's assiduous kneeling, her well-fondled rosary. "But then, who is to be one's true king? God?"

She laughed. "Oh, no, my darling." She leaned over and stroked my hair. "Your own desire. Your own wishes, aims, ambitions. Those are your king. Marry them."

"But I thought you loved Papa," I said. "You're always tending to his wishes."

She made an indelicate noise with her lips. "Ay, no," she said. "That's part of being a wife, of playing the queen. You make yourself recall the smile you smiled when you loved him, and you put it on your face. You recall the things you did then, and you do them again. And you can see—how marvelous!—that he has utterly no idea how you actually feel, the coldness you carry inside—that he has no notion at all that your love is dead and he has killed it, that you've cauterized the wound like surgeons do when they cut off a limb. It is a false, deceptive phantom hovering in the place love used to be."

She poured another brandy for herself, and another for me.

"And this is why men are so scared of women, ultimately," she said, "and where the sad source lies of any power we have in this world."

"Men? Scared of us?"

"Oh yes, my daughter. Because they cannot tell whether or not we truly love them. And they know they cannot tell."

I thought of the young heroes in novels and their fine sensibilities, the swift lines of the romantic sonnets they composed on the spot, the way their dark eyes noticed everything, the way their long fingers roved nervously over objects when they were thinking.

"I don't think so," I said. "I don't think that's true."

"Of course you don't," she said, and her smile was soft but with a cool little twist in the corner, and her eyes were faraway, like a ship you watch dwindle and disappear over the horizon. "Of course you don't." She stirred herself enough to pat my hand. "But you will."

The maid came in with tea and inquired about the next day's dinner, and we answered her, and she left. The night wound its way into a very late hour, and we felt fatigued, and the maid came back and cleared away the things. My mother and I took our candles and went upstairs and embraced in the corridor, murmuring good night, and entered our separate bedrooms and closed our doors.

I sat with my candle before my vanity and practiced my mother's cool, sad, furtive little smile in the looking glass until I got it right.

19

CHAVETA

My father was a blunderbuss, all noise and explosion. But harmless, on the whole. Never beat us. A playful man—or used to be. Played loudly, sang loudly, yelled. I tried to imagine him as a teenager wooing my mother in Havana—and to imagine her, quiet and shy, pious, lifting her eyes for a moment and then turning back to whatever chore she'd been assigned at the small café her widowed father ran. She married at fifteen. My father, loud even then, drew the notice of the Spanish soldiers, so my parents fled in the dark of night. Not long afterward, I was born here in Key West, and this house had grown smaller with the years.

"She was a flower!" my father liked to say. "A shy flower. But she wanted to be plucked, eh?" And he'd nudge and cajole my mother into a blush, and she'd slap his hand away from her waist or hip or wherever it had settled.

"Hush," she'd say, shaking her head. "Show some respect."

"Respect? For you, my angel, I have nothing but respect. Is there a ring on your finger? A roof above your head? That is respect made real, my turtle dove. Respect made real."

This was the contrast that fueled our home. The tensions between them burned hot but not dangerous, an engine that kept my father working hard and the babies coming every couple of years, a perpetual-motion machine, a factory.

Now my mother was thirty-three, like Jesus, and she'd lost more children than she'd kept. Her exhausted eyes rarely rose from her work, as if even her lids were too heavy.

Sometimes I thought she'd like to climb up on a cross of her own and hang there, just to get some rest.

20

SOFIA

"I'm not sure I should enter the pageant this time, Mamá," I said. I had won the previous year's. "It seems unkind to the other girls."

My mother caressed my cheek with a soft laugh.

"Oh, my angel!" she said. "What a generous soul you are. But only think how proud your father would be, dancing the winner's waltz with you again, and think how beautiful you'd look."

I stood up. It was true that my dress would be the most beautiful. And my elocution was perfect—for the acceptance speech.

"I am blessed to have inherited your beauty, Mamá," I said, "and as for grace and comportment . . ." I gave a little twirl around the drawing room, raising my arms, admiring their smooth pale roundness. Before the long mirror, I turned back and forth, pulling my hair up, back, to the side—there was no angle that didn't show me to advantage. I could see, behind me in the glass, my mother's approving smile. Often had she exclaimed, "I see so much of myself in you, my dear!" "Truly, Mamá. Who could compete?"

"Be that as it may, Pura Salazar will still have an elegant gown—you know her mother will spend a fortune—and there are other pretty girls in town. Rough around the edges, perhaps, but still pretty. If you don't enter, everyone will say you're either snobbish or scared."

The thought of Pura in a new gown irked me. And Chaveta could actually look quite pretty when she was clean—and not sporting menswear. Not that she'd ever enter. Or would she? For the money, she might. If she ever put her hair up properly . . . If Zenaida were light-skinned, she might have been serious competition, too, but no one really looked at her.

I turned again in the mirror, envisioning myself in ruby-red silk, or emerald-green—or palest cream, for innocence.

Yes, palest cream.

The afternoon sun glinted most becomingly upon my hair. I imagined the crushed smiles of the other girls as I ascended the dais at the San Carlos to take my bouquet of white gardenias and be crowned.

"Perhaps you're right, Mamá," I murmured.

ZENAIDA

At dusk on Thursday, my mother and I walked to the beach. The rope soles of our sandals slapped the street. Red streaks dripped into the sea.

"You should enter the pageant, my daughter."

I glanced over. It had been a long evening already, and I didn't feel like arguing.

We'd finished serving ropa vieja, one of my mother's specialties, along with sides of fried yucca, rice, and black beans. Seventeen men devoured it all, and once their plates were cleared, my mother and I ate in tired silence, and then, while I began to wash that brutal stack of tin plates and cups and cutlery, she ladled the good leftover food from the pots into the pail, grabbed a spoon, and set off for Beggars' Corner.

Each evening, she carried our leftovers there, where the hungry lined up for scraps from those of us who were more fortunate. I knew she worked so hard because she feared standing there herself one day. She never let me go instead of her. "Rough customers," she said. My mother wore a Bowie knife around her waist in a leather sheath, and she'd used it more than once. "Pirates come to land sometimes," she said. If anyone managed to disarm her, she wore another, smaller knife strapped to her thigh.

Tonight's delivery had been uneventful, which meant the pail and spoon would be sitting on our porch by dawn, scrubbed as clean as ditchwater could get them.

When she got back to the kitchen, she took the brown sponge from my hand.

"You dry," she said. "Keep those hands pretty."

I took a folded flour sack from the neat stack on the shelf, and we worked in silence together.

Once everything was put away, she said, "Let's go bathe, girl."

Her smile was soft, and we headed for the shore with towels hung around our necks. When we arrived and took off our shoes, we were alone. The sand was cool. We stripped off our dresses and waded in, wearing only our white chemises. The water, still warm from the day's sun, slid around our shins.

"I mean it," she said. "Enter that pageant. Win that money."

"I want to be a schoolteacher at the San Carlos, Mamá. I don't want people talking about what I look like."

"They're talking whether you want them to or not. Might as well make dollars."

"I don't want to parade around, showing off."

"You already are, girl. You don't think about it that way, but you are. Every time you walk up Whitehead or Duval, you think every man and boy in town don't look at you? Only now they're getting it for free." My mother shook her head. "Make them pay, girl. Make them pay."

We were in up to our knees, and she reached down, lowering herself with a groan to sit in the salted waves. I sat beside her. The water lapped at our ribs as we faced the wide horizon. Each wave lifted us, pushed us backward a little toward shore, and dropped us softly on our behinds. It was a good feeling, like being rocked in a rocking chair or cradle.

"Beauty's no blessing, girl." She cupped her hands and poured water on her chest, her face. "Beauty's a curse. Might as well make it pay."

I knew how she'd gotten her first two babies, a bad and frightening way, at fourteen and fifteen. Some masters used all the girls on their plantations, like spittoons, but hers had singled her out, given her little gifts, made sure she had light work. The white mistress had stood watch when, seven and eight and nine months pregnant, my mother had been lowered screaming into the belly pit, dug in the dirt so unborn babies wouldn't be injured by the whippings.

In the twilight, I could see the thick twists of scars that roped my mother's back and shoulders, familiar and terrifying.

She hadn't told me how she'd lost those children, or if they were still alive somewhere in Cuba, or what she felt when she thought about them.

I knew I was not allowed to ask.

No, beauty had not been kind to her.

We watched the dark, slow shadow of a sea turtle paddling past.

"I will do it," I said. "If you tell me to."

"Then I am telling you," she said. "Make that money. Make them pay. Make every man in this town consider you for a wife. A prize. Lock yourself up a proper future with a good husband."

I nodded, though I had no intention of marrying anyone on the island. I would enter the pageant, though, if the money would make her happy.

"Okay, then," she said.

We sat in silence as the last slivers of light faded from the sky. She waved her hand toward the horizon.

"You see how the sun sets? But tomorrow, the sun will rise again. This is a symbol, girl. A Bakongo symbol. The indestructibility of the spirit."

"Bakongo," I repeated softly.

"I got Bakongo on my father's side. On my mother's, Lucumí. Yoruba people. In the homelands, they would not know each other, but enslavement makes strange bedfellows. You love who's there. So my father's Bakongo fire met my mother's divination, her orishas, trying to understand the world, comprehend it, move through it smooth. The Bakongo aim to fix it, change it. Fire and thunder, hail and guns." She shrugged. "How could I not possess rare power?"

I felt small fish nibbling my toes. The wind on my shoulders began to feel cool.

"And you got that power in you," she said. "Get clear on this. I don't want you ever doing sugar work." She meant bordellos, not the cane fields. "But if you ever got to—let's say I'm dead, you're on your own—"

"Mamá—"

"No, just listen. Let's say you got to. Well, know this. It doesn't matter what they do to you. Your body's just a shell. You'll still be clean inside."

"Mamá—"

"You getting grown now. You need to hear this. Your body, your freedom: they can take that from you, anytime. Only thing they can't take from you is your heart. So guard it. Your heart's the only thing that's yours. You the one who chooses when to give it away. So guard your heart, baby. Don't give it away easy. Because if you ever get it back, it comes back broken."

I stared down at my hands. She was talking about Maceo. I didn't want to think about him, didn't want to hope.

"I only ever gave my heart away one time," she said. "To your papa."

I glanced over at her, disbelieving. After my father died and we'd lost the small income his newspaper had brought, economy dictated that we share a room so she could let my room to boarders. Sharing a room, even with the curtain that she hung between us, meant I'd seen many a man share her bed over the years. Sometimes they were boarders. Sometimes Sofia's father. Sometimes it was too dark to tell. Through slitted lids, I'd watched their activities in the moonlight. The man on top, shoving and panting, or my mother on top, writhing and twisting, sliding her hands over herself like a fine dance. I studied them. Sometimes I felt sickened, sometimes I felt stirred. Sometimes both. After the man left and her soft snores blurred the night sounds from outdoors, I'd slip my hand between my legs and twitch my finger in the place that makes the gold explode.

All these years, we'd honored an unspoken pact of pretense: I'd pretended to be asleep, and she'd always pretended to believe I was.

With one sharp glance from me, that fell away.

Her laugh was soft. "That's not love, girl. That's just pleasure."

I looked at her, astonished.

She laughed again, shrugging. "What can I say? You got to keep things in order. Like you got to exercise a horse. Like you got to keep a carriage oiled if you want the wheels to turn." She laughed and patted herself softly between the thighs. "This here is the center of a woman's power, girl. Not power over men, though some use it like that. No. Power in yourself. Power for your life. If that goes, your joy goes."

"Mamá." I didn't know what else to say.

"Your father understands."

She always spoke of him in this way, in the present tense, as if he were still alive and aware somehow.

"He don't want me lying alone every night, like nuns at the convent. There's some things you can do for yourself, and some you need another warm body for."

We sat there in the dusk, caressed by the water, staring out at the dark horizon gilded with a last thin line of the sun's blood-red.

"Speaking of your father, child," she said.

I waited.

"I know a teacher's not all you want to be." Her gaze was soft.

I'd tried to be hasty, slipping all those scribbled sheets of foolscap beneath books, beneath table linens, beneath folded clothes on my shelf when she'd walked into the room.

"No," I agreed. "It's not all."

"I know, baby. You can do that, too. You got your daddy in you." She reached over to stroke my hair. "But just keep it to yourself for now." She rocked back and forth a bit. "For now, just keep it to yourself. We on our own here, girl."

My chest felt suddenly full, aching, heavy with guilt. I would never understand her life, her pain, her grief, her fear. I looked at her, my eyes filling, and nodded.

A slow, calm smile broke across her face. She stroked my hair again. "Baby," she said.

The incoming waves pushed us gently backward, inch by inch, toward the shore. Our bodies drifted in the same rhythm, in the same slanted direction. Side by side, we were lifted and dropped, lifted and dropped by the ocean's force.

We smiled at each other until it was too dark to see.

22

ZENAIDA

Friday morning after chores, my hair was smooth and braided, and I donned my pale-blue linen dress, starched and ironed. My white kid boots bore no smudges, and my white reticule hung from my wrist. Though my mother claimed there was no need to spend good money on a corset when my figure was so slim, I held myself erect and stiff and breathed in tiny sips, as if I were tightly laced, as I walked up Emma Street and then veered right on Front Street, another of the town's thoroughfares. I looked the lady.

Still, when I got to Sariol's General Merchandise at the corner of Front and Duval, my fingers twisted nervously together as I entered, and I browsed for long minutes among the bolts of fabric, pretending to be a normal young woman longing for a pretty dress, imagining how I'd look in a gown of shimmering gold silk or white muslin sprigged with rosebuds. I wandered the aisle of china dishes, letting my glance linger on the wedding sets, in case anyone was watching. Finally, I wound my way to the stationer's corner. Señor Sariol came out from behind the front register to serve me. His smile was polite enough, but he said nothing, glancing me up and down.

"Fifty sheets of white foolscap, please, sir." It was the commonest, cheapest kind.

His thick eyebrows rose toward the shiny dome of his head.

"Fifty? Still drawing, eh? That's a lot of pictures for a young girl like you."

I'd prepared myself for this question. I knew that some parts of it had not been spoken aloud. *Young*, yes, and *girl*—already those things made my request suspect.

But *like you*, I knew, meant *colored*.

I smiled my prettiest smile, the one I practiced in the looking glass and on my mother's boarders when I had to ask them to do something they did not want to do: remove their shod feet from the furniture, or aim their spew into the spittoon. The more innocent and friendly you looked, the more apt they were to obey. That was the smile I gave Señor Sariol. I dropped my eyes as if I felt shy.

"I'm still just learning," I said, "so I ruin a lot. I'm trying to make botanical sketches."

He frowned.

"Like Mr. Audubon," I said. "But just plants. I have no ability to hunt—as he did, to kill his birds." Señor Sariol still looked skeptical. "The flowers are just for decoration, to beautify my mother's boardinghouse."

I had in fact done three rather clumsy sketches—our ceiba tree, a pineapple plant, and a green avocado hanging from its twig—and patiently colored them in. They hung on the walls of our parlor, in case anyone should ask. They were so dreadful that it would be easy to claim I used many sheets of paper trying to improve.

"Hmm." He nodded and turned to the shelves where various sorts of paper lay stacked. He began counting the sheets, flipping them against his thumb. I glanced around the store.

He wrapped my stack in brown paper, tied the parcel with string, and named the price. My coins dropped into his pale palm.

"Here you are, then, miss," he said. "Enjoy your sketching."

"Yes, thank you, sir," I said, taking the parcel. "I will."

I dropped a little half curtsy and kept my face pleasant and still (another expression I had practiced; I employed it at home when my mother berated me for some housekeeping lapse). Holding my back very straight and measuring my steps, I left the store and descended the wooden stairs, my parcel tucked under my arm, the heels of my boots tapping the boards.

On the street, my pace quickened.

23

SOFIA

Gastón's beef bourguignon fairly melted on the fork, and my father poured the claret freely, his black hair and mustache so heavily pomaded that they glistened. My mother ladled sauce and her smooth talk over everything like a benediction. My silk dress, cut low to show my shoulders, was so pale a pink as to shimmer almost white in the lamplight's glow, and my corset carved me into pillowed curves. My maid had coiled my hair into a heavy black chignon and pinned white gardenias behind my ear.

And Señor Feliciano Galván responded as every man did, his dark eyes fastening on me again and again, gleaming, his talk quick and delighted, delicately teasing, hinting at deeper longings. It was just the four of us at dinner—well, five, including my grandmother, but she sat like a toad, as usual.

Señor Galván wasn't like one of those soldiers, however handsome, who'd sat at our table in the past, much less one of Papa's dull business friends. He could talk. He spoke with my mother about Rome and the Jesuits, and with my father about Cuban independence and the civic pleasures of Havana—Grandmama snorted at that—especially in the Barrio de San Lázaro, where he'd dwelt with his patrón.

Señor Galván seemed to like it when girls were bold and free, so I said, "I wouldn't mind moving to Tampa myself." My father nodded his approval.

Señor Galván looked at me strangely and was quiet for a moment. "Tampa is the South," he said. "The American South." He took a drink of wine. "I've lived in Tampa," he said. "I've worked there. I've walked the streets as a Cuban immigrant. Don't wish for it."

Switching the subject, he waxed gallant about the lush charms of our island: the graceful palms, the fragrant blossoms, the wild and vivid birds, the ripe red mangoes plump and pendant from the trees, the melting sunsets unmatched by even those he'd watched from the Malecón—coded compliments, all. I fluttered my fan and my lashes to let him know his arrows had found their mark. Yet it wasn't all performance on my part: I couldn't keep my lips from smiling or my heart from beating fast. He was far more handsome than people had said. I felt the heat in my cheeks. The force of his attention made the breeze along my collarbones feel like the stroke of one of his long fingers.

After he left and Mamá and Papa had gone up to bed, I waltzed alone around the drawing room, humming, replete with happiness, imagining myself in his arms.

Señora Galván, I thought. As one does.

24

FELICIANO

No small amount of trepidation had plagued me as I climbed the bright tiled steps to the wide veranda of the Robles mansion. Though wealth no longer intimidated me, I knew my political views would likely clash with those of any factory owner, and three hours of a dinner could feel like an eternity when tempers flared. I wondered what Robles had heard of me thus far. Factory owners were powerful men, and rumors of Robles's ruthlessness had reached me even in Tampa. Though he couldn't sack me from my post as lector—only the cigar workers could do that—he could make me want to leave.

At my knock, a dark-skinned young woman answered the door. Funny: even in the United States, where the scourge of slavery was finally illegal, some people liked to reproduce the look of it. The girl led me to the drawing room and gave my name.

Everyone looked up from their sofas and comfortable armchairs. Señor Robles rose and shook my hand with unfeigned heartiness. Whatever he'd heard of me, it had not predisposed him toward ire. His thick mustache wagged as he greeted me ("Call me Narciso, my boy,

I implore you!"), and I went in turn to the stout elderly woman (his mother, a widow all in black), his beautiful wife with sad eyes and a dark-red velvet gown, and the daughter, also very pretty. I dropped a kiss on each (respectively smoother) hand.

Robles held out a small wooden humidor, and I selected a cigar.

"And some sherry?" he asked. "I have an Osborne, a fine old solera."

"Please."

He turned to a wheeled mahogany cart and poured for both of us. Placing the goblet in my hand, he said, "To your health!"

I nodded and touched the lip of my glass to his. "As to yours. And to a free Cuba."

The old woman loudly cleared her throat.

"Ah! Of course, Mamá," he said. He took a hasty drink for the sake of the toast and went to pour her a glass. "How very thoughtless of me."

She took it and turned to me. "To a free Cuba," she croaked, "or whatever you like." She sipped it and set it down. Her milky eyes crawled over me.

We drank and smoked, and he asked me about my impression of Tampa.

"A fine place," I said, "and growing, but the Americans control it. We Cubans are welcome only on our own side of Nebraska Avenue. The Americans call us"—I glanced at the ladies—"the Americans call us the vilest names, whether we are white or brown or Black." I shook my head. "I'm accustomed to Havana, to Rome. A man is a man. He should be treated as such."

"Folly," snorted the old woman. "A dreamer's dreams. But dream them if you like."

"Grandmama," said the girl.

"Don't shush me, child. I know what I know."

Robles puffed his cigar. "I've heard these things about Tampa. I've heard about the prejudice there. It is the American South, after all. But if one keeps to his place—"

87

"The whole world is everyone's place," I said.

The old woman snorted again; the surface of her sherry rippled. The wife smiled at me, her expression warm and shy.

Robles's eyes were thoughtful. "Yet the cigar factories in Tampa are quite orderly, I hear."

The maid came in and announced dinner. We rose, I gave the daughter my arm, and we moved through the wide doorway in two pairs behind the old lady.

In a large dining room painted the color of chocolate, we took our seats around a fine table that glittered with silver and crystal. The porcelain plates and bowls were a luminous soft turquoise, and a chandelier twinkled above our heads.

"If by order, sir, you mean suppression. Law enforcement, the sheriff—all are in the owners' pockets, and they don't hesitate to break a strike before it even starts." I glanced at the ladies. "By brutal means. It's not safe for any lector who makes too free from the platform."

"This, too, I've heard about Tampa," said Robles. "Lectors who are too disruptive do not last."

"It's true," I said. While the maid poured red wine and served some kind of onion soup, I told the story of a comrade who'd been bound, gagged, and beaten one night, then thrown in the hold of a ship bound for Guatemala.

"What was his fate?" asked Señora Robles, her eyes compassionate and troubled.

"He was lucky," I said. "A sympathetic sailor found him and tended to his wounds. He is well now. And he will return. He will fight on."

"Yet Tampa is an orderly place." Señor Robles helped himself to more wine. "The economy is growing."

"They beat workers in the streets," I said.

"Yes, I've heard those rumors."

I laid the spoon down in my empty bowl. "They are not rumors, sir, but fact."

One Brilliant Flame

"Indeed, my boy. Indeed. But, ah!" The little maid entered, weighed down by a tray and accompanied by a man in a chef's costume. "Look. Here's our dinner."

"Beef bourguignon," the chef said, and laid before me on a shining porcelain plate a thick slab of steak. Small potatoes nestled at its side, flecked with some green herb.

"Exquisite, Gastón," murmured Señora Robles. The chef and the maid disappeared.

"We don't stand on European ceremony here," said Robles. "None of this seven-course business. I like the taste of French food well enough, but I can't stand all the fuss."

"Let me give you some of Gastón's sauce," said his wife, ladling it out herself from the porcelain boat. "It's heavenly."

I shaved off a sliver of beef, and indeed it was. "My compliments to your chef," I said. "This makes my board thus far here in Key West pale by comparison."

Señora Robles sighed with pleasure. "I am so gratified to know it," she said. "But tell us. Where is it that you've been dining?"

"At the home of my kind acquaintance Eduardo Salazar," I replied, "and very fine it is. I make no complaints. I only claim that this is better still. Superb."

Had my beautiful hostess been a cat, she would have begun to purr.

"But to be frank," I continued, "I now seek lodging elsewhere, and perhaps you can help me with a recommendation. I want somewhere simple and economical so I can pay my own way and impose no longer on the family of my friend."

"Ah!" said Robles, leaning forward, his elbows on the table (which drew a quick glance of reprimand from his wife—a glance he either did not notice or ignored). "I can recommend most highly the boarding-house of Señora Baliño. The food is hearty well-cooked Cuban food, and plenty of it. The rooms are clean, and the beds are comfortable." All three women's faces swung toward him. "So my workers tell me," he added. "And my business visitors from Havana, the ones without the means for a hotel. The rooms, they say, are quiet and neat, and Señora Baliño is a thoroughly respectable lady."

"So true," volunteered the girl. "Her daughter is a great friend of mine."

"Yes," said Señora Robles. "Zenaida, her name is. A most sensitive girl."

"See if it suits you, my boy!" said Robles. "Why not?"

"Perhaps I shall," I said, and I thanked him. The potatoes melted, hot and salted, in my mouth.

"People say," said the girl, "that you are a poet."

I nodded, swallowing. "In Rome, they taught us to write sonnets," I said. "And in truth, I found I had some facility for the task."

"Don't be modest, my boy," said Robles. "In Tampa, your poems are the talk of the town. They call you the Spanish troubadour, penning tributes to every Cuban in a skirt."

"Narciso!" cried his wife and mother simultaneously.

He chuckled. "But is it not so?"

"It is my blessing and my curse to find inspiration in beauty," I replied, "with which the ladies from Cuba are exceptionally graced." I hoped it sounded gallant and sincere. "And I should add, sir, that though it was my fate to be born on Spanish soil, I cast my lot with Cuba many years ago."

"Is it very difficult," the daughter asked, "to write a sonnet?" She fluttered her pink fan. "Does it take a very long time?"

"It depends," I said, "upon whether the muse visits me or not. If she does, then the rhymes flow like wine, and a sonnet appears on the page in mere minutes. Other times it can take many days."

"Could you write one"—her eyes were cast down, her long lashes black against her rosy cheeks—"for me?"

I lifted my glass. "Already my mind begins to compose the lines."

Pleased feminine laughter rippled around the table.

"A book!" Robles cried. "You must publish a collection of your work. There are many fine printers here in Key West."

"Oh yes," said his wife. "Oh, you must. You truly should." The dark crimson of her well-formed lips matched the hue of her velvet dress. "There's nothing so magical as holding a book in your hands."

"Yes, there's always a market for such things," her husband said. "The ladies love to read such stuff, of course, and the men . . . Well! The men might borrow your lines to woo their own dames. Most of us have no gift for flowery words."

The dowager cleared her throat. "For most women, I've observed, a way with numbers does just as well, or better."

"Oh, Grandmama," said the girl.

"I know whereof I speak, child," the old lady said. "A wife might complain about having no flowers, but if the gold is there, she'll stay. By God, she'll stay. Flowers with no gold, on the other hand, soon wilt, and love wilts with them."

The daughter shook her head. "Grandmama, you make ladies sound so mercenary."

In reply, the old woman only pursed her lips, training her gaze first on her daughter-in-law, then on her son, then on the ceiling.

Señora Robles quickly began to query me about Rome and Spain. She wondered if I hailed from Barcelona, or Madrid, perhaps, or Seville, her eyes lit with more eagerness than I'd previously observed. *Alhambra,* I wanted to say, to please her.

But I could not.

"I was born in Galicia, in the province of Lugo, in the small town of Villalba." Watching her face fall, I felt the sting of pride. Galicia, as everyone knew, was one of the poorest regions in Spain. "My family lives there still, on the farm of my grandfather and his grandfather before him. The land is barren, and they struggle." Along with Asturias, Galicia sent the greatest numbers of immigrants to the New World— desperate men, mostly, uneducated and hungry for any kind of work.

"They gave me to my godfather when I was a boy of seven, and he took me to Havana. When I was twelve, he sent me thence to Rome, to the College of Saint Joseph. The Jesuits educated me there until I was nineteen."

I told the merry story, which served so well at parties, of playing tag and hide-and-seek upon the rooftop of the Palazzo Altemps, darting among marble statues commissioned long ago by the Medicis. The ladies laughed, as ladies do. I didn't mention, as I never did, the crueler games that left me torn and shaking, sobbing into the crook of my bent arm at night—silently, lest I wake my tormentors. Their taunts rang in my ears. *Feliciana, Feliciana.* They laughed, holding me down. *Pretty boy. Girly boy.* I had gone to Rome with my hair curling over my collar, as was the custom in Havana.

It was no use telling the priests; some of them did it, too. When I grew older and stronger myself and could have taken my turn, I had neither the desire to get my own pleasure that way nor the courage to suffer the consequences of intervening. I lacked the method and the means. It was a system far larger than I, unstoppable, a great machine of savagery, and I could not bear the shame of uttering what had happened to me. I simply grew up knowing how vast the limits of the possible could be.

When I attained my manhood, I pretended never to have been hurt, never to have been vulnerable. I swaggered like other men, held forth loudly like they did. But fear dogged me. I did not care to walk alone at night, or sit with my back to the door, or sleep in an unlocked room. Some nights I woke with a cry and lay in the darkness, drenched in perspiration, reminding myself I was safe.

"Yes, Latin and mathematics and geography—all of it," I affirmed, agreeing with Señora Robles about how fortunate I'd been. "The Jesuits are strict yet excellent educators." I'd long ago made friends with the looking glass, which taught me how to pretend to be the man I wanted to seem. I'd learned how to make myself smile, how to make my eyes light up as if I were having a very good time.

She asked me about Tampa, and I reported that the grass was broader of leaf and thicker upon the ground than the grass in Key West, and that the trees were taller, more varied, and thickset, such that the riverbanks, viewed from the deck of a boat, looked almost like pictures of the Amazon, and that the dances at the social clubs (Cuban, Spanish, Italian) were lively and full.

"And are the women very beautiful?" the daughter asked.

"Of course." I smiled. "Though not so beautiful as here. Perhaps it is your tropical clime, more like Cuba's own. Just as blossoms bloom more beautifully and emanate more fragrance in Cuba, so, too, are the ladies I have seen here on Key West more lush and lovely than those in the North."

It was sheer nonsense, hand-fashioned for society—but for just an instant, the face of one of the Key West factory workers flashed onto the canvas of my mind. It wasn't that she was exceptionally beautiful— though she was, in all the ways that make a sonnet flow so smoothly from the pen: dark eyes rich with secrets, lips curving like ripe fruit, dark hair that escaped its braid to frame her lovely face as the hours of work wound by . . . Yes, she had all those things, and a lithe body under her shapeless work dress or the men's trousers she sometimes wore. But it was her temperament that struck me: the passionate strike of her knife against the wood when I read particular passages by Tolstoy or Bakunin—or how, unlike most women, she didn't fear to be the first to rap or to leave her chaveta dormant on the table when others were banging theirs. She had her own mind. The swift way she rose when lunch was called, threading her way through the bodies of the workers who milled about to chat—Where did she go with such certainty of step? Her section of the long table was always left pin-neat, as if no one had been there at all. And the fiery way her gaze met mine—just a quick glance, but burning—when I said something that stirred her. The faint curve at the corners of her lips: hard-won, so different from the easy smiles of admiration that so often greeted a man of my age, appearance, and wages. Hers was a smile one had to earn.

And already she had begun to influence me, which was what I'd heard happens to men when they find the one woman who will be theirs. Yesterday, after reading a passage by Proudhon, I spontaneously cried to the crowd of workers, "Every man has nobility in him! It may lie dormant, it may be a latent quality within that has never yet been provoked by dire necessity. Yet it lies there, strong and patient, waiting for us to call it to life in our hour of need. These true tales of other men who rose to the occasion with their full humanity can spark our own nobility and fan it into flames."

Knives were pounding the wooden workbenches; the room echoed with thunder. I looked out over the rows of workers. Some had risen to their feet. A heady feeling rushed through me. Glory.

My eyes swept the crowd, seeking the approval of the girl. But she sat immobile, expectant.

"Do you hear me?" I raised my hands high. "Every man—free or slave, Black or brown or white, rich or poor—every man has nobility in him!"

The wave was rising, cresting—I felt as if I could throw myself down from the tribuna and they would catch me and carry me aloft, all of us triumphant and aflame.

But her knife held still against the board. Her dark eyes gripped mine. Waiting.

I raised my hands again for silence.

"And every woman!" I cried.

Her knife struck wood. My heart resounded. Her dark eyes smoldered, burning mine.

"Yes, we find that orchids thrive in our garden," the Robles daughter was saying. "It is the heat, surely, and the tempests that cross our isle, leaving the soil so soaked with rain." Her cheeks gleamed pink, and she fluttered her fan near her lips.

"I shall have to see them some afternoon," I said agreeably.

The maid cleared our plates and brought out a pale-yellow cake on a platter. When she sliced thick wedges, I could see the dozen layers of thin pastry interleaved with cream. It was beautiful, but my belly was already full, and I thought of all the time that Frenchman must have spent on it, how many of the island's hungry his skills could have fed.

We spoke for a while of Cuban politics, of Spain's efforts to cling to its last colonies, the way the Spaniards imprisoned and shot and hanged any who rebelled. We talked of America's desire to claim Cuba and make it into a state, to avail itself of its rich sugar plantations and tobacco fields, its cattle ranches and coffee farms, its surfeit of skilled laborers.

"I love Cuba," said Robles. "But, though I still have interests there, I will never return for good. She was my home. She made me rich. I love her like I love my mother."

The old woman muttered something into her cake.

He shrugged. "But in the United States, I am free."

"Yes," I said, "but, loving freedom ourselves, we must set Cuba free as well."

"I support the insurgents," said Robles, "in word and in dollars." The old dowager rolled her eyes. "But I'm a businessman. I hedge my bets, but I bet on the winner."

"They win who are helped to win," I said, and the talk went on in that fashion, anarchist against bourgeois, but in truth I knew how dependent I was, a luxury item (a reader of novels, after all!); I knew whose oven baked my bread. I was no soldier, and I had no wealth to give. My patrón had left me penniless, and the battlefield frightened me, as did the barracks. I'd known too much of pain. My gallantry was all in words, ideas.

We finished our cake. Leaving the women to do whatever women do when dinner ends, Señor Robles and I rose and retired alone to the veranda, where we drank our after-dinner port and smoked the evening's last cigar, the palm fronds softly clacking in the night breeze full of salt. We spoke amiably of the production of many little newspapers in Key West, of the fine bordellos of Havana ("Don't bother with the ones here, my boy," he said, "unless you want the clap"), of the shipping firms in New York that grew wealthy handling the finances of the cigar industry, including those of Robles's own factory.

When I felt it was polite to do so, I took my leave, thanking him and shaking his hand. Like most bourgeois I had known, he lacked imagination, but he was not a bad man. He was affable, friendly, generous, shrewd. I respected him—the way one respects an opponent in chess who has far more pieces on the board.

I walked slowly toward the Salazar home, easy in mind because the streets were still lit and full of people promenading, like any town in Cuba or in Spain. Whole families walked side by side in the streets that were now empty of carriages. Friends called out to each other or stopped to chat.

Thinking of my mother and father back home in Villalba, I felt that sharp contraction in my chest that sometimes came. I remembered the way my mother used to hold me on her lap, kissing my forehead, and how my brothers and sisters would fall asleep next to me on our straw pallets on the floor, our arms thrown loosely over each other. At seven years of age, alone in the cold, soft, clean-sheeted bed in Barrio de San Lázaro, confused by the rocking sensation that still plagued my body, though I'd left the ship that afternoon, I'd sobbed into my pillow.

My patrón came in. His hair was thick and gray and hung wavily to his shoulders, and he wore a thick robe of some soft red cloth. He bent to lay his hand on my shoulder. "Here," he said. "Come over here, boy."

Crying, I let myself be led to the window. It was strange to feel the smooth cloth of a nightshirt floating around my legs.

My patrón pointed. "See that tower?"

I looked, sniffing, and nodded. It was huge and made of stone.

"That tower," he said, "has stood right there for two hundred years, guarding this city from pirates."

I glanced up at him. I had a boy's typical interest in all things piratical.

"Now it guards you," he said. "Do you understand?"

I didn't, really, but I could feel the pressure of his expectation. I nodded again.

"It is right to miss your home, your good parents. But when you are sad, look at this tower. Think of this tower, strong and tall. Be like the tower. Very strong. Very tall and very straight." As if by the magical command of his voice, I felt myself straighten. My tears stopped. "Can you see anything inside the tower?"

I shook my head.

"No. No one can. No one can see what is inside the tower. What's inside is yours and yours alone. That's no one's concern. Stand firm."

At home on the farm in Lugo, I had never heard such words. We ran with the animals, cried when we hurt, ate when there was food.

I looked at him in wonder. "Is that what you do?" I asked.

The creases around his eyes deepened. His smile was proud but sad. "Of course, my son," he said. "It is what all men do."

I nodded again. He led me back to bed, tucked me in, and left.

I'm not your son, I didn't say, because I could tell he was trying to be kind.

At Eduardo's, where the vast house was still and silent, I shot a game of billiards by myself, drank a whiskey, and went to bed.

I was lying there on my back in the dark, full of good food and good drink, my head pillowed on my crossed arms, listening to the wind and recollecting the events of the evening, when it occurred to me that I could not recall the daughter's name.

ZENAIDA

I was old enough to understand that everything had its natural arc; I'd read Shelley's "Ozymandias." All things arose, flourished, and fell away: plants, beasts, people, power, passion, empires. Everything was impermanent, the Buddha taught, but because we humans were so terrified of change, we sought to cement everything that was good by creating institutions. If there was land we loved, we made a state. If there was work we loved, we made factories. We took spiritual ecstasy and made church, with all its rules and hierarchy. We took love itself and made marriage. And then we were trapped in the terrible game of preservation and defense, unable to let a dead thing die.

In a book I found in the library of the San Carlos, I read about the nomads of Mongolia, and in truth I believed I'd relish such a life: all of one's belongings in small sacks that could be strapped to the back of a Bactrian camel; a yurt, like a tent, round and snug, made of hides, with a fire inside for cold nights, and thick rugs on the ground; everything mobile, light and quick, making it easy to leave a place, to move, to go. A life to match the wild restlessness I felt inside, my impatience with anything less than perfect justice, perfect dignity, perfect equal-ity—which meant, inevitably, impatience with everything, at least as I'd experienced the world thus far in Key West, which was no Shangri-La. And to ride horseback! Galloping wildly across the steppes at top speed—What freedom and joy that must be! But my mother. My mother. I could never abandon her.

On Saturday as dusk was falling, after the evening meal, I walked my mother to the San Carlos for bolita, as I always did. We arrived early and watched Señora Socarrás light, one by one, the gas lamps that jutted from the wooden walls. (The debates about whether or not to switch to electric-ity raged on and on: it was unnecessary and too expensive; gas worked fine. No, gas flames were dangerous, old-fashioned, a fire hazard; electric-ity was modern, and we must move with the times. No, the ambience from flames was warmer, more humane, while the glare cast by electric bulbs was garish. Somehow Cubans always managed to draw a simple argument out over many months, as if arguing were itself the point.)

My mother chose our seats and drew out her printed ticket: eighty-three. For her, bolita was a chance to win as much money as a boarder paid in a week. For me, it was a chance to sit with girls and gossip and to glance shyly at any handsome boys.

The bravest ones were in short supply. As soon as a boy grew strong and tall enough, he usually joined the resistance as a guerrilla fighter, and then he'd disappear, perhaps never to be seen again. Most of the Cuban men I knew on Key West were middle-aged, or running necessary businesses, or simply too old, too slight, or too cowardly to do well on the battlefield.

Unlike many other boys, Líbano, the cafetero, had never returned to Cuba to join the fight, but though handsome and well built, he attracted little feminine interest. Too serious? No swagger? He just didn't seem like the kind of hero we'd been schooled by romantic plays and poems to want. I liked him, but not that way.

Due to this dearth, any young man who arrived on the island was cause for celebration and speculation, no less than in the Jane Austen novels I read in English. I was still curious about the new lector. All the seats were filling up, and the crowd grew loud and boisterous around us. Señor Robles and Señor Salazar mounted the stage. As proprietors of the two largest cigar factories, they usually served as the masters of ceremonies at the bolita games.

Both factory owners stood at the edge of the stage looking out over the audience to choose the eight young men—boys, really—who'd toss the sack. Arms waved wildly to be chosen. Eight lucky, grinning boys ascended the stage.

Then Señor Salazar looked around the audience, slowly, slowly, letting the anticipation build. Who would be chosen as the selector? It was always a pretty single girl—and usually light-skinned, though I'd done it twice in the past.

"Celida Boza!" he cried, and everyone clapped. Blushing and smiling, Celida rushed down the aisle and climbed onstage, dressed in pink. We always took care to dress nicely for bolita in case we were called. No one really knew for sure if the two factory owners decided in advance upon the selector or made a last-minute decision, influenced by how pretty we looked when they scanned the audience. I myself did not care for the attention, so I'd begun dressing plainly on Saturday nights, despite my mother's urging, and never wore a flower in my hair. It had been nearly a year since I'd been chosen.

As Celida crossed the stage, the eight throwers laughed and joked, playfully shoving each other and stomping the boards. Celida stood between Señor Robles and Señor Salazar.

From his chair down front, pudgy old Plutarco Alfaro, the keeper of the balls (and also our pharmacist), ascended the stage with his heavy leather sack. He set it down with a thump. His gray mustache drooped with wax, and his bald head shone in the gaslight. From his jacket, he pulled a folded linen sack. He held it up and shook it so we could all see that it was empty.

Then, with the assistance of one of the throwers, he poured all one hundred ivory balls from the leather bag into the linen, pulled the drawstring tight, and tied a knot. He held the sack high and shook it. Everyone cheered. A few good shakes would be enough to mix the balls sufficiently, so it was never clear to me why eight boys needed to stand in a circle and toss the bag back and forth, but they did so every week, faster and faster, laughing, the heavy sack flying between them, as we cheered and clapped and stamped our feet and yelled from below.

"Cease!" yelled Señor Robles. "Silence!"

Everything grew still. The thrower who'd caught the sack handed it to Señor Alfaro, who carried it to Celida and held it out. She curtseyed once to him and to us, the audience, before running her hands over the linen. Smiling, she grasped one ball. Señor Salazar whisked over, producing a pair of silver scissors from his breast pocket, and carefully clipped the linen. Señor Alfaro stepped away, holding the sack so no other balls could fall through the hole.

Celida raised the ball high, still clutched in the scrap of fabric so we could all see that no substitutions had been made. All the men stepped away from her. Alone in the center of the stage, she lowered her arm, pulled away the scrap of linen, and looked at the ball. She raised her face to us. "Thirty-six!" She held it aloft for all to see, though of course the tiny painted numbers were invisible to most of us.

The usual eruptions of joy occurred around the auditorium, and the winners held up their tickets.

My mother's elbow gently nudged my ribs as she folded her number away.

"Maybe next week, eh?" she said, as she almost always did.

"I'm sure of it," I replied, like my part of the catechism.

Walking home together, arm in arm, my mother and I turned down Southard Street and came upon a strange man. He was talking loudly to no one, and people had drawn away from him, staring. I did not recognize him. His back was crooked, his neck twisted. He bent forward, his arms working at awkward angles as he tried to retie the lace of his boot. He could not manage it; his hands were bent strangely at the wrists, his fingers oddly gnarled. People looked away as he grew more and more agitated, muttering imprecations in a voice that grew steadily louder. My mother let go of my arm, went to the man, and laid a hand on his shoulder. Instantly, his body calmed. He twisted his head to see her, and she spoke to him in a tender voice. She knelt and tied his boot for him. I saw her rummage in her reticule and tuck something into his pocket, saying quiet words. He blessed her and kept blessing her, and then he quieted and began to limp away.

She retook my arm, and we continued up the street.

"Mamá."

She said nothing.

"Mamá. You need to be careful."

She glanced at me.

"Mamá, he could have been dangerous. You don't know him. He could be anyone."

"Exactly," she said. "He could be anyone."

I did not know quite what to make of this, so we walked on in silence in the dark.

I was not sure what I would do without my mother. Where I would go. I had slept in a bed across from hers every night for years now, ever since my father died—had spent each day working at her side, cooking, cleaning, performing the endless routine of meal-making and housekeeping for the stream of strangers who stayed a night or a week or a year, substitute fathers and brothers—and, for her, lovers—who melted in and out of our lives.

They were the changing scenery, the backdrop. My mother was the constant, the anchor, the compass rose by which I steered.

Though I daydreamed sometimes—like every girl, I supposed—about love, marriage, a life that would take me glamorously elsewhere, like the heroes and heroines of the novels I devoured, my mind was so accustomed to her, so rooted like a little plant in the soil and structure of our daily life together, that I found it impossible to imagine my life without her. Her moods, the scent of her sweat, the rhythms of her hands and body. We bled at the same time, laughed at the same things, remained stoic in the face of almost any pain—but cried (those rare times that we cried) just the same, in loud, helpless sobs we tried but failed to stifle. She was like an older sister, a temperamental friend, but with a whole lifetime's worth of suffering and wisdom I didn't have. She was the Zeus from whose forehead I had sprung, the ground I touched again and again to stay strong.

I'd yet to read a poem or story about a daughter who loved her mother this way. Perhaps such things didn't really signify and were not worthy of literature. Most mothers in books were just—*mothers*. Not really quite full people. Just vessels who were there to love and give and sacrifice—or who failed to do so sufficiently, and hence were damned, either by their sons or by the gods.

In my observation, most daughters—in literature, as in life—didn't dwell in this kind of awed and loving thrall; rather, they viewed their mothers with amused frustration, as obstacles to their romantic free-dom, or as simple cushiony backdrops, reliable as an old couch.

My mother was a person, warm and real and kind and unpredict-able, rock steady in some ways and mercurial in others: her evanescent moods, her tempers, the flash-fires sparked by nothing I could see, the storms of sobbing that blew in like an afternoon thunderstorm and disappeared as quickly, leaving her fresh and cleansed.

A person, vulnerable and real—yet she felt inescapable.

My mother was a tempest. A saint.

The ocean.

A plague.

26

SOFIA

Feliciano said in Tampa the white North Americans called us names. Racist names. Us! Fine white Cubans! (Spaniards, really, with the blood of Spanish aristocrats.) This must have been an exaggeration.

But he said I wouldn't like it there: the roughness, the roads not yet paved or lit with streetlamps. In Tampa, he said, one must carry not only a lantern at night but a rifle, too, because dangerous animals prowled. Jaguars. Wild, aggressive, shaggy boars with tusks like knives.

My father winced when Feliciano said it, but my mother nodded along, for she loved proper cities. In addition to the grand tour of their honeymoon—Paris, London, Venice, Florence, Rome, and all the great cities of Spain—they'd lived in Havana and visited New York. But Cuba had been too dangerous my entire life, she said, for me to go even there. So I moldered here on this stupid little spit of sand.

To me, Tampa was one step closer to New York. The trains already ran there—unlike here, where one must take a ship to go anywhere at all.

And what no one knew but me—thanks to my regular rifling of his locked desk drawers, that old and useful habit—was that my father had already purchased land in Tampa. After the cigar rollers' strike last year, he purchased it, but he had said nothing to us.

I did not know if construction had begun, but the drawings in his drawers showed a factory even larger than the Flores Cubanas—and made of sturdy brick, not wood, which was much better if there was a fire or hurricane. What's more, the drawings showed two hundred tiny houses, each one identical to its neighbor, each with its little backyard the size of a handkerchief. In Tampa, my father would be boss and landlord both, like the feudal lords of Russia. He'd even be the bank, if he let the workers lease to own. Here in Key West, the "bloody sympathizing slumlords," as he called them, would forgive a month or two of rent when the cigar workers would strike, until they got back to work and on their feet. "At my expense," he growled.

In Tampa, he'd be the slumlord himself, I supposed—though *slum* was hardly fair, for the houses looked neat and orderly, though small, with little parks and plazas scattered in among them. He'd be like some benevolent member of the gentry, and his tenants would be his laborers, as in novels about the English countryside.

Tucked alongside the plans was a letter with a red wax seal from some important Tampa official:

> *As per our recent conversation, I remain very happy to assure you of Tampa's strong commitment to law and order. My men are well trained and will not hesitate to use all means at their disposal to quell any labor uprisings. I tolerate no unions in this town, and particularly—you'll excuse my speaking frankly, man to man—no unions of foreigners. My men will back me. Your workers will cease to give you trouble here. Given the infusion of economic energy your investment in Tampa will bring, I anticipate this agreement serving as an arrangement of great mutual benefit.*

And his illegible signature, with a grand inky flourish.

It was quite an interesting feeling, knowing something my mother did not—something important that could change all our lives. What I did not know was if the ground had yet been broken—if these plans were becoming reality even now, or if they remained in the realm of dreams.

It was the plan for the large house that most intrigued me, of course: grand and gorgeous like any plantation mansion in the American South or Cuba, with stables and a broad curving drive shaded by oaks. I could rather see myself swishing up and down the veranda in a silken gown or dancing in the large first-floor room that was surely meant for balls.

Or so the plan suggested. I had to roll everything quickly back up and slip it away when I heard that damn maid's step in the hall.

27

ZENAIDA

On Sunday morning, I woke, lying stock-still in the strange luxury of a quiet bedroom, my mother already downstairs cooking, the breeze filtering through white muslin curtains that veiled our window. Palm fronds smacked softly against each other in the yard. My minded drifted pleasantly.

One bright, cool Sunday morning a year or so ago, tired of all things Cuban and curious about the other cultures on our cosmopolitan little island, I drifted into the Black Episcopal church and sat down in a pew near the back. Church was a foreign place to me; my mother had no time for it. Since she had left Cuba, the orishas were all she needed, she said.

Around me on the long wooden benches, smiling ladies fanned themselves. The sounds of English flooded like a warm tide—but a very different English from the tongue the white North American shopkeepers spoke. Rather, the sounds were melodic and warm, for the church's congregants came from Nassau, Jamaica, and the Bahamas.

The priest came into the pulpit, like a lector mounting his tribuna. He read scripture and talked of heaven to come—quite like a lector indeed, I realized. Perhaps all people craved a man on a tower telling them what was right and what to desire.

Then he began to preach against jezebels and harlots, those women who used their beauty to tempt good God-fearing men away from their wives. The fanning ladies around me nodded, murmuring assent. Some glanced at me. I shifted on the unforgiving wooden bench, beginning to see why church was not my mother's favorite place to go.

The priest then began to prate about the future and paradise, which we all would earn after we died, he said, if only we were good enough. Lifting his hand high, he read to us from the New Testament. "'And it shall come to pass in the last days, saith God, I will pour out of my Spirit upon all flesh: . . . and your young men shall see visions, and your old men shall dream dreams.'"

All the ladies were saying "Uh-huh" and "Preach," and I found myself wondering what flesh felt like when God's spirit was poured upon it—if God made it throb and tingle and glow the way my flesh did at other times.

Your young men shall see visions, I thought, *and your old men shall dream dreams.*

But what about women? What would we get to see and dream?

Church interested me no longer.

For a while, I just lay peacefully in bed, willfully immune to the looming day, listening to a cock crow, watching a tiny green lizard roam the unpainted tongue-and-groove boards of our ceiling, wishing I could dwell forever in this lull of peace, this bliss that always lay within the reach of each of us. But I knew my mother was waiting downstairs. I felt obliged to take up the mantle of responsibility, like Arjuna. To play my role. I'd been reading the *Bhagavad Gita*. Arjuna, though born into the warrior caste, saw through it all. He didn't want to fight. But all the world's a stage, et cetera, and his great blue god urged him back out onto the battlefield—but with a wisdom and detachment that allowed him to slip fluidly between dangers, like the knife of an enlightened butcher slips between the bones and sinews of the meat.

To triumph without effort. I'd also been reading the *Tao Te Ching*. And Sun Tzu's *Art of War*. Unusual choices, perhaps, for a girl not yet sixteen, but these were unusual times (the grown men liked to say), and the lending library at the San Carlos was open to all, and my mother did not interfere with my choices. Many girls read novels, after all, and sometimes, to allay suspicion, I read romantic poetry aloud to her in the evenings when we'd finished all the chores. No more could my father have interfered, once himself a brave agitator for liberty, a printer of Havana's and then Key West's boldest cries for insurrection. I believed he looked down from heaven with approval.

But take care, my daughter, I heard him say. *Do not meet my fate.*

28

SOFIA

Women could not become scientists, of course—not the kind that mucked about all day in laboratories with chemicals and machines—yet I had come to consider myself a scientist of nature, like the lady naturalists in England, but of human nature, not foxes and fens, for I liked to observe my fellow creatures and experiment upon them to learn how they work—a great advantage being that any drawing room or social occasion could be my laboratory.

A strange and paradoxical phenomenon I had observed regarding house animals such as dogs, for example, was that if you petted them and fed them and spoke to them affectionately until they loved you most devotedly, and then, for some minor infringement—or for nothing!—you slapped them and said a harsh word, they would not abandon you. Not at all. Rather, they would love you all the more and try much harder to please you. It was very illogical, yet it was true.

With servants, I had employed the same practice. It was most effective.

Beside me, my mother prayed and crossed herself again and again. The bishop prayed from his pulpit. Church was most tedious and yet relaxing. One just knelt and let the mind roam free.

At play with other children when I was younger, my methods had worked in quite a similar manner, though of course I could not slap them if their fathers were gentlemen. Subtler cruelties were required. But again, once the cruelty occurred, they sought your approval, playing whatever game you wished and attempting to curry favor with you by saying aloud the opinions they supposed you to hold, glancing over to see if you were pleased.

Yes, cruelty was surprisingly effective in many realms.

How strange God's creatures were!

CHAVETA

As soon as I heard the news at the San Carlos, I took off running up Duval, made a quick right on Southard, and then raced left on Emma. When I got to the corner of Petronia, my breath was coming hard. I vaulted up the boardinghouse steps.

Inside, the long table was full of men drinking coffee, talking and waiting for their Sunday breakfast.

In the kitchen, Señora Baliño was frying bacon. I grabbed a slice before she could slap my hand away.

"Where is she?"

Her head shook. "Still upstairs."

Crunching the bacon, I took the steps two at a time. Ran down the hall. Swallowed. Opened her door.

"Oye, Zena."

She sat up fast, clutching the sheet.

"Ay, Chaveta, you scared me. Can't you knock?"

"Maceo's back," I said.

SOFIA

It was not that I longed, necessarily, to inflict pain, as such. It was more that I craved the infliction of sensation—any sensation at all. I wanted to make myself felt—not make myself *known*, the thing so many people claimed to want. (There was nothing really here to know, I could calmly attest: only an emptiness, an observant, alert patience, keen with pleasure.)

Not known. Felt.

I longed to exert myself upon the senses and minds of others, to be recognized as a force to be reckoned with. To make people do as I wished. My mother, my father, my friends. Servants were too easy; they were required to obey. It was just . . . the days were just so monotonous. I sought an outlet for my considerable energies.

Strolling downtown this morning with my maid at my side to carry my parcels, I saw a worthy target, an opponent, a vision of power incarnate in masculine flesh. Sleek, tall, muscled, he was abetted in his perfect beauty by the glossy steed on which he rode. The horse trotted, and the man posted admirably—unlike most of these leaden lumps around here who just jolted about on their horses' backs like sacks of corn. Thud, thud, thud.

This man's shoulders were thrown back, his spine straight as a flagpole, his lean waist an advertisement for what it narrowed toward, his bulging thighs gripping the horse in a manner that made one's thoughts stray quite nicely. And his face. A vision of manly beauty: proud eyes, full lips, tough jaw.

But dark, alas! And hair like a black sheep's wool. For me, he could be only a plaything, no more.

But what a plaything . . .

The horse's tail swished, and they rounded the corner, lost to sight.

"Do you happen to know," I said lightly to my maid, "that young man who just rode by?" I always said *young man* when pretending disinterest, as if I were a dowager aunt gossiping over crumpets.

"Yes, miss," she said. "His name is Maceo, after the great general, and he is a soldier for free Cuba. They say his mother named him after the general in rebellion against her master, his true father, and was severely punished for it. He comes to Key West only to recuperate from skirmishes."

"But I have not met him."

"No, miss. He always stays at the boardinghouse of Señora Baliño, in the Fambá quarter." *The colored section,* she meant. I felt a flare of irritation spark my throat. Zenaida surely knew him, then. Had probably sat next to him at dinner. Had edged past him in a narrow hall. I took a calm breath and lifted my hands in front of me to inspect their creamy smoothness unmarred by labor. She'd no doubt scraped dishes from which he'd eaten, too, and cleaned the privy after he'd shat. My back straightened in its corset.

My maid shifted the packages in her arms. "In the past," she said, "he has always kept his presence very quiet."

"Hmm," I said. Usually I forbade her to speak unless spoken to, but this piece of intelligence intrigued me. "Well, there's nothing quiet about parading up Duval Street on a horse like that."

"No, miss," she agreed.

"I wonder what happened to make him change his ways."

"I wonder, too," she echoed.

31

ZENAIDA

Outside the tall windows of the galera, I stood with my mother and other women who were free from work in the afternoon and who arrived at the factory to gather in clusters, our parasols jostling, and listen to the latest installment of the Russian novel the new lector had brought. Ostensibly, I, too, was there to listen—to better myself, as my mother said: to get an education—but, as always, I stood where I could watch Chaveta.

Nimble, swift, and slim, her fingers flickered as she twisted the tobacco into a tube, wrapped it, and slicked it down with resin; her hand on the knife trimmed the ends with a certainty I envied, the way my mother chopped an onion or the head from a hen: utterly free of hesitation, sure of purpose, as if doubt were unknown to her, as if she never wondered what to do. The new lector's voice described the vacillations of Anna Karenina, who seemed far more comprehensible to me: driven by desires, acting, then drawing back, anguished, judging herself, trying a different path, stumbling . . . She felt more real than the people I knew in my own life, who never seemed to question what they did, all so committed, so passionate, so sure—whether wresting Cuba from Spain's grasp, or marching in a strike, or making fistfuls of American dollars. They all seemed to know what (and whom) they wanted, while I watched and longed and wondered, unsure of what was right, unsure of what to do. And so I did nothing. I obeyed my mother. Observed. Listened. Played it safe.

Though Maceo had arrived on the steamer from Havana, he had not yet come to the boardinghouse, which was strange. Chaveta said he was staying a few nights with the Bozas first and was said to be unwounded. (I felt a spasm of anxiety, remembering Celida's beauty onstage when she chose the bolita ball. Was she the reason he stayed with them?) He had come to rally troops, Chaveta said, to raise funds, to inform us of the progress in the field, and to wait for secret instructions from the Cubans in New York. He didn't yet know how those instructions would arrive, and he was seeking a way to smuggle them back to the guerrilla fighters—a way that could not be detected if the Spaniards captured him.

Bent over her workbench, Chaveta blew a dark strand of hair from her face. Her cheeks were flushed with the heat of the galera. Outside, a breeze cooled us. The shade of my pale-yellow parasol shielded me from the sun. But still, it was hot. The full feeling from the good food at lunch made me drowsy. The handsome new lector read on, but my mind drifted from the story of Oblonsky and Levin and Anna and their lusts and woes as Chaveta's hands twirled and spun the brown leaves into objects men would kiss to life and suck and burn, her head bowed over her work, a quick smile flashing on her face from time to time when some line from the lector pleased her.

"Girl." A deep voice, above and behind my shoulder.

I turned.

His eyes were dark and steady, and he wore a soldier's garb: mended, clean, a rebel fighter's clothes, the color of forests. He smelled of leather, soap, and horses. Hot flutters beat in my belly.

"Maceo."

"Drink coffee with me." His voice stayed low, but still the other women glanced, cutting their eyes at each other. My mother's face was very still but for a tiny twitching at the corner of her mouth.

"No," I said. "I'm listening to this."

"You're listening to fiction." His dismissive smile was faint. "I'll tell you something real."

My mother looked at me, her eyebrows arching so high they nearly hit her blue headwrap.

"Leave me alone," I said. "I'm busy."

"I'll call on you this evening."

I shrugged. "Do what you like."

His breath stroked the nape of my neck, and my hairs quivered, electric.

"Always."

Without turning to stare, I knew everything about Maceo by heart. His skin, smooth and fine and easy to covet, like polished teak. Touchable. Sleek. It sloped up over his cheekbones, which my fingertips hungered to trace. His brown-pink mouth was candy, ripe fruit, obscene and sweet, as if his lips were plump with juice. In comparison, I felt my own ugliness, all my features just slightly shy of perfect harmony, just close enough to beauty to fool others but madden me when I prodded them with my fingers in the looking glass. I had studied him for hours while he slept in the sickbed at my mother's boardinghouse, fevered from his bullet wound.

I stood stock-still, letting the moments pass, staring hard at the lector on his high platform to keep from swaying. As if he could feel my gaze, the lector read a sentence directly to me, his eyes on mine, but the sense of it did not penetrate my mind. Chaveta pounded her knife on the table in approval. Other rollers followed her lead, and a thunder of metal on wood filled the air, deeper and stronger than the applause of clapped hands.

When it faded, I felt cool emptiness behind me where Maceo's body had been, and the air no longer bore his scent. I glanced back to confirm the truth. He was gone.

My mother's elbow nudged my ribs.

"Mamá, stop," I said. "It's nothing."

She laughed.

32

SOFIA

But who could say? Perhaps I would not marry at all. In New York, single ladies could open tea shops. I read about it in *Peterson's Magazine*. It was quite respectable. Their clientele comprised mostly ladies, who craved a place to sit in public with their friends, and the owners hosted them with grace and charm. Ladies liked to stroll about in their best dresses, and tea shops gave them a destination, a place to rest after shopping.

Hosting little teas at home for one's friends was all very well, but one couldn't make a living at it. I poured tea excellently and knew all the graceful things to say and do. With Papa's fortune, I could easily buy a charming storefront and equip it. What fun it would be! Ordering all the little chairs, the tablecloths, silver cake stands, the pretty porcelain cups and plates and saucers . . . (Flowers and birds, probably. Like everything. I'd rather have china patterned like the Brooklyn Bridge, all thin silver lines like steel.) I'd stock a shelf or two with books so solitary ladies wouldn't need to fear appearing lonely, and my shop would have large bay windows facing the street so my patrons could showcase themselves for passersby. Gentlemen would find excuses to dawdle outside . . . window-shopping, as it were. I'd hire a French pastry chef and a girl or two to do the washing up, and I'd wear the most beautiful gowns. Yes, that would be a lively occupation.

Not here in Key West, of course, where everyone prefers coffee anyway—and what would be the point? So that a lot of tobacco strippers and cigar rollers would clomp in, wearing their flat shoes and gray work dresses, blathering on about wages and strikes?

No, New York was where I'd go. I'd wake each morning in my lovely flat overlooking Central Park, open my tea shop at ten, close at five, and then go home and dress for the theater—the opera—the symphony—

If I were to marry, I'd get a substantial dowry but immediately lose all my rights to it; I'd become my husband's property forever after. But if I did not marry, then all of Papa's fortune would come to me (when he died), and I could do as I liked.

A tea shop in New York. Or anything at all.

I wouldn't want to deal with his horrible cigar factory, of course. The smoke always clung to one's clothes. I'd leave that to the managers, or sell the whole enterprise. And perhaps even the same with the estates back in Cuba. Cash out the lot.

A wealthy heiress. I liked the sound of that.

Men would, too. And if I remained a spinster, I could do what I liked—not only with my money, but with them.

CHAVETA

"But why would you, of all people, want flour?" Loud, stout, and red-faced, the baker's boy had eaten too much of his own product.

I glared. "Why ask questions?"

He rolled his eyes and took the tin cup from me. Handed it back full.

"What I mean to say, Chaveta, is that no man would ever picture you over a stove, baking like a good wife."

"Mind your own business," I snapped. "Girls don't picture you at all."

His dumb laugh followed me out the door.

ZENAIDA

Late that Thursday evening, after Maceo had moved his things into a room at our boardinghouse and dusk had fallen over the city, he came into the kitchen and invited me for coffee. All my chores were finished.

I looked eagerly at my mother. "May I?"

She nodded her permission, and though she did not speak or raise her head from the garlic she was mincing, her eyes gleamed.

"I'll wait on the porch," Maceo said.

In the front hall mirror, I smoothed my hair and ran my hands down the bodice of my pale-yellow dress. My dark eyes shone, my lips were pink and plump, and all the curves of my face tilted toward joy.

As Chaveta knew and my mother surely intuited, I had been in love with Maceo since I was fourteen, since he came to us one night straight from the countryside of Cuba with a bullet in his shoulder and a fever. My mother had removed the bullet and sewn shut the wound; I'd made poultices from the live-forever plant that grew in our backyard and kept them on his shoulder, sponging his forehead with cool water as he ranted. Once, he woke, desperate and crying, delirious with fever. "Mamá?" he kept saying, clutching my hand. When the last fever finally broke, he opened his eyes and gazed upon me. "Are you an angel?" he asked. A cliché, it moved me deeply nonetheless, and I had thought of him ever since.

Our bond—if it was one—had been utterly chaste, and since then, I'd had only a schoolgirl's fantasy spun from glances and gossamer: a handsome soldier, fighting bravely far away; a besotted girl, waiting— no more than a storybook romance.

Yet here he was, in the flesh. Tall, muscled, quiet.

He gave me his arm and we walked along Thomas Street. I quivered with pride to be seen with him, with excitement to feel his body's warmth so near.

I imagined we'd stroll to some staid establishment open late: Armonía's Sweet Baked Goods, or one of the tiny Jamaican or Bahamian corner shops where everyone spoke English but still welcomed Cubans, or even the restaurant at the Hotel Russell.

Instead we turned right on Southard and then left onto Duval. Next door to the San Carlos was a café that served spirits. Light and laughter always poured from its door. I'd never been inside.

"Come," he said.

I hesitated.

"What?"

"They gamble in there."

He laughed. "They gamble everywhere."

Still I hung back. "My mother might not like it."

"Your mother doesn't gamble?"

"Of course not."

"She doesn't play bolita?"

"Of course she does." She set coins aside each week as religiously as some mothers set aside coins for the collection plate on Sunday. But bolita was hardly gambling, in the sinning sense. All the families went to the San Carlos on Saturday evening for the bolita drawing. Grandmothers, little children—it was all quite wholesome in Key West.

We were proud of our clean bolita games. There was none of the deception that clung to bolita in the gambling dens of Tampa and Havana, where the winning ball was weighted with lead or placed in ice all day so it could easily be detected by the rummaging hand of the selector. "That's not the same," I said.

"Gambling is gambling," Maceo said. "Anyway, we're not here to gamble. We're here to get a coffee, be part of life."

Part of life. Yes, I hungered for that. I looked at the open door of the café. Red laughter spilled out into the street. Perhaps it wasn't quite the Club des Hashischins in Paris, where authors like Hugo and Dumas (along with other men of letters) were reputed to eat hashish resin crushed into a paste with honey and pistachios, and then share their wild visions late into the night on the banks of the tree-lined Seine. But it wasn't nearly as dull as darning boarders' socks at my mother's wooden table, either.

"Okay," I said. "Just for a while."

I took his arm again, and we went in.

Inside, the wood-paneled room was clouded with cigar smoke and crowded with mostly men, though a few women sashayed around in bright ruffled dresses and perched on various laps. Each wooden table bore a glass-shaded kerosene lamp or a flickering candle. The smoke was so thick my eyes began to sting. A violinist fiddled loudly in the corner, his brisk melody punctuated by the dominoes' clack, the roll of dice, and the quick slap of cards on the tables. At every table, a boisterous argument was in full flower.

At one of the large round tables, Feliciano Galván was waving his cigar about, debating with two older lectors. All three had small notebooks rife with inky scribblings in front of them. Half-full whiskey glasses littered the table.

Maceo tugged me toward an empty table at the back.

In the corner, Líbano the cafetero sat methodically playing chess with old Señor Gutierrez.

"Líbano!" I felt suddenly shy, as if a different slice of him had just been revealed.

He smiled amiably up at me.

"I didn't know you gambled." *Oh, Zenaida. What an awkward, judgmental thing to say.*

His smile widened, and he shrugged. "I don't play for money. I play to learn."

"Ha!" said Señor Gutierrez. "He plays to win! He plays to grind old men like me into the ground."

I laughed. Maceo pulled out a chair for me at the next table, the two of us sat down, and I had hardly smoothed my skirts before young Valdés was there to take our order.

"Two coffees," said Maceo. He turned to me. "Cream?"

I nodded.

"Sugar?"

Smiling, I nodded again. At my mother's boardinghouse, cream and sugar were luxuries reserved for the boarders. My mother and I drank our coffee black: a cup in the morning, a cup at noon, a cup at three o'clock to get us through the evening's work.

Young Valdés whisked away.

"But this Thorn, this mystery poet, is clearly a man of learning," Feliciano was saying in his loud, deep lector's voice. "His rhymes are unpredictable, his vocabulary broad and deep."

"But I don't care for all this aesthetic innovation," said one of the other lectors. "The Spanish sonnet is a perfect form. It needs no so-called improvement."

Young Valdés placed the cups down in front of us, frothy and hot. Maceo paid him, and he must have given something extra, because young Valdés gave a little whistle, and Maceo, seeing that I'd noticed, smiled that small, proud smile men get when they've been admired.

He began to describe the recent raids and skirmishes in which he'd fought, and the room melted away.

35

CHAVETA

Full of Friday-night dinner at the boardinghouse, I slapped a nickel on the table.

Señora Baliño clucked her tongue and pushed it back at me.

"You're my daughter's friend, child."

She carried the dishes away.

I left the nickel there.

In the parlor, two cigar workers slouched in chairs, playing checkers and arguing about which Spanish governor of Cuba was the biggest bastard.

Zenaida came downstairs, glancing around.

"No one's looking," I said.

She handed me the wrapped stack. "You're sure you don't mind?"

I touched her blackened fingertips and smiled. "I'm sure."

She walked me out onto the porch that ran the length of the building.

"Don't get caught, Chaveta. If you get caught, they'll make you tell."

Her soft whisper. My name on her lips. Her dark, worried eyes: they were all I could see.

"Never," I swore.

I walked home in dusk.

36

ZENAIDA

After Chaveta left, I sat at the long table doing the books by lamplight. My mother was rearranging the sacks and boxes of provisions in the pantry.

"Everything all right?" she asked.

"It all adds up. Good profits this week." I turned the book around to show her.

She leaned to look and nodded. My mother liked the way our ledgers looked in my school-neat hand.

"But, Mamá?" I hesitated.

She turned back to her work. "Speak, child. Closed mouths don't get fed."

"Mamá, I think we could make more."

"Why do we want to do that?"

"You always say you're tired."

She straightened the sacks of black beans on a shelf. "I'll rest in heaven, child."

"If you charged just a little more money per room, though, and a little more per meal, you could take some time off once in a while. Even hire another girl to help."

"What am I going to do with time off?" She laughed. "Go to the opera? Girl, running this place gives me purpose. We make enough to get by, and we do a service for our fellow man, and for Cuba. Only thing I got to save up for is you, and there's money under my mattress for your future."

"Oh, Mamá, you know that's not—"

"You're my child. You work as hard as I do." That was far from true. "You got a right to be secure." Smiling, she came over to where I sat and laid a light hand on my head. It gave me a holy feeling. "But I won't be charging more."

We stayed that way for a moment, like flesh turned to statues, the pen in my hand, her palm on the crown of my head, as if setting her stance and my acceptance in stone.

"Okay," I finally said, breaking the spell. She stroked my hair and moved to the other side of the table, dragging out the long bench to sit down.

"Look," she said, facing me. "On the plantation, I was raised to be a Christian." I didn't interrupt. "In Havana, when I met your papa, I became a socialist. Okay? So I believe in Jesus, and I believe in Marx. They got plenty in common. But I'm also a daughter of Yemayá, which means I don't have to wait for no man to make the world right. Waiting takes away your power. I can live the right way now."

She took a guava from the wooden bowl between us and bit into it, watching me as she chewed.

"This is my ability." Her gesture took in the guavas, the oil lamp, the long wooden table, the whole room, the boardinghouse itself. "This right here. From each according to her ability. So I give it."

I nodded, rubbing my finger across the dried columns of ink.

"And the men who stay here, who eat here—they need this. Not every good man can afford a house and a wife. So I give them a roof over their heads, food in their bellies, and a smile and soft word when they feel low. To each according to his need." She took another bite and stared off, chewing. "I can't throw the yoke from the shoulders of Cuba, and I can't kill the masters of the plantations. But the men who stay here? One way or the other, they can."

She finished the guava and smiled, licking her fingers.

"If I ask a higher price than I need, I'm fast on my way to becoming a bourgeois. Your papa wouldn't like it."

My father's dead, I didn't need to say. I knew what her reply would be.

Not to me, girl. Not to me.

"You're a real radical, Mamá."

"Your father didn't love me for my looks alone." She laughed. "Who do you think came up with half those crazy ideas he used to print?"

This startled me. "What?"

She laughed again. "Yes, my daughter. Sometimes, lying there in bed together late at night, all tired after loving, I would just start talking. Just idle crazy talk, you know? Whatever wild notion came into my head. And your papa would lie there listening with his arm around me, saying next to nothing, or once in a while asking a little question. And I'd ramble until we both drifted off to sleep—just beautiful dreams of the way the world could be. A better way.

"Then we'd wake up the next morning, and I'd forget all about it. Just late-night nonsense after love, you know?

"But then, three, four days later, your papa would sit down at the table, proud as a cat with a lizard in its mouth, shake open the latest edition of his paper, and start reading his column to me—full of my own ideas! But sounding much more learned, of course. Big words, long sentences. I was so surprised. First, second time it happened, it almost shocked me out of my shoes. Then I got more used to it. I'd just smack him on the arm or something. *Go on, you.* It got so I had to be careful what I said at night." She smiled at me. "I didn't want him getting killed over some wild notion of mine." Her face fell. "Not that it did any good."

We sat in silence.

"Did he ever put your name to any of it?"

"My name?" Her laugh was soft and wry. "Oh no, sweet girl. Never."

I frowned. "That's not fair."

"Zenaida, no. It was fair. Ideas are free. If he liked them, they were his to take. A gift. And putting his fine language to them and putting them out in the public world: well, that was his gift to me. No one would have listened to the half-baked ramblings of some . . ." She settled her cheek in her palm and gazed off. "Maybe in future days, daughter. Maybe in future days."

"But he kind of stole them."

She gave me a stern look. "No, he didn't. It wasn't theft. Don't let me hear you say that. It was mutual—a mutual gift. Mine to him, his to me. Ours to the world. Besides," she said, tucking hair behind my ear, "if he'd wanted to steal from me, he could have just kept quiet and not read his columns out to me. I never would have known."

I nodded. It was true.

My mother could not read or write.

37

Sofia

"But can't you make it just a little looser down the sides?"

Frowning, our dressmaker, Hildita, muttered something under her breath, her brow riddled with wrinkles. We stood in my dressing-chamber before the cheval mirror. She had draped me in light linen but pinned it tight as a corset.

It was a bright Saturday morning, and she had come to cut and pin my gown for the pageant, all creamy silk satin imported from Seville, while my grandmother, propped in an armchair in the corner, had delivered her entirely outmoded fashion opinions until she'd fallen asleep.

Truly, *irascible* was far too slight a word for the years of assiduous effort my grandmother had devoted to developing the trait. I did not know her before she was old, of course, her voice rasped and croaky; her fingers swollen with fat and permanently curled, their nails thick and yellow; the flesh collapsed in folds around her sharp eyes, brown and shiny as coffee beans, missing nothing. Perhaps she was lighthearted once, or generous, or pretty. Perhaps she used to dance, when she could wear those clothes that filled the attic trunks.

To me, she'd always just been Grandmama, grouchy and complaining and clomping about the house in her tightly laced black boots, reeking of too much orange-blossom perfume, as if she were trying to smother the scent of decay.

My mother avoided her—and no wonder. I could not imagine permitting my husband's mother to live in my own house, even if she were an angel, which Grandmama most decidedly was not. She picked at my mother constantly, calling her clothes too showy, too pretty, too romantic "for a woman of your age," her hair not scraped back tightly enough against her skull. It was as if she wanted my mother to dress like another widow in the house. One was enough, in my view—or one too many, even: the drab black clothes, the tedious piety. Grandmama did spoil me a bit, escorting me to Delaney's or White's or Ferguson's and telling me to pick what I liked, telling the shopkeepers to put it on her account. But it wasn't worth it, having to listen to her dour remarks and walk so slowly down the streets.

Grandfather was a tyrant, Father said—I had never met him; he died in Cuba—as strict with his wife and children as he was with the slaves. "We just dressed better," Father said, "and ate more." Perhaps it explained why Grandmama was so bitter, so sour. The strange, stooped defeat of her gait. I couldn't imagine letting a husband beat me, but apparently it was the custom then.

I'd kill him with poison or ground glass. I'd serve it sweetly, and then he'd be dead.

As soon as my grandmother's snores rattled loud and regular, signaling a brief respite of privacy, I had prevailed upon Hildita for another project—but she was being most uncooperative.

"Just a day dress," I whispered again, wrenching the linen away from my ribs. "But even looser. Not a gown. I want something a bit more free, you see—something that lets me breathe." *Like a worker's dress,* I thought but did not say, thinking of how easily Chaveta moved. "And much less fabric in the skirt," I said. "I want it to flow as I walk, not hamper me with all that extra draping."

"Señora Robles!" Hildita called down the corridor in a tone of panic. "Señora Robles?"

My grandmother startled in her armchair. "What? What's this?" I sighed. "Oh, for heaven's sake."

My mother's steps came up the stairs and down the long hallway. "What is it?"

"Young Señorita Robles wants something very different," said Hildita. "Very new."

My grandmother snorted, crossed herself, and closed her eyes again. Hildita repeated my requests.

"But this seems very strange, my daughter."

"I just want it to be modern, Mamá."

Hildita was shaking her head and murmuring to Jesus.

"It's only one dress," I said, "and only for the day. Of course I'll still wear proper gowns to dinner and when we go out in the evening."

"Nonsense," said my grandmother.

"It's simply practical," I explained.

"Practical?" my mother echoed. "For precisely what activities do you require this practicality?"

True enough. I inspected myself in the looking glass. I couldn't very well tell her about my tea shop dream, much less explain that this dress was my way of practicing to be the proprietress of such a place, the way Zenaida and I had once dressed up in Grandmama's finery as opera stars and queens.

"A dress with less cloth would cost less," I said.

She stared at me. "Since when has money ever crossed your mind?"

"It crosses it quite often," I said. "Just because I do not practice small economies doesn't mean I'm unaware." Indeed, I had drawn up two different budgets for my future: one for my tea shop and apartment

Joy Castro

in Manhattan, if I remained unmarried, and another for my wedded bliss (a pied-à-terre on Central Park, with our main estate back in Oriente or Andalusia or wherever my husband happened to be from). I'd read plenty of real-estate advertisements in Papa's copies of the *New York Times*, and I'd labored, too, over the long gray columns of the stock market, trying to master how it all worked. Sometimes I thought I had inherited my mother's form and my father's mind. (Much better than the reverse, to be sure.)

"Do let me try it," I said. "Just this once. I want something more comfortable." I gripped the sides of the dress and shook the fabric where it was pinned so close to my ribs. "More freedom."

"Freedom?" My mother laughed. "Comfort? You forget yourself, my daughter. Which day in my life do you suppose I've felt comfortable or free?"

"But my life will be very different from your life, Mamá."

Hildita crossed herself and clutched her heart. "Oh, Señora Robles. These young people. She doesn't know what she's saying."

My mother's eyes fixed on mine.

"Oh, I think she does," she said. "I think she knows quite well." She turned to Hildita. "Make her any dress she wants," she said. "Do whatever she asks." She looked at me, her face transformed into the stiff, beautiful mask she so often showed to Papa. "See how you like your freedom when you get it."

She spun and stalked out of the room, her spine straight with whalebone and fury.

136

38

CHAVETA

Friday night.

Black heat rising from my brothers' and sisters' bodies. Mosquitoes' sharp whine. Symphony of snores. Smell of dried piss.

I rose, slid the broadsides from my crate of clothes, slipped out to the kitchen shed.

Poured flour in a small pail, took it to the yard.

Pumped. Used a stick to mix the water in.

Grabbed a paintbrush, the paste, and the broadsides, and slipped into the dark streets.

The next morning, my mother had to prod me from bed. I walked to the factory in a fog. My thoughts slid thick and slow as snails.

But in the galley, my fingers moved as quickly as ever. One leaf for strength, one for fragrance, one for combustion. Roll each leaf into a tube, roll all three of them together, chop the ends. Wrap them in binder leaves. Roll the whole thing in a wrapper. Smooth and seal it all together with tree resin from the little pot. Shape it, press it, roll it smooth. Pinch the tip. Trim, trim, trim, smooth. Do it again. And again. And again.

But fog rolled through my brain. My eyelids sagged. Even my shoulders drooped forward.

The morning's readings from *El Yara* did nothing to wake me up, nor did the earnest chapter by Proudhon.

"You need extra," whispered Líbano when he came with his urn and poured my black brew.

Even smiling back took work.

Lunch at Zenaida's mother's boardinghouse only made things worse. Back at my bench, heavy with goat meat and plantains, I tried to focus. Roll each leaf into a tube, roll them together, chop the ends. Wrap them. Seal it all together with resin from the little pot. Shape, press, roll. Pinch the tip. Trim, trim, trim, smooth.

Anna Karenina, Anna Karenina—Who cared? A woman's so-called virtue was an overrated thing.

But at the windows, townswomen clustered, straining to hear each word, Zenaida among them, twirling her yellow parasol.

I felt surly. No lines made me rap my chaveta on the table.

Whenever I mustered the energy to glance up, Feliciano's dark eyes swung to mine. Strange.

The day wound on. Late afternoon. Gold light slanting in.

Roll them each into tubes, roll the tubes together, chop their ends. Wrap it. Seal it with resin from the little pot. Shape, press, roll. Pinch the tip. Trim and smooth. Ninety-seven cigars sat stacked on my table. Feliciano's voice droned on until, thank God, the chapter ended. The book snapped shut.

"I'll close a different way today," he said, "for a new voice has arrived in Key West."

I glanced up.

"A powerful voice," he said. "The voice of a poet and a patriot. His majestic words have appeared around the town, yet he cloaks himself in mystery."

I looked out the window. I could not see Zenaida.

"This stranger calls himself The Thorn. I have been observing his work, and I am greatly impressed. If one of you knows him—if one of you *is* he—I invite you, I implore you, to make yourself known to me, to tell me. I will reveal his secret to no one. I long only to make his acquaintance, to clasp his hand in fervent friendship, to celebrate our brotherhood, to learn the workings of his mind."

He pulled a folded paper from his pocket.

"This very dawn, as if by a genie's magic, this new poem appeared on walls around the city."

He read to us:

Whose Jungle?

Some men proclaim the whole wide earth
belongs to mighty Spain,
that roaring beast with flashing eye
and glossy golden mane.
They say Spain is the jungle's king,
its paw upon the globe.

But I call Spain a house cat,
wrapped in a threadbare robe.

Some say a conquered country
must learn to love its chains.
Humility befits the ruled,
the schoolmaster explains.

But Cuba is a mighty dream,
just waiting to be born.

The lion's paw can't crush me,
because I am
The Thorn

A hushed moment, and then chavetas thundered on the wood.
An elbow nudged me. Graciela whispered, "Are you okay?"
I looked down.
On the table, my hands lay still. My fingers empty.

39

CHAVETA

Just before dusk, like every Saturday, I swung by Soto & Sons' Butcher Shop as it was about to close. Ramón, the second son, took off his apron, got his rope and pole and gutting knife, and locked up. I had my father's pistol. We set off on foot for the groves of buttonwood trees.

I was not fond of Ramón. At all. He bored me and had a nose like a potato. But I needed his help. And he knew it.

Outside the town, I found the direction of the wind. *Crepuscular.* That's the word for deer, said Líbano—for all animals that come out at dawn and dusk. I found a place downwind from where the deer would appear and scraped a spot with my boot on the dusty ground. Ramón did the same. Scorpions scuttled. We lay down on our bellies.

"No," I said. "Don't touch me."

He pulled his hand off my hip.

I watched for deer.

It was meat for my family, yes, but it was also practice for Spaniards. Each deer was a Spaniard. I aimed for the heart.

The butcher's son tied its back legs to a branch to gut it and let it bleed. He cut it down. We tied its forlorn ankles to the pole and hauled it back to his shop. He severed it into cookable portions, wrapped the best cuts in paper for me, and put the rest on ice for tomorrow's customers.

In the back room of the butcher shop, surrounded by dead dangling beasts and blood, we sat on the bench against the wall.

I paid him with my hand. His eyes rolled back in his head.

At home, my mother cooked the venison, a late feast, in time for my father to stagger in from the weekly bolita game at the San Carlos. Everyone went to bed happy and fat.

When I have no luck with the deer, we eat rice and beans, and the young ones stare at me. Then I go out Sunday morning to hunt up a brace of wild doves.

Little Spaniards of the air.

40

ZENAIDA

"What do you think your mother would want to be," I asked, "if she didn't have to be your mother?"

It was late on Sunday afternoon. The three of us walked along the seashore where the road broke off from Front Street, north of the Marine Hospital. Sofia had linked her arm through mine and was talking ad nauseam about her tea shop in New York.

"If she weren't my mother?" Sofia wrinkled her nose and laughed. "What else would she be?"

Down along the water's edge, Chaveta kept pace with us, pitching shells and rocks into the sea, her trouser legs rolled up and her boots dangling from her neck by their tied laces.

"That's what I mean," I said. "If your mother could be anything she wanted to be, anything she was good at." A brisk wind blew. "Like a man."

Sofia looked at me strangely. "I've never thought about it. What would my mother want? All she wants is for my father to be more romantic. Serenade her and so on, like when they were courting in Havana."

"But your mother likes poetry a great deal," I said. "And novels. Maybe she would have wanted to be a teacher." I gazed out at the vast blue horizon. "Or even a writer herself."

Sofia gave a perturbed little snort. "What an absurd thing to even wonder," she said. "What mothers *want*."

"My mother could be a tailor," called Chaveta from the water's edge. "She sews all our clothes, and they always fit."

"In a manner of speaking," Sofia murmured.

I nudged her ribs and gave her a warning look.

"Well, what about your mother, then?" Sofia asked. "If she didn't take in boarders, I mean." She kicked a little rock. "I suppose she could work in a grand house, or in a hotel."

"My mother does seem happy, doing what she does," I said. "Though she's often tired." Out in the sea, two dolphins broke the water, their arched gray bodies gleaming. "But to tell the truth . . ." I hesitated, feeling shy. "I think she could have been a doctor."

Sofia laughed, then looked over at me. "Oh," she said, dropping my arm. "You mean it."

"She knows how to cure almost anything," I said. "Tea from the gumbo-limbo tree for infections, and its bark for insect stings."

"Everyone knows that," called Chaveta.

"Well, and princewood bark to cure malaria, too," I said, "and mangrove leaves for healing wounds." I thought of Maceo's fevered brow, his restless days spent twisting and tossing in the bed. "And the live-forever plant for nearly everything."

"Just because she knows a lot of plants doesn't mean she'd be a good doctor," said Sofia. "More like a witch, if you ask me. Doctors have to train in hospitals and so on, and cut people open and chop off legs and learn anatomy."

I didn't really have an answer to that, so I fell silent. We walked on. I watched Chaveta walk along, her easy rhythm next to the waves.

More than once, I had wondered if such a diagnosis could be exactly right: if my mother truly was a witch. She seemed so wise, so powerful, so mysterious. When she took off her blue headwrap, wild snakes of her hair twisted around her shoulders, and I'd often wondered if it was an encounter with a woman like my mother that had made the ancient Greeks devise the myth of Medusa. My mother's muscled arms and healing potions—the knife strapped to her thigh—would surely terrify those pale ancient men afraid of thunder, who needed their women tame and docile by the hearth.

My mother said that many women back in Cuba knew which plants could cure, which plants could kill. They had to, when there was no pharmacy within a day's ride, and when white Creoles enacted cruelties on their flesh for sport. Women had to heal the sick and mend the wounded with the plants that grew nearby.

Our garden behind the boardinghouse was not as beautiful and groomed as the Robleses', but we had a mango tree, an avocado tree, pineapple plants, guava trees, and coconut palms. My mother tended a kitchen garden, too, where she grew garlic, onions, tomatoes, and herbs, as well as the botanicals. The live-forever plant grew there—the one I had bound Maceo's wounds with. But more dangerous plants, as well.

One day a year or so ago, I had been out noodling in the yard, crouched down among the herbs, picking posies, humming a little tune to myself, and thinking vague romantic thoughts about Maceo.

A strong hand gripped my shoulder, and I cried out.

My mother. I hadn't heard her approach. She shook me, her face stern and angry. I lost my balance and fell onto the earth.

"Never touch that plant, child. Never. This plant is only for the direst need." She pulled me to my feet and shook me again. "Are you hearing me?"

I nodded.

Her face softened. Her grip on my shoulder eased.

"Only the direst need," she repeated. "If an evil enemy threatens you and you have no other way, make a tea from these leaves. Sweeten it with extra sugar. Lots of sugar. Your enemy will soon be gone."

I nodded.

"If you have a baby in you and it can't come out, take one section of one leaf, no bigger than your littlest fingernail"—she held hers up to show me—"and drink the tea yourself. The baby will leave you."

I looked toward the gate. Sofia was waiting.

"I have to go, Mamá."

My mother looked up. "Did you hear what I'm just telling my daughter?"

Sofia's smile was immediate and sweet. "No, ma'am. What was that?"

"Never you mind. You girls go enjoy yourselves."

And we did.

Beside me at the shore, Sofia took my arm again.

"But, Zenaida." Her voice was low and confiding, with an oddly vulnerable note. I glanced over. "Let me put a question to you." To my surprise, her eyes and face looked naked, her expression more honest and confused than I'd ever seen it before. She glanced at Chaveta, who was some distance away pitching shells into the waves, and looked back at me. "A private question."

The change in her startled me. My heart filled with sympathy, which it did too readily, and I melted, as I so often had with her. There was so much Sofia didn't understand—because she'd never had to.

"Yes, of course," I said, my voice gentle. "What is it?"

"How will I ever know," she said, "if a man loves me for myself, and not for my father's money?"

It drew me up short. It was a question I'd never have to face.

"Oh, Sofia!" I said. "But you are pretty! And accomplished. You dance well, you have a good education . . . you know French. You play the piano—"

"Only passably," she muttered.

"Oh, but come now, Sofia. You sing, you can embroider—"

Her laugh was harsh. "Do men really care about stitched pictures?"

"Yes, all right. But still—"

"And even all these things you list: they are just things *about* me. Things I've been taught because my parents paid the tutors. The accoutrements of a rich man's wife." Her clenched fist struck her chest. "They are not *me*. How will I ever know if a man loves *me*?"

I fell quiet. I felt sad for her—and startled. I'd never before considered the benefit of poverty, of having nothing but oneself to offer. If Maceo were indeed to love me, it wouldn't be for the hope of future gain.

"I do see what you mean."

"And even if I do go to New York and start my tea shop," Sofia continued, "and if it were to become a success—which I'm quite sure it would, incidentally—then, even so, a suitor might want me only for my wealth, however independently gained."

"Indeed," I reflected. "For men are no more virtuous than women, and greed warps people's hearts."

Sofia twisted her hands. "But what can I do?" she asked. "I mean, aside from giving my fortune to the poor, or something equally mad." She shook her head.

"I suppose," I said—my mind veering from Sofia's plight and toward a larger realization, the words coming slowly from my mouth as my mind groped to find them—"this is the torment men must always face." Again, I felt startled. Never before had I considered such a thing.

She looked at me, impatient. "Whatever do you mean?"

"This torment of not knowing," I explained. "For men can never be certain if we truly love them for themselves, or merely for the creature comforts they provide."

Sofia stared at me as we walked in tandem. An abrupt laugh barked from her lips.

"But that's what men are *for*." She laughed again, waving her hands as if to wave away flies. All vulnerability had disappeared from her face.

I felt foolish and naive, as I so often did with Sofia. I looked down toward the water. Chaveta was ankle deep in the waves. Sofia's eyes followed my gaze.

"Are you going to enter the pageant, Chaveta?" she called.

Chaveta made a sound difficult to categorize but not at all polite. "Don't be ridiculous," she called over her shoulder.

"Turning yourself out to your best advantage isn't ridiculous," Sofia objected. "It's a skill, a talent." She already knew I'd promised my mother I'd enter. She'd reacted effusively and with great curiosity, asking about what I would wear, how my hair would be done, and so on.

Chaveta veered up the sand toward us. "But the girl who can pay to have the most beautiful dress made," she said, "can still lose, if she's too skinny or too fat for the judges' taste. The girl who can pin up her hair in an elegant way still loses if the judges think her features too thick, her eyes too small."

"Yes, but of the true beauties—"

"The ritual itself breeds an ugliness in women," said Chaveta. "I'd rather have a friend with small eyes than one with a small soul."

I smiled. "Better a weak chin than a weak mind."

"Exactly," said Chaveta. "It's all just bones, inherited from our ancestors and shaped by evolution."

"Chaveta!" Sofia fluttered her fan. "There's no need to blaspheme."

Chaveta just laughed.

We'd drawn near a manchineel tree. I stopped and pointed up.

"You know," I said, "my mother knows which plants are dangerous, too. Like those. The tree of death, the Spaniards call it. Just one leaf from it boiled into tea can kill a man." We gazed up into its harmless-looking leaves. Black-spined iguanas lounged on the branches. "And those fruits."

"The little green apples?" Sofia said.

"Yes. Iguanas love them, but for people, a single bite is fatal. They say one apple can kill twenty men."

Chaveta had drawn close to us. "Don't touch the bark, is all I know," she said. "The sap will burn your skin."

"In the olden days, the Calusa people would put the sap in their enemies' water supply," I said. "And they'd tip their arrowheads with it. That's what my mother says, anyway. And if you're foolish enough to burn the wood," I added, "the smoke can blind you."

"It all sounds so *Count of Monte Cristo*," Sofia murmured, staring up. "One single leaf can kill someone?"

"Yes, if it's boiled in tea. Of course, you would have to add a great deal of sugar, I think, to disguise the taste. Or honey. Or sweet sherry, perhaps. And you would need to collect the leaves with a little cloth to protect your fingers." I thought about how careful one would have to be. "And not breathe any of the steam."

"Sailors who touch the bark and then take a piss—well, they remember Key West, that's for sure."

"Oh, Chaveta!" Sofia cried, slapping her arm. "Why must you always be so vulgar?"

Chaveta laughed. "Why must you be such a prude?"

We turned away from the manchineel tree and walked on, past Fort Zachary Taylor, as the sun sank toward the waterline.

41

MACEO

I wasn't born disloyal. My mother birthed me in her parents' hut on the sugar plantation in Camagüey owned by the man who'd gotten her with child—with me. She was thirteen.

I was four when I fingered the ridged flesh lacing her back, not knowing what it meant. Eight when she showed me the whipping pit, the belly-shaped hole in the dirt that had protected my unborn self when they beat her. Eleven when she died of fever. Fourteen when I escaped.

Until she died, my mother would smuggle me each extra scrap of meat she could, whispering that I was her boy, I would always be her boy, that the Virgen de la Caridad del Cobre watched over me, that I would become a man and deliver us from our oppressors, that I was a son of Chango. She had named me for a great warrior, she said, a great Black warrior. With cowrie shells, with herbs she gathered and ground into paste, she rubbed my collarbones, my shoulders, the little swells of muscle in my arms.

Hungry, I devoured all she gave. Her food, her touch, her murmured words of love, her promises of the power my future held. Growing fast, I strutted around the cooking fires at night with the other boys. We swung our little machetes, forged small so that we, too, could cut the cane all day.

At night, in our huts, two (or even three) boys to a hammock, our arms flung across each other in sleep or wrapped around each other for comfort, we discovered the tender root of bliss that lay between our legs, taking our pleasure with each other's bodies until sharp slaps from an auntie parted us. We began to know the furtive hand of shame, the soft, shy breath of our kisses replaced by a dance of secret glances and averted eyes until we could slip off into the trees.

Absorbed thus by my own cares and pleasures, I didn't know what it signified that my mother's face grew sharper, her dark eyes flamed brighter.

I didn't know she was wasting away.

When I escaped, I joined the rebels in the hills. Muttering around our small fires at dusk, we seethed for the demise of both slavery and Spain. Free Blacks, free Cuba. Never one without the other. We'd heard what happened in Santo Domingo, the fierce and bloody birth of Haiti. We knew the plantation owners in Cuba feared the same—and we knew Spain stoked those fears.

I grew to manhood. My machete was large and sharp; I carried a pistol and rifle. I'd proven myself in battle many times before I dared suggest a target. "This particular plantation has much wealth," I said, "and two hundred Black souls suffer there."

Two hundred meant liberating perhaps fifty strong men to join our forces, and women and children to stay behind, farming crops for us and caring for the elderly and sick. All we needed was to exterminate the overseers and the family. We rode west.

Few pleasures outranked that of shooting dead an overseer, and when it was a face one knew, the pleasure was twice as sweet. But we soon ran out of overseers, and we were running out of ammunition. "I'll take the master!" I yelled, racing up the stairs. I ran down the corridor to where I knew he'd retreated. "I'm here, sir, with reinforcements," I shouted, as if I'd come to save him. Then kicked in the door. His pistol was raised, aiming, but when he saw my face, he frowned. His arm wavered and fell to his side. He glanced around the room, confused, and my eyes followed his gaze. The leather chair where he'd dandled me on his knee, run his hand over my head, called me *a good-looking little chap, if woolly.* To him, it must have felt like fondness. Pride, perhaps. The crystal bowl on his desk—he'd fished hard candies from it and put them in my mouth.

I lifted my machete high.

"But—my son!"

"But my mother," I replied.

And cut him down.

42

Sofia

That cafetero came again, bearing a message for my father. The girl showed him into the drawing room, where I was embroidering another stupid tea towel for my trousseau.

"Go," I said.

She went. I set my stitching aside.

He stood in the center of the room, clutching the note from his employer.

I rose and held out my hand. "I'll take it."

He bowed slightly and gave me the envelope, which I laid on the credenza.

"Take my hand," I said.

His eyes crimped with confusion and fear. "Oh, miss. I could not."

"Don't be afraid." I laid my hand on his. "Go ahead," I said. "You may."

Slowly, glancing about, he took my hand and lifted it.

"Kiss it."

His dark eyes darted all around. "I dare not, miss. I could not."

"But you must. Kiss it, I say. I insist."

He bent his head and pressed his soft lips nervously against it. I turned it over in his hand.

"Again."

His breath trembled hot in the cup of my hand. His mouth pressed my palm.

My thumb and fingers gripped his jaw. I squeezed. I dug my nails into his flesh so hard he whimpered. His hurt, soft eyes met mine, questioning.

"Tell no one," I said.

He nodded in my grasp. "No, miss," he whispered.

I released him.

"Now go." I waved toward the back of the house—a graceful little wave, like a duchess's, dismissing him. "Tell the girl I said she's to give you something to eat for your trouble."

He backed out, bowing, not daring to meet my eyes.

I sat down, smoothing my skirts over my lap, where a pleasurable heat had begun to pulse. He was good practice for larger game.

43

ZENAIDA

Thursday. Laundry day. All the sheets and towels and pillowcases billowed on clotheslines in the yard, along with all the clothes—pants, shirts, socks, ragged underwear—of the men who lodged with us. My back ached as proof, and my hands were sore, the skin dry. Scrubbing the sweat and stink out of strangers' clothes was a future I did not relish.

After we washed the supper dishes, I sat with my mother on the front porch, my eyes closed, neither of us speaking. We were too spent. Our hands lay in our laps. Dusk rolled in, then night.

I heard the sound of hooves and opened my eyes. Maceo trotted up on his brown mare and slid to the ground.

"Señora Baliño. Señorita Baliño." He nodded to each of us in turn. "With your permission, ma'am, may I take your daughter to the café?"

She glanced at me and gave a little laugh. "It looks like it," she said.

Apparently, I had not concealed my smile. All my exhaustion had mysteriously disappeared.

At the café, the lectors were debating. Feliciano sat at the central round table with Señor Casuso, Señor Lacedonia, and Señor Ruiz—together with young Eduardo Salazar and Señor Robles, who got to sit there, I suppose, by virtue of being rich.

Around the table stood various workmen, crowding close to listen. Chaveta stood there, too, hands on hips, hair knotted in a low bun. I touched her elbow as Maceo and I passed; she gave me a smile and nod.

Maceo and I settled at our small table nearby, where we could hear the lectors easily, and he ordered us two cafecitos and a whiskey for himself.

In the corner sat Líbano, playing chess with Señor Gutierrez again. Líbano glanced up at me and smiled. I liked his smile, because it always filled his eyes, too, and made the skin around them crinkle. Señor Gutierrez, following his gaze, turned around, saw me, gestured at the chessboard, and shrugged, raising his eyes heavenward. I smiled. He was such a gentle old man.

The lectors were arguing about the Grito de Yara as if it had happened yesterday next door, though it occurred in Manzanillo, in the east of Cuba, on October 10, 1868, two full years before I was born. I'd heard it a thousand times: Carlos Manuel de Céspedes freed all the slaves on his own sugar plantation and called for Cuba's freedom from Spain.

"Céspedes looks noble, certainly, from our vantage point. But to be fair," said Señor Casuso, "it was much simpler for someone like Céspedes to free his slaves while declaring independence. He knew landowners in the east would support him."

"But how can you say that?" asked one of the workmen who stood in a circle around them.

"In the east, most rich Cuban landowners raise cattle, coffee, and tobacco. There are few sugar plantations. Only ten percent of the population suffers in slavery. It is not like in the west."

"Exactly," said Señor Ruiz. "No labor is so brutal and intense as working the sugar cane fields. No free man wants to work like that, and no plantation owner could afford to pay him enough to do so. Therefore, nothing is so profitable for the sugar plantations as slavery."

Our drinks arrived. Maceo paid.

Señor Lacedonia nodded. "Most Blacks in the eastern provinces are already free men: farmers, artisans, small merchants. If the enslaved population rebels, it is not such a vexing matter. But in the west, where the seat of power resides—and where the sugar plantations dominate the landscape—half or more of the population lives under slavery's yoke."

I sipped my coffee.

"Precisely," said Feliciano. "And if they rebel—especially if they rebel with violence against the masters, as the Africans did in Saint-Domingue—western Cuba will be bathed in blood. The plantation owners know that. Even if emancipation were peaceful, the plantations would collapse."

"Yes," said Sofia's father. "Without the high profit margin that slavery creates, the sugar plantations become just another business, and not a very sound one." He used his cigar to punctuate his point.

"Whereas now Cuba's sugar plantations generate a king's ransom every day," said Feliciano. "When slavery ends, the wealth that pours from Cuba into Spain's coffers will dry to a trickle, and the Pearl of the Caribbean could become just another piece of flotsam floating on the sea. The Spanish crown knows that, and those wealthy western Cubans know it, too. Today, Spain lines their pockets well. White Cubans in the west live in splendor, so they support continued Spanish rule, and slavery, because they love their own balances. But the white Cubans in the east are fighting to end both, with their Black brothers alongside them."

"Spain is pro-profit and pro-slavery," said Eduardo, "and so are its Cuban minions. Cowards they may be, but there's an economic logic to their backward ways."

"It's why Céspedes was right," said Feliciano. "Emancipation from slavery and freedom from Spain's colonial rule must go hand in hand. Independence from Spain means independence for all Cubans, not just those of fairer blood. All Cuban men must be free, or none of us is free." All of it had been said so many times before. My life had been saturated with such rhetoric.

"And all Cuban women," shot Chaveta.

"Yes, of course." Feliciano turned to her with a smile. "I am no ogre from the Stone Age. All Cubans."

"Ah, speaking of the women!" said Señor Lacedonia. "What is this new Russian novel you're reading at the Flores factory, young Galván? All the ladies in town are talking about it."

"As well they should!" said Eduardo. "It is highly romantic."

I didn't want their opinions to spoil *Anna Karenina* for me. I turned to Maceo. His whiskey glass and coffee cup sat empty.

"What do you think of all that?" I asked quietly. "The politics. The violence. You've seen it all up close."

"What the lectors say is true." His eyes did not meet mine. "In the east, there are few cane plantations. There is some violence. But not much," he said. "Most of the blood stays on the battlefield." He hailed the waiter and ordered more. His face was a handsome mask, a door that had closed.

44

MACEO

I wasn't born disloyal. These idealists in Key West, building their little utopia of racial harmony—they don't know what it's really like.

When I got back to Cuba, healed by Señora Baliño's potions and poultices and the love in Zenaida's eyes, I joined a new battalion of rebels, thinking I would be respected as an equal. But they had begun to institute the same old hierarchies: the whites in charge, the rest of us as servants.

At least the Spaniards were honest about it.

These Key West utopians haven't sweated in the stocks, been bitten by flies, broiling all day under the fucking Cuban sun, dragged there by their new white brothers in freedom—and for what? For taking a break to stretch my aching back when digging latrines for white men's shit? These Key West Cubans: they haven't been publicly beaten by their new white so-called brothers for "impertinence to an officer." I have a mind and spoke it, for which act I got thirty lashes in front of my supposed brethren. How different from slavery was that?

To hell with it. To hell with Cuban freedom and its lies of equality.

When my back healed, I stole my mare and struck out on my own. I wanted real freedom, with my own people, away from Spaniards and white Creoles and their plantations and their speeches and their proclamations and their whips. All I wanted was to find a palenque in the mountains, one of those secret communities of African fugitives who'd escaped from slavery. I wanted to be out of it all: I didn't give a damn about the "Free Cuba!" insurgents and their dream of freedom that still kept me doing their laundry and working their fields.

A small band of white Cubans found me in the forest. Freedom fighters, so-called. Overtook me, stripped me of my rifle, my pistol, my machete, my clothes, my dignity. Beat me ruthlessly. Kicked me until I bled. Six of them. Or five. Or six. I cannot say. I fainted. Woke. Lost consciousness again. Heard their laughter as they rode off.

Bleeding, smeared with mucus, drenched in my own piss, I limped to the river. My mare lifted her muzzle, dripping, and gazed at me with her benevolent dark eyes. I crawled into the water. I bathed and prayed to Ochún. I closed my eyes and saw my mother's face and cried.

I was eighteen.

45

ZENAIDA

At the lectors' table, Eduardo was describing Oblonsky, Anna Karenina's brother, who had made love to his children's governess and thrown his household into disarray when his wife found out.

"Women are beautiful, yes!" Eduardo said. "And very tempting, to be sure. But why do men so often break their marriage vows?"

"Why do men cheat?" Señor Robles laughed. "Wait until you're married. You will see. This is no mystery. Wives turn it into an anguish, an opera, an excuse for suffering. But there is no cause to suffer, and no mystery."

"But why?" persisted Eduardo.

"Look," Sofia's father went on. He stubbed out his cigar and leaned forward. "You have food at home in your pantry, right?"

Eduardo nodded. Around him, most of the others did, too.

"It's good food. If you were hungry, and your wife cooked it for you, you'd eat it, no?"

The workers laughed, agreeing.

"But then, let us say, for the sake of argument, you go on a trip. You travel all day. You are tired. You are hungry. Someone offers you a delicious piece of cake. Do you accept? Or do you say, 'No, thank you, there's food at home in my pantry, many miles from here'?"

Most of the men laughed and shrugged, nodded, glanced at each other. Feliciano's face was still.

"Of course you take the cake!" said Señor Robles. "And you enjoy it. Going hungry when you have a beautiful piece of cake in front of you—well, this makes no sense! Only a fool would refuse good cake out of loyalty to food back home in the pantry."

Feliciano's eyes were on him, softly glowing, but he said nothing. I felt sad for Sofia's mother, and for my own.

"You speak a sound logic!" said Señor Ruiz, laughing. "Though don't tell my wife I said so."

There was laughter. We all knew Señora Ruiz, formidable and stout.

Señor Robles continued. "And no man wants to be called a fool by other men." A smattering of applause rippled through the crowd. He looked around, satisfied. "I rest my case."

"There is one problem with your theory, sir."

Señor Robles, eyebrows raised, located Chaveta. "And what is that, girl?"

"Do I look like cake to you?"

A loud, lewd worker smacked his lips.

She lifted her chin in a quick jerk. "Eat me," she said, making a gesture with her hands that managed to be at once both vulgar and dismissive. The men burst into laughter. "But, sir," she said, turning back to Sofia's father. "To be serious. Women are not food."

Everyone's eyes swung back to Robles to see how he'd respond, but Chaveta went on, her cheeks flushed, her dark eyes bright.

"That sack of flour in your pantry?" she said. "It has no feelings, knows no tenderness. It made you no promises, feels no pain. And if another man came and took your flour, you'd call him a thief, but if he baked bread with it or poured it on the ground or set it on fire, the flour itself wouldn't care." She glanced around at everyone. "But women love, and we are loyal. Our feelings are the same as men's. And when someone betrays us"—she squinted directly at Robles—"we hate him."

"Ha!" exclaimed Robles. "A spitfire in our midst. Who are you, girl?"

"You well know, sir, that I am Chaveta. I have made cigars in your factory these four years."

"A chaveta, indeed. But you trim the point too fine." He glanced around, making sure his pun was appreciated. The men laughed; half of them were employed by him. "You work in my factory?"

"I am among your best rollers, sir, and a friend to your daughter."

"Well, no more!" He laughed again. "You can keep rolling cigars for me, since you say your work is good, but leave my daughter be. She needs no bad influences. She is trouble enough as she is."

The men laughed again, long and loudly. Many had daughters, and most had admired Sofia—from a careful distance.

In the corner, Líbano had stopped his game and was watching.

"Insurrection on the factory floor is bad enough," said Robles. "Insurrection at the dinner table I will not have."

The faint smile flickering at the corner of Chaveta's mouth went out.

LÍBANO

In 1512, before the Spaniards executed him, the priest asked Chief Hatuey if he would accept Jesus Christ as his savior so he could go to heaven.

Chief Hatuey asked if there were Spaniards there.

The priest said yes.

Hatuey said, "Then I would rather go to hell."

When I thought of this, I always laughed. Such gallantry and courage. I liked imagining the Spaniards' faces when he said it.

I could easily imagine Chaveta saying something of that nature.

The way her shoulders always were flung back, the swift way she walked. The way she spoke her views, no matter what. Her eyes defiant, if a little scared. The firm, quick way she wielded her knife at the workbench.

Sometimes when Chaveta's eyes flashed, I wondered if she was somehow descended from Chief Hatuey's line—in spirit, if not in flesh. (I did not know if Hatuey had left any children behind when the Spaniards bound him to the stake.)

I hoped Chaveta would never have to burn.

CHAVETA

Maribel. Tomas. Lisabeta. Jaime. Victor. One good thing about working in the factory was not caring for my little brothers and sisters all day. In my mother's face, my mother's body, loomed a weak, disheveled echo of my own. Once, she had looked like me.

I sat at the kitchen table studying a map of Cuba. She stood behind me loosening my braid. The little ones were asleep. Papi could have been anywhere.

"Do it for us," she said.

"Do what?"

Exasperated sigh. "The pageant, of course. What I told you before. Enter the pageant."

I twisted my head around to glare. "I will not."

"For the little ones. Think what fifteen dollars could do."

"I'm no prize cow," I said. "No girl is. It's a stupid custom, and everyone who submits to it is stupid."

"Fifteen dollars isn't stupid." Her hands smoothed my hair. "And you're such a pretty girl."

"I don't need fifteen dollars. I work for my money."

"Victor and Jaime won't grow right without more pork on their plates." Her fingers stroked my temples, my neck, made small firm spirals on my scalp. I couldn't concentrate on the map. My tired eyes closed. "Mari and Lisa need schoolbooks."

"I already give you money each week."

Her hands let me go. "Ay, why do you have to be so selfish?" Her footsteps behind me, up and down. Irritation. "It would take you two hours. Put on a dress, let me put your hair up, stand there and look pretty. And there's two weeks' wages in your hands."

"No."

"Even if you don't win, maybe some nice man sees you, some man with money, and—"

"No. Mami, no. Forget it. It's not happening."

She stepped around the table and stood across from me. Leaned on the table. Over the kerosene lamp, her eyes were dark slits.

"We'll see about that."

48

ZENAIDA

Both Feliciano and I had been invited to Sofia's house for dinner, so we walked there together as the sun set.

It was a great honor to have a lector staying in our boardinghouse, and I was grateful for the opportunity to linger over his slim leather-bound volumes of poetry when I cleaned his room, though I did wonder why he didn't stay at the Hotel Russell or some other hotel more befitting his station.

But if Feliciano had been troubled by the discrepancies between the accommodations at our boardinghouse and the luxuries to which he'd been accustomed at the mansion of the Salazars, he was far too much the gentleman to mention it. We had only checkers and dominoes to offer, not a billiards table, and while my mother was rightly proud of the two privies (one for the men and one for us) that stood in our yard—each with its stack of clean, rinsed leaves from the live-forever plant, so much smoother and fresher-smelling than old catalogs or almanacs that rested in other outhouses (and no less interesting: if you paid careful attention, you could read the green language of their veiny growth)—they were nothing like an indoor water closet with a chain you could pull to flush everything magically away.

Feliciano offered me his arm as we walked along, and I took it. Unfortunately, he made several poetical remarks about the sky's being set aflame, et cetera, which made the walk seem significantly longer than it was.

At last, we climbed the tiled steps of the Robles mansion. The maid Magdalena greeted us at the door and showed us to the dining room, which was laid in all its customary glory. Eduardo Salazar greeted Feliciano with a hearty embrace, his sister, Pura, smiled and curtseyed, and Sofia's sad-eyed mother embraced me warmly, as she always does. Sofia herself was draped in burgundy satin, her lips and cheeks so bright they looked rouged. Her grandmother, already seated, grunted by way of greeting. She and I understood each other: she knew I had no place at their table, and I knew she'd prefer to see me in a servant's dress, if there at all. Sofia's father pressed a quick drop of sherry upon both young men, and we all took our seats.

Julieta came around to pour wine, Magdalena and Gastón brought in dishes full of food and began to serve, and the general mood was convivial. Everyone was discussing the police arrest of some youths who had tried to set fire to a church, and how dangerous it could have been with the cool, dry winter we were having, the high winds that blew at night.

"With Key West's only fire engine up in New York for repairs, it's most fortunate those boys were caught," said Señor Robles. Sofia's grandmother muttered something about young people nowadays.

"But let us shift to happier topics," said Feliciano, drawing a folded paper from his breast pocket, "and consider another sort of flame." He unfolded the page. "I took the liberty of composing a sonnet in honor of Señorita Robles."

"Oh my!" Pura fluttered with excitement, blushing as furiously as if the poem had been penned for her. "Oh, Sofia! Did you hear?"

Sofia's smile was smug and cool. "Do read to us," she said.

"If my host will permit me," said Feliciano.

"Have I any choice in the matter?" exclaimed Señor Robles, laughing, casting his gaze at the chandelier as if entreating the heavens for help. "If I refuse, I shall never hear the end of it!"

Feliciano cleared his throat. "For Sofia Robles, then," he said, and read:

> I should like to shine like the sun upon your days,
> to be the angel that admires your every charm,
> or the bird that sings of nothing but your beauty,
> or the zephyr playing sweetly with your curls.
> I should like to give you joy with my singing,
> —if it should chance that my verses contain
>   joy—
> and to gather all the scepters from across the earth
> to lay as offerings upon your altar.
> I should like to uproot a lovely laurel,
> and throw it in the path before you pass,
> as a lyrical carpet of tenderness,
> because you are a prodigy of beauty,
> because you keep the lily's purity,
> which is the endless fountain of loveliness.

Applause broke out around the table. "Hear, hear!" said Eduardo, and his sister clapped and clapped.

"It does me more than justice," said Sofia. "I am well pleased, sir."

"My daughter, your praise is too faint by half," her mother said. "The verse is very sensitive, invoking the classical Spanish sonnet—yet diverging from the standard form in ways original and strange." She looked at Feliciano in genuine admiration. "It is both familiar and yet like a dream, delicate and surreal."

I didn't think nearly so much of it, myself. *Lyrical carpet of tenderness?* Señor Robles was rolling his eyes, and I felt myself rather in his camp.

"Exactly!" said Eduardo, ever the kind enthusiast. "Quite good, my friend. Quite good. You'll have the ladies fainting in the streets."

"Hardly a desirable outcome," croaked Sofia's old grandmother, scraping the last bit of soup from her bowl.

"Oh, but, Señora Robles," murmured Pura. "Have you no sense of romance?"

The old woman chuckled. "Ask me about romance in five years, girl. Let me know where it's gotten you."

Sofia's mother turned firmly away from her mother-in-law and spoke in a voice like velvet. "But truly, Señor Galván," she said, "it's a very fine poem. Very fine."

"We have a Spanish Dante in our midst!"

Really, Eduardo could be a bit much.

SOFIA

Papa was arguing politics with Señor Galván and Señor Salazar again. (Feliciano and Eduardo, I usually called them privately to myself, for fun, but sometimes one must be proper even in one's mind.) It was entirely dull. Having flattering poems about oneself read aloud was an infinitely superior pastime.

"Of course I want a free Cuba," Papa was saying. "But I'm a businessman. These rebels hurt their own cause by giving so much power to the Blacks. Maceo, Moncada . . . What sensible plantation owner wants another Haiti?"

Eduardo spread his hands in a soothing way. "But Cuba will never be like Haiti. My father says so."

"Free us from the yoke of Spain? Very well," said my father, sipping his wine. "But enslave us to these African savages? Never."

Zenaida had gone very still. Well, if she wanted to move in our circles, she needed to hear the way people really talked.

"All men must be free, or none," said Feliciano. "It is a simple law of justice."

"You may be a bit idealistic, my young friend," said Papa.

Feliciano shrugged. "What is a man without ideals?"

"Or a woman, either, for that matter?" I said quickly. I wanted his eyes back on me, not on my father.

"Oh really!" Eduardo laughed. "Come, Sofia. And what are your ideals, pray tell, besides a fine house, a fine carriage, and a very rich husband?"

His sister softly slapped his arm. "Oh, Eduardo, do stop."

"I want my independence," I said. In unison, my mother and grandmother gasped and crossed themselves, like God's own puppets. "My financial independence," I said. "I can add and subtract and read the newspapers." I met my father's frown. "If you can run a business, why can't I?"

If I'd wanted eyes upon me, I certainly had them now. Everyone stared, agog. Only Zenaida's brow looked mild.

"And what business would you run, my daughter?" My father's mouth was pursed halfway between amusement and annoyance.

"A tearoom, I believe. In New York City." My mother gasped again. "For ladies," I added. "Cuban ladies, mainly, but others could come." I flicked open my fan. "Cuban ladies would appreciate a warm oasis of civility and grace amidst all that cold cement, and the rest could learn much from us, as regards beauty and refinement."

Eduardo and Feliciano made the proper admiring noises.

"But your ideals, then," persisted Eduardo, "are simply those of your father, but dressed in crinolines?"

The three men loudly laughed.

"A capitalist in lace!" shouted my father. He was on his third glass of wine.

Zenaida covered her smile with her napkin, and somehow that irritated me more than the open laughter of the men.

"There's nothing wrong with wanting to earn one's own living," I said. "Particularly given the other liberties it affords."

"Other liberties?" asked wide-eyed Pura. "Such as what?"

"Once we're the minders of our own wallets," I said, voicing it aloud for the first time, "then we needn't depend on a husband. We can marry whom we choose—for love, instead of for an income." I looked at Feliciano directly, feeling bold, and tossed my head. "Indeed, we needn't marry at all."

Pura's gasp joined those of my mother and grandmother.

"Oh my God," murmured my mother, eyes closed, crossing and fanning herself. "Dear God."

"What rubbish," said my grandmother. "If you're the sort of girl who doesn't want to marry, we can pack you off to Saint Ursuline's tomorrow. That's what convents are for."

"Oh, Grandmama," I said. "I've hardly said I never wish to marry. Only that financial freedom furnishes us with freedom of the heart as well."

"My God," my mother said again.

"Here, I agree," said Zenaida quietly, speaking for the first time. "What good is it to free Cuba, and even to free us Blacks and coloreds"—here she looked steadily at my father—"if every woman is in bondage in her home?" She took a quick sip of water. "We deserve the right to work, to earn, to own property."

"And so a woman may, if she is widowed, with nothing else to do," said my father, waving an expansive hand toward my grandmother.

"I well know it, sir," Zenaida said, "for my mother, widowed these several years, owns outright the boardinghouse she runs." She blotted her lips. "As you may know."

My father reddened. He was unaccustomed to impertinent speech from anyone but me.

"Yet I would not want to have to watch my husband die to gain the right to my own purse strings," Zenaida continued. "The great José Martí might like the Cuban woman soft and yielding, but she acts so only because she must. And even so, not all women do. The mambisas fight in battle."

Feliciano had laid down his fork and knife and was studying her. "And your ideals, Señorita Baliño?" he asked. "What would those be?" "I claim nothing so grand as ideals," said Zenaida. "Just to be permitted to do everything anyone else can, in peace and safety."

"Hear, hear! Those sound like ideals to me!" said Eduardo, flourishing his hands gallantly over the table, nearly knocking a decanter down.

"Yes, yes," echoed tedious Pura. "Noble, indeed."

I'd had enough of Zenaida. My error was becoming clear. It was one thing to turn a stray into a pet but quite another to watch it eat from your own dish.

I reached across to my mother's place and swung the little bell. The girl appeared. "Can you not clear the things?" I made my tone sweet. Gentlemen didn't like it when you were sharp to servants. It bespoke domestic disharmony, even jealousy. Many men, Grandmama had told me, took mistresses from among the house staff, and they wanted a wife who'd look the other way. While I'd hardly permit such a thing, it never hurt to practice grace. "The hour grows late," I told the girl as she began to gather dishes. "The men would no doubt like to smoke."

"Ah yes." My father had relaxed against his chair, his hands comfortably folded over his paunch. "And sherry."

The girl, arms full, disappeared.

"Before we split into our separate camps," said Feliciano, "does anyone know this new rival for the poet's crown?"

We all looked at him blankly.

"A new poet has been posting work around the town, someone who calls himself The Thorn."

"Ah yes!" said Eduardo. "I saw one of his poems on the wall near the stables. Quite good."

"Quite good, indeed," said Feliciano, pulling a tiny notebook from his breast pocket. "Listen. I copied this one down." He read aloud:

All nations crave the Caribbean Pearl—
Why should they not? As lush as any girl
in nature's prime, borne on the ocean's breast,
Cuba croons to sailors, promising sweet rest.

But stop your hungry ears and sail on past,
lashed tightly to your galleon's stalwart mast:
for Cuba's not for you, O nations
of the earth.

She is her own.
Attend her glorious birth.

My mother was leaning forward, her eyes half-closed. "Wonderful," she murmured. "Quite strong. That allusion to Homer . . ." She judged herself a connoisseur of these things.

"And that's just one," said Feliciano. "I've seen others equally impassioned and eloquent." He rubbed his jaw. "I would learn this man's identity. He has a muscular line and a fine mind. I'd like to meet him."

"Could he be a new arrival from Havana?" asked Eduardo. "Or some well-known lector or journalist here in Key West?"

Pura blinked. "But why give himself a false name, though?"

"To protect himself," said Feliciano. "Some of his verses don't merely border on sedition; they cross that line. He could be tried for treason. If he's writing in Cuba or must go there for business, he's courting a firing squad. For example, listen to this one." He flipped the pages of his notebook, stabbed one with his finger, and read:

I dream of freedom deeper than the sea—
a grace and wisdom born of liberty—
for I, like all my brethren, crave
the self-rule sought by Hatuey.

'Tis easy to condemn the Spanish knave
with words—but not enough. We must be brave
in battle, the arc of history to bend,
if Cuba's future we would save.

If Cuba's destiny we'd mend,
our soldiers to her shore we'll send.
Our funds will light the cannon's fire,
our homeland's honor to defend.

'Tis useless just to pluck upon my lyre
and sing pale hymns of bold desire—
Inside our hearts does Hatuey's image burn:
To Cuba we must all return.

"Oh, my, my! Now that's inflammatory stuff!" my father said. "Inflammatory?" He glanced around the table, waiting for our approving laughter. "Burn . . . ?"

I sighed. "Yes, Papa. We all caught your witticism." He was painfully fond of puns, a most unfortunate trait of which neither my mother nor I had, alas, been able to break him.

My mother shook her head. "But still: to be shot for a poem." Her hair had come loose from its chignon, and tendrils curled around her throat most fetchingly. What a shame she was old. "What kind of mad world is this?" she said.

"It's understandable, though," said Eduardo. "Poets are powerful! Poems infect men's minds," he said. "And hearts."

"That's what we poets aim for at any rate," said Feliciano. "We can only watch, and speculate, and try to weave a spell—for humans do crave spells, the lot of us, whether our preference is politics, or God, or a lover's gaze, or the stories that unspool from the pages of a book."

"This is so true," my mother murmured.

He took a drink of wine. "One way or another, we all long for hypnosis, for something to make sense of it all and soften the pain." He shrugged. "Those sages who can bear to walk this earth with naked minds are very rare."

I stifled a yawn.

"So we aim, and we keep shooting, though most of our arrows fall short." He stared out the window into the darkness. "But not The Thorn's. He strikes true."

One of our peacocks shrieked.

50

ZENAIDA

"Yes." Feliciano's face was pensive. "I would very much like to meet this man."

"But perhaps," said Sofia's mother, her soft voice tentative, "it could be a woman?"

The table burst into laughter.

"I'm sorry. I'm so sorry, Señora Robles," said Eduardo. He burst into helpless laughter again. "But surely: what nonsense!"

"No, truly." She turned to Feliciano imploringly. "Think of Sor Juana, for instance, or Carolina Coronado, or Gertrudis Gómez de Avellaneda—or Rosalía de Castro, from your own province, Señor Galván."

"But those hardly signify as women at all," said Eduardo, still laughing. "Nuns and so on."

Sofia's mother turned to him. "Women's opportunities are not the same as yours. Sor Juana became a nun so she could continue her studies—the only way she could. And Rosalía de Castro, by the way"—she gave him a withering look—"was married, with six children."

"Well, let's not sell the fair sex short," said Señor Robles. "Of course women can write drivel about flowers and love, if they're inclined toward poetry—but politics?" He laughed and waved the maid over with a freshly opened bottle of claret.

And so it went. While Sofia's grandmother dozed in her chair, they debated for an inordinate length of time a woman's ability to write poetry.

I mentioned Phillis Wheatley and Elizabeth Barrett Browning, but no one recognized their names.

51

SOFIA

Patience, patience. You catch more flies with honey than with vinegar, or so my mother liked to say (it was a Bible verse or something)—though she had thus far failed to explain why any reasonable person would want more flies.

Annoyed with my father for pouring more wine—thus prolonging the time Zenaida might use to compel the young men's interest—I concentrated on imagining Feliciano and Eduardo as flies, their tiny faces stuck on little black bodies with ink-line legs and buzzing wings, hovering over the dinner table. This vision made the entire enterprise less fraught, for though I had absolutely no interest in joining my destiny to Eduardo's—and joining his family's tobacco empire to ours, as my father had more than once hinted—I might very much have enjoyed a handsome poet on my arm in New York City—a poet, that is, who was well aware of who controlled the purse.

Recalling how my latest kitten curled and purred, I shifted in my chair and stretched languorously.

"Your own poems do infect our minds, Señor Galván," I said, smiling. "The ladies' minds, at least. But the hour grows late."

"A contradiction in terms." My father snorted. "Ladies' minds."

Feliciano frowned. "It's one thing to charm a woman with blandishments—"

"Ha!" broke in Eduardo. "All women love to be told they're pretty. Eyes like the moon and so forth."

His wide-eyed sister, Pura, tilted her head, as if knocked by a sudden revelation. "This is true," she said. "We do."

"But to fuel a revolution," Feliciano continued, "to keep pouring oil upon its flames, after eighteen long years of battle, when the fire in many men's souls is flickering . . ." He rubbed his brow. "For a poet to find that fire within himself, and stoke it, and keep stoking it, and use his pen like a bellows to blow that spark in others back to life . . . I bow to such a man."

Eduardo clapped him on the shoulder. "Ah, you sell yourself too short, my brother. Your verses inspire us all. And each day from the platform, you inspire hundreds of workers to revolt."

"Revolt against Spain, I hope," said my father.

"Against Spain, sir, I mean," Eduardo said. "Of course."

"Six of one," my father said. "Once they smell their freedom, they're halfway to mob rule."

"Oh, I hardly think so, sir," Eduardo said. "When they're donating all their extra pay to the Cuban cause for weapons and so forth, they cannot shore up sufficient funds to see themselves through a strike." He shrugged. "That's what my father claims, at least. He hopes our fight against Spain goes on forever."

My mother gasped. "Oh, surely not," she said. "To make light of the loss of Cuban lives, the destruction of the countryside—"

52

ZENAIDA

The hour had indeed grown very late, and generous quantities of evidence in favor of masculine literary superiority had been proffered by the three men at the table. I eyed Sofia's snoring grandmother with some envy.

"Well, you Robles ladies soon will have a break from patriarchal authority," said Señor Robles. His mother startled awake—Had she been pretending all along?—and all three of his relations' faces turned toward him. Sofia's mother's face, in particular, was rigid with anticipation, as if bracing for a blow. "Yes, tomorrow I go to Tampa," he said. "On business. For a week."

"Your business takes you for so long?" said his wife.

"I'm afraid so, my dear," he said, patting her hand as one pats a dog. "Tampa holds the keys to the future. The tobacco triangle, they'll call it one day: Tampa, Havana, and Key West."

"A whole week," she murmured.

"Zenaida, you look tired," said Sofia, when we had all risen and made our way toward the door. "You work so hard, after all. Pura and Eduardo, you have your carriage, don't you?"

"But I walked here with—"

"Oh yes!" Pura turned to me. "Ride with us, Zenaida. You must."

"Most certainly," Eduardo said. "It's no trouble at all."

"You're very kind," I said, for nothing else was possible. "I would be most grateful."

"Stay and have a last cigar, my boy," said Señor Robles to Feliciano. Sofia smiled.

53

CHAVETA

No moon. Pitch black. Perfect night for it.

I was brushing glue on a wooden fence slat when someone grabbed my arm. I jerked, but he held fast.

The damn new lector. Our eyes locked. His fingers gripped my arm.

"Who is he?" he said.

I laughed. "Get lost, Galván."

"This Thorn," he said. "Who is he? I must know."

I shook my arm from his grasp. "Why? So you can report him?"

He stepped back, stung. "You know I am no traitor."

"You are a Spaniard."

He drew himself up. "I am Galician."

"As if that makes a difference."

"Havana is my home. I give my whole life to the cause. You must see that. You must respect my commitment."

I spat my respect in the dirt.

"Come, Chaveta. I beg you." His voice softened. He took hold of my arm again, but gently. "I must have his name. Not to report him—not at all! Just to meet him. This Thorn is a finely skilled poet and a gentleman of principle. I want to make his acquaintance. Just give me his name." His hand caressed my cheek. "Chaveta. How beautiful you are." His face lowered. "Come, beautiful Chaveta." His lips brushed mine. "Darling Chaveta. Bold Chaveta. Tell me, my love."

"Bastard!" I backed away and spat the taste of him from my mouth. "I would die first."

Clutching my brush and glue and stack of broadsides, I spun and ran into the dark.

SOFIA

"Mamá," I said. The furniture and rugs of the drawing room lay gilded in late Saturday sun.

She looked up from her embroidery.

"Mamá, you're humming."

"Oh." Her cheeks pinkened. "Was I?"

"You never hum."

"Well," she said. She dropped her eyes to her embroidery again, a long pale-green table runner decorated with golden pears and arabesques. "Is it annoying you, my daughter?"

"No," I said. "Hum all you like."

But she fell silent.

We continued stitching.

ZENAIDA

When Chaveta and I arrived at the Robles mansion for our usual Sunday-afternoon visit, the front door stood propped open, and Sofia was playing the piano, plucking out an unfamiliar song.

I knocked my knuckles against the white doorjamb.

"Oh, come in, come in!" called Sofia, waving to us both. "Listen to this."

Beginning again, she swayed back and forth on the bench in a sinuous way, like a snake, and pounded out a series of notes that managed to sound both triumphant and sly.

Finished, she rose with a flourish.

"It's from the new French opera by Georges Bizet," she told us. "You'd like it, Chaveta."

"Would I?"

"Oh yes," Sofia said. "It's set among the cigar rollers of Seville, the women, and the heroine is a cigar roller who incites the lusts of too many men—and pays the highest price." She glanced down at the sheet music. "*Carmen*, they call it. It's a scandal in Paris and Vienna. The

Germans adore it." She twirled, and her full skirts flared around her. "I do wish it would come here."

"Got any cake?"

Sofia glanced at her impatiently. "Of course." Her eyes drifted until they found the little bell. She rang it, and the older maid appeared.

"Bring out the tea," Sofia said.

We settled on the veranda, enjoying the afternoon sun—and, before long, Gastón's latest creations.

"This tea, you know," Sofia said, "came all the way from India."

Chaveta rolled her eyes. "Doesn't it all?"

Sofia frowned. "Of course not. Much of it comes from China, and now Ceylon—"

"Good Lord," Chaveta said, helping herself to another pastry.

"Fine," Sofia snapped. "What would you like to talk about, then? Anarchism, I suppose? Revolution? How to kill Spaniards?"

They went on at each other like that for a while, sharp little smiles flickering on their lips, as if they were whetting their daggers and enjoying it. When we'd gorged ourselves into a near-stupor, Sofia rose.

"Come," she said, smoothing down her skirts, "we've just had a shipment from Rome. Let me show you my new shoes."

Chaveta and I glanced at one another. Like most people, I had one pair of real shoes that buttoned—the leather kind with closed toes—for important occasions at the San Carlos or shopping downtown, and just a pair of rope sandals for everywhere else. Chaveta shrugged.

We followed Sofia inside and upstairs. Her closet, as I well knew, was as large as the room I shared with my mother.

At the top of the stairs, she turned back with a smile.

"What a lovely dress, Zenaida," she said.

56

SOFIA

On Sunday evening, after a visit from my friends and a pleasantly dull supper on the veranda, my mother was reading Cervantes aloud in the drawing room when my maid came in.

"Your grandmother's asking for you, miss. She wants you to bring her sherry up."

I looked up from my sketch pad, surprised. Grandmama never asked for me. She liked to sit up there in her four-poster ebony bed and drink herself to sleep.

"Are you sure?"

"Yes, miss."

I was loath to leave, for I'd been hard at work drawing a floor plan for my tearoom—where I'd want the tables to go, and so on. It was most absorbing, imagining the conversations people would have, and how they'd praise the exquisite little cakes, and how much profit I would make each week.

"Yes, all right." Reluctantly, I set my things aside and rose. "Bring me the tray."

"Yes, miss."

She disappeared and reappeared. I took the tray from her hands and climbed the stairs.

At Grandmama's door, I knocked with my foot.

"Come in, child."

Opening doors while carrying a laden tray wasn't easy. I went in. Old people were most tiresome.

"You wanted to see me, Grandmama?" I brought the tray to her side and set it on the nightstand.

She stared at me.

Good Lord, she wanted me to pour the sherry for her as well.

I did so. She took it from my hand.

"Have a seat, girl."

I pulled the little pink armchair close to her bed and sat down.

"What are you doing with that cafetero?"

"What?"

"I saw you. I know what you've been doing."

"Oh." I laughed and tossed my head. "That's nothing. Harmless. A little flirtation."

"Don't try to fool an old lady," she said. "Watch yourself, girl. Three times now I've seen you with him. I've seen what you do. You've got the old Robles streak." She shook her head in warning. "That's what slaves are for, girl. Not white people like that coffee boy you're playing with. Not here in North America, where everyone is free now. Slaves can't fight back. They can't tell anyone." She sipped her sherry. "Oh, you should have seen the things my father did to the pretty little Black girls back home. Couldn't walk, sometimes, they couldn't. And his father before him, my mother said. That's what the Blacks are for, she said. Stay out of men's way and count yourself lucky."

She chortled, the dry interior of her throat rubbing against itself.

"Fine gentlemen! Cultured gentlemen! Paragons of empire. They studied law in Madrid, genuflected to the Pope at the Vatican, and then came home and carved up little Black girls. When I read that French fairy story about Bluebeard and his hidden torture dungeons, I thought, *Oh, the whipping shed.* There were two on our estate: one the overseer used, for actual whipping, with the post and belly pit—though most overseers preferred to whip outside, as an example to the others."

She paused, took a drink of sherry.

"And then there was the other whipping shed, the special one reserved for the paterfamilias. It had a bed with iron rings so wrists and ankles could be tied, and a table full of wicked-looking instruments like surgeons use, and all manner of leather and metal devices hanging from hooks on the wall. Splatters of blood in the dirt. Like something from the Inquisition. It's no accident we're descended from Spaniards. I went there only once as a girl, alone, when no one was about, but the shock of it never left me. Think of it! My own father, who led me on my pony and tucked me in at night. My grandfather, who sang me old songs and brought me toys from Paris. I never went to their shed again, but dreams of it haunt me to this day."

She leaned close.

"We are monsters," she said. "You bear the blood of monsters." She nodded, and her yellow teeth showed when she smiled. "Powerful monsters."

She fell back against her pillows.

"But here you must be careful. On the sugar plantations, we were gods. Undisputed gods. Here, we are only citizens."

"Grandmama, you make too much of a little—"

"This penchant for the exploration of pain," she croaked, "this curiosity about what the body can bear, the mind—the pleasure of enacting it, like God, or like the Devil—it's not an acquired taste, girl. You have it or you don't. I myself do not, thank God, though I well know what it looks like. It's a powerful force, and you must be careful."

"I don't think you know what you saw, Grandmama. We were just playing. Your eyes are getting so bad now, you know."

"Don't bother with your lies, child. You've got the Robles blood in you, all right. Never seen it in a girl before. Your own father doesn't have it. Skipped a generation, I guess. He is a simple man, thanks be to Jesus, and his pleasures are the normal pleasures of men: a whiskey, a smoke, diverting company from time to time. But watch yourself. This Key West is no place for carrying on. Your father can't afford a scandal."

"There won't be any scandal, Grandmama. The boy won't talk. He's practically mute."

She shook her bloated finger at me, its nail as thick as the shell of a crab. "I might be fond of you, child, but it's my son's fortunes to which I've tended all these years. It's his riches and his reputation for which I've sacrificed, and you'll not threaten those. North Americans have institutions for girls who don't behave, and all it takes is a stroke of your father's pen." She drained the sherry from her glass. "Watch yourself, girl. I've got my eye on you."

I smiled sweetly.

"Yes, Grandmama," I said.

ZENAIDA

I overslept. When I woke, hot and sweating, my mother's bed on the other side of the room was already neatly made, its corners tight. The sky was white and empty, and no breeze stirred. From below rose the smell of coffee and the clatter of dishes. I dressed in haste and hurried down.

I took the plates from my mother. "Why didn't you wake me?" I said under my breath.

She only glared. One of her stormy moods was upon her.

"They say there are Spanish Autonomists here in our midst," Feliciano was saying to the men as I carried in a platter of fried eggs and thick slices of buttered Cuban toast. The workers fell upon the food like the starving, and I took my time refilling all their coffee cups, lingering to listen. "They say they're plotting a bombing soon. Or arson."

"They'd love to see this city burn," said Señor Gandarán through his white mustache. "Cowards. They were never happier than when the hurricane flooded us in '70. They ran stories in the Havana papers saying we'd all been washed away."

"Dream on!" said another man. "Key West is here to stay, and so are we. The Spaniards are the ones who need to go."

"Cuba for Cubans!" Señor Gandarán thumped his coffee cup on the table.

"All Cubans," put in Maceo.

"Ay, all Cubans. Naturally." The men stuffed their mouths and swallowed coffee faster than I could pour it.

"It would save the Spaniards much trouble, to be sure," said Feliciano, "and I speak as a man born on Spanish soil whose heart belongs to Cuba nonetheless. With Key West wiped from the map, New York would be the only source of funds for the insurgents. You here in Key West contribute twice as much or more. A new staging ground would have to be found to mount the military campaigns, and munitions would have to be stored farther away—Saint Augustine, Jacksonville . . . Nowhere is so close as here, so well positioned."

"Ninety miles," someone chimed in, a mantra we heard often.

"An easy sail," agreed Feliciano.

"Legends say the Indians used to paddle it in canoes."

"That's no legend," said Señor Gandarán. "My great-grandmother in Havana saw them with her own eyes."

"Your great-grandmother," teased another of the workers. "What else did she most definitely see? Tell us the gospel."

"Don't mock what you don't understand," snapped Señor Gandarán, "which leaves you almost nothing."

The men laughed.

"There always have been traitors among us, though," said one of the cigar workers who'd come back from Havana only the previous week. "You never can tell."

"Mostly you can," said Líbano. I was surprised. He seldom spoke.

Maceo looked up from the bacon he was devouring. He swallowed and wiped his mouth with the back of his hand. "What do you mean?" he said. "What do you mean, mostly you can tell?"

Líbano glanced up for only a moment and then dropped his eyes back to his plate. He shrugged.

"No, really. Tell us." Maceo's tone took on the sharp edge of a superior officer commanding his troops. "What do you mean?"

Forks paused in the air.

"Just a feeling," said Líbano, clearly bewildered and already looking like he wished he'd said nothing. "The way you know a new man will want sugar in his coffee or not." He shrugged again. "You just know."

"You missed your calling, then, Líbanito," mocked Maceo. "Serving coffee isn't enough for someone of your keen observational skills. You should work in espionage."

"More men's lives," interjected Feliciano smoothly, smiling, calming the room, "have been saved by coffee than by spies." Líbano shot him a grateful glance. "But tell us, cafetero: Have you spotted any secret servants of the Spanish flag within our midst?"

Everyone stared at Líbano, waiting. His eyes lowered again. He pressed his lips together hard and stared down at the food he'd barely touched. I felt a sudden pang. He was just a boy.

"Anyone could be a spy for the Spaniards," I said, leaning to clear away soiled dishes, hoping to draw the men's attention from him. "Just as anyone could be a true son of Cuba. What men proclaim about themselves can be a lie, and much noble behavior happens behind closed doors."

Feliciano clapped twice. "Brava," he said. "Indeed. Or daughter."

I looked at him, confused.

"Or true daughter of Cuba," he said. His eyes were amused, locked on me and dancing with a curious intensity.

"Just so!" said one of the cigar rollers, and the others banged the butts of their knives against the table.

"Hurrah for the daughter of Cuba!" said Señor Gandarán, lifting his coffee cup like a beer stein.

In the doorway, my mother was standing very still, her eyes wide and fixed on me.

"And bring more toast!" someone cried.

58

SOFIA

"Mamá," I said. A soft little smile played on my mother's lips. Breakfast had been cleared away, and she toyed with her coffee cup. "Mamá."

She looked up.

"I think I might go for a walk," I said.

She sighed. "Yes, my daughter." She folded her napkin on the table and made to rise.

"By myself," I said.

Her eyes widened, and she sank back into her chair.

"I just want to walk a little on my own," I said, prepared to argue at length for permission.

"Are you sure, my daughter?" She seemed strangely placid. Ordinarily, she would have begun to talk about my virtue or suggest which servant could accompany me or suggest that I call for Edmund to bring the trap around.

"Yes," I said, rising and folding my napkin on the tablecloth. "The fresh air will suit me."

"Very well, my dear," she said. "Don't go far."

"Just to Zenaida's for a while," I said. "Or perhaps down to the shore."

59

Chaveta

All the tamales were gone, the tin plates glazed with sauce. The rice and beans, gone. The little ones squirmed to be excused to go play.

Papi turned to my mother. "Very good meal."

"Thank you, my dear," she said.

Something in the room was crackling. The air. I could feel it.

"Chaveta," he said, turning to me. He laid his fork down. "Chaveta. My daughter. You are going to enter that pageant."

"Papi, no!" I shoved back my chair.

"Your mother wants it."

Her eyes down on her plate, all modest like some Virgin Mary.

"Fucking martyr," I muttered.

The little ones gasped. Mari and Lisa crossed themselves like automatic machines, and my father's hand lifted to slap me.

"Do it," I said, jerking my chin up at him. "Go on."

His hand dropped. He shook his head. "Don't fight me on this, Chaveta."

"But, Papi, listen to reason," I said. "You know me. You know me better than that."

"Your mother wants it. She's a good woman. She asks for nothing. She's been a good wife to me all these years, and she wants this from you."

"Papi, it's ridiculous. I can't stand onstage like livestock. You know I don't belong in some stupid pageant, all dolled up like one of your—"

"Ay, watch your mouth, girl." His eyes angry, his voice loud. He shook his head again. "No, my mind is made up."

"Papi."

"You're still my daughter." His jaw was set, his thick face stubborn. "And my word is final."

I looked at my father. His face of stone.

Finally, I nodded.

"Good," he said.

My mother looked vindicated, sitting there like she was waiting for her halo to appear.

I stood up.

"But take note," I said. "This is how it happens. This is how you lose a daughter."

I walked out. The door banged shut.

60

SOFIA

After dinner, it grew dark, and the lamplight glowed around us. Mamá sat across from me on the other sofa, embroidering gold pears onto her table runner. Everything was very peaceful with Papa gone. I pulled a strand of emerald floss through my own cloth, where the plume of a peacock's tail was slowly accreting. One day, it would be a pillowcase on some bed.

The girl came in with the tea tray.

"Julieta," I said, setting my sewing down on my lap. "You look a bit tired this evening. I'll take the tray up to Grandmama again."

She stared at me. So did my mother.

"Really," I said. "It's no trouble. You may retire early."

"Yes, miss." Eyes wide, she laid the tea tray down on the little table and backed away. "Shall I set out the things in the kitchen for you?"

"I'll do it," I said. "You take the evening for yourself."

The girl evaporated backward into the darkness, curtseying and nodding. I rose and folded my embroidery away into its basket.

"What a kindhearted mistress you've become," said my mother, her glance full of approval. "And a kindhearted granddaughter, too."

I smiled.

61

ZENAIDA

On Wednesday morning, after serving breakfast to the men and washing all their dishes, my mother and I wheeled our little wooden handcart to the market. Groceries for twenty hungry workers and ourselves were far too much to carry in the woven string bags other women used.

It was a cool, sunny morning, and a brisk wind blew. I loved the crowded marketplace: all the bright marquees fluttering over the booths, the chattering throng of housewives and servants, the great stacks of mangoes and avocados ripening in the sun, whole forests of pineapples, vast tubs of coconuts and guavas, fat bulbs of garlic, onions galore, pyramids of yams and potatoes. Women gossiped together and argued with the merchants for a lower price. Wooden barrels stood full of rice, black beans, black-eyed peas, coffee beans—and the spice shop! Cinnamon sticks and cardamom pods, black peppercorns and red threads of saffron in a clear glass jar . . . And in the fish aisle, all the seafood you could ever want, caught fresh that morning: stone crabs and mangrove snappers, pink shrimp, red grouper, spiny lobsters, huge silver tarpon laid in shimmering rows, yellowtail with their bright stripes and spots, long thick cobia fish, and blackfin tuna from deep at sea.

We took our time among the open-air booths, chatting and comparing, choosing our food. Then we headed for Soto & Sons', where my mother chose six nude slaughtered hens and a thick slab of salted bacon, and from there we went to the bakery.

As I was choosing the fresh long loaves of bread for dinner, the second housemaid of the Salazars walked in. Clotilde Corrales was a tall, plump woman, very dark, who always wore a purple headwrap, smelled of rose water, and left a tangy scent on your shoulders when she embraced you.

She clasped my mother's arm. "Have you heard?"

My mother smiled. "Only praise for this fine weather."

Clotilde leaned close, though there was no one else in the bakery. "Old Señora Robles passed on in the night," she said.

"Oh no." My mother crossed herself, and I quickly followed suit, my wrist stiff with shock. I'd just seen the old woman myself not long ago. How very strange I felt—a little dizzy. I had never liked Sofia's grandmother—and yet, to imagine her so suddenly gone—

"Oh yes. Some kind of terrible stomach trouble, very quick, and then a heart attack, they think, for the old woman kept clutching her chest and was dead before the doctor could get there."

"Oh no," my mother said again, in a tone of great and genuine sadness, shaking her head. She held both of Clotilde's hands. "I'm so sorry," she said. "The family will suffer so."

Clotilde snorted. "I don't know about that." Her eyebrows lifted. "But Señor Robles will be called back early from his business in Tampa, they say."

"Oh yes, of course. He must come back. He loves his mother."

Clotilde shrugged. "What man doesn't? Mothers are easy to love. They dote on their sons." She laughed, chose her loaves, and handed her coins to the baker's boy. "It's us wives men find so hard to love."

My mother smiled. She had been well loved as a wife, but it was not polite to say so, when most wives suffered one way or another. "This news of the old woman's death will spread like wildfire," she said.

"So it will," said Clotilde. "I must go." She nodded in farewell. "Free Cuba."

"Free Cuba," replied my mother.

We paid for our loaves and headed home. I wheeled the handcart alongside her. The white sun climbed high toward its zenith.

"Poor Narciso," she said. "He loved his mother so. I never met her, myself, but he always said she was a good and tender woman."

I refrained from sharing my opinion. We walked on together toward home.

62

ZENAIDA

At four o'clock in the afternoon on Thursday, I joined the great mass of mourners congregating on Duval Street outside the Robles mansion. Sofia's grandmother already lay in the back of a wagon, her pine box laden with heaps of white hibiscus blossoms.

Behind the wagon, Sofia was climbing into her family's barouche to join her mother and father. I stood amidst the crowd. Most were probably there to pay their respects to Señor Robles rather than from any genuine affection for Sofia's grandmother, who had largely kept to herself—and was not, moreover, known especially for her charm. My mother had not wanted to come.

When Sofia got her skirts settled, she looked up and saw me.

"Oh, ride with us, Zenaida!" she cried, reaching out a hand. Black lace lapped at her wrist. "There's plenty of room. Mother, may she?"

Señora Robles nodded, invisible behind her dark veil. I drew close to the carriage's side.

"Can she, Father?"

Señor Robles's eyes were shot through with bright-red sprawls of blood vessels, and the flesh around them was puffy and pink. He glanced at me distractedly and waved a hand. "Yes, yes," he said. "Where's the damn priest?"

Their groom, Edmund, sat on the box, dressed in Sunday whites, holding the reins and whip (just for show: he only flicked it in the air above the horses, he'd told me). We nodded to each other as I climbed up, surprised not to have to walk in the long parade of mourners who had gathered.

The priest arrived on his horse, the wagon driver cracked his whip, Edmund clucked to the Robleses' fine pair of glossy chestnut geldings, and we began to move.

I'd ridden in Sofia's carriage a few times before—she'd order Edmund to fetch it, and he'd drive us around the island, as far as roads would go, or up and down past all the shops on Front Street. Still, it felt strange to move so effortlessly through the air, aloft, above all the trudging mourners. It was much more pleasant to ride down Angela Street in the smoothly rolling carriage than to walk behind it in the clouds of dust churned up by its wheels—and the wheels of six carriages that followed us, bearing the wealthiest families in town. A number of young men rode horseback behind them, too, all in their Sunday whites or uniforms.

"It's so terribly tragic," Sofia kept saying, her hand pressed to her breast. She wore no veil, and her black gown displayed her décolletage to fine advantage. "I am most stricken." Her eyes kept darting to see who'd gathered at the roadside to watch us pass.

The way to the cemetery was not long. A brisk, dry wind blew, which was helpful as we followed directly behind the wagon with Sofia's grandmother—a sign of respect that was not particularly practical, in my view, as no one grows more fragrant in death.

Edmund's shoulders were broad inside his white jacket and shirt, and the muscles of his neck shone dark. When he'd first gotten to Key

West, he'd boarded at my mother's for a few weeks until he could find a small place of his own. He kept charcoal and paper next to his bed, and he sometimes sketched vehicles of various styles: barouches like the Robleses', landaus, traps, and so on. He had driven a landau for a rich family back in Havana.

I knew a little about a lot of men on the island—and a strangely intimate little, owing to the nature of my acquaintance, like whether they made their own beds in the morning or left their sheets tempest-tossed, whether they kept their personal effects in tidy stacks on their nightstands or scattered them in a whirlwind across every available surface. What their pillows smelled like once they'd lain their heads on them all night. The odd little things that usually only a wife would know.

It put me in a strange relationship of knowledge, I'd noticed, particularly regarding those men who affected a public persona quite different from how they spent their solitude.

There was once a young soldier who stayed with us, for example, who polished all his brass buttons, combed his hair with military precision, and strutted about like a stallion, shoulders back and all that. But his sheets always lay in a twisted mess, and his underclothes would molder in a heap in the corner before he'd take them to On Wo's Laundry. (He claimed my mother and I didn't use enough starch or iron his collars stiff enough; I remembered she was most offended.) Sometimes he missed his spittoon, which was very disgusting to clean up, all those shiny gobs on the wood. He went back to Cuba and fell in combat. I could not remember his name.

Or Señor Torres, who was always very gruff when he came down to eat with us or when he sat in the parlor playing dominoes, as if he were just another mean old man with no heart. But propped on his nightstand, he kept a photograph of a beautiful woman with dark eyes and a tender smile, and next to it a stack of letters tied with white ribbons and a much dog-eared copy of *The Count of Monte Cristo*.

Or Líbano, whose room was always filled with books—books stacked on the windowsill, stacked on the floor: books about history and science and places far away—but who almost never spoke, and when he did, his speech was very plain and simple, like that of a child or someone uneducated, or he would say some odd phrase that made a kind of sense but seemed plucked from another plane. If indeed he comprehended all he read, he wore his learning very lightly, unlike most men, who seemed unable to utter a sentence without citing the latest expert or mentioning the newspaper in which they'd unearthed their opinion.

The carriage rolled on toward the cemetery.

CHAVETA

Robles closed his factory for the day so we'd come to his damn mother's funeral, so there we all were, trudging along like herded sheep. Zenaida got the smooth ride, but you couldn't have paid me to squeeze into that capitalist cart.

A strong wind blew my hair back.

But not strong enough to kill the smell.

"Chaveta." A whisper at my side.

"Líbano!" I smiled, happy to have a companion to trudge with. "But you don't have to show up for this, do you?"

"Señor Picasio told me I must. It would reflect badly on the coffee roastery if I didn't."

"Oh, sure." I nodded. "Did you know the old lady?"

"A little," he said. "I would see her in the drawing room sometimes when I took messages to Señor Robles. Or sitting in an armchair in the shadows at the top of the stairs."

I laughed. "Like a spider."

"Shh," he said, glancing around, smiling. "Did you know her?"

"Please," I said. "Who can know a lump of granite?"

"Or a ship wrecked on a sandbar."

"An iguana in a bog."

"The bog itself."

We laughed. An old lady elbowed my ribs.

64

ZENAIDA

Due to our island's high water table, our cemetery was a city of stone, a labyrinth of crypts above the ground—quite similar to graveyards in the great city of New Orleans, I'm told.

My mother says the dead in Cuba are buried in the dirt, where they rot—unless cursed by vodou, in which case they rise back up smoothly dripping from the mud as zombies, hollow-eyed.

I felt safer knowing Señora Robles would be entombed under a heavy slab of stone. In truth, she was no pleasure in her normal state; I would not like to meet an undead version.

Edmund clucked at the horses, and we rolled down a little street between various tombs and mausoleums, the differences in their sizes and elaborate carvings distinguishing no less among the rich and poor in death than their various trappings had in life. Some were plain stone boxes with only names and dates. Others had arches and curlicues and melancholy angels, their hands clasped in grief.

At the new crypt for the Robles family—for Sofia's grandmother was the first Robles to die in Key West—Edmund helped us down from the barouche, and we stood there respectfully, letting all those behind us catch up and gather around. Wind whipped up clouds of chalky white dust from the shell-strewn street.

While the priest said his necessary words, only Sofia's mother crossed herself—and then Sofia, too, once she felt her mother's glare through the veil. Chaveta caught my eye and winked. The cigar workers and servants bowed their heads in a show of respect but shuffled uncomfortably at all that talk of heaven. No one cared much. Why should they, when paradise was only ninety miles away?

Men slid the box into the crypt and closed it, and Señor Robles wiped his eyes and loudly blew his nose. Feeling embarrassed, I looked down. My black shoes were coated with a thin film of white powder.

Then Edmund helped us back into the carriage, and we rolled back the way we came.

CHAVETA

"Will you go to Sofia's now?"

"Yes," said Líbano. "To pay my respects."

"To eat the free food, you mean."

He laughed and said nothing. We walked down Elizabeth Street together amid the throng.

Feliciano waved from the Salazars' carriage.

Maceo trotted by on his horse.

ZENAIDA

Grief is another nation, my mother used to say, and the bereaved are citizens of another world. Their behavior is not always rational, so one must not judge them too harshly.

When we arrived back at the Robles mansion, Edmund handed us down from the carriage, and Sofia and I, arms linked, climbed the steps to the veranda and went inside, her parents following closely behind us. The cook and maids had remained at the house, laying out spreads of food and drink.

"I'll be right back," Sofia called, disappearing up the stairs, the soles of her black boots tapping the wood.

I stood awkwardly as the guests began to filter in: the rich, well-dressed ones who'd ridden in carriages or on horseback.

Sugar is the national food of Cuba, people say, and arrayed across every visible surface were silver trays of small lemon meringue tarts and miniature key lime pies and dozens of little ramekins filled with perfectly browned flan. Coffee urns stood ready on the sideboard. On long porcelain serving platters, Gastón's éclairs and napoleons lay in neat diagonal rows. When we mourn, we sweeten the pain.

And soften it, too. Bottles of sherry and rum stood aerating, attended by rows of shining crystal goblets.

Tasting Gastón's delicacies was always a pleasure of mine. I took a small dish of his flan and a silver spoon, and I settled myself on a settee in a corner of the drawing room to watch the people share their condolences with Señor and Señora Robles.

My feelings for Sofía were so mixed; I often wondered why I remained friends with her at all. She sometimes treated me with hostility or disdain, as if she were simply using me as a companion because no one more desirable was at hand.

Yet I was using her, too, and I felt guilty about it sometimes. No other mansion in Key West had opened its doors to me. No one else had invited me to ride in a carriage. Sofía's home, her parents, her wealth: the bookshelves full of leather-bound volumes, the gleaming grand piano, the arrays of elegant food and drink—they revealed a way of life so lush and different from the bare wood of my mother's boardinghouse.

I knew this was a cheap and shallow reason to remain Sofía's friend. But nowhere else had I spun a globe. In Sofía's house, the world opened up.

We'd had real moments of intimacy, too, over the years—shared laughter, shared tears. I sometimes wondered if, had we not been divided by the hierarchies of race and class, we could have been truly close.

Moreover, she provoked my curiosity, intriguing me with her peculiar ways, offering me the chance to observe a complicated character, the way a novelist might become fascinated and study someone compellingly odd. She was like one of the Chinese puzzles the traders brought: strange shapes one must struggle to put together.

When Sofia reentered the room, she poured herself a cafecito and came over to sit beside me, arranging her black taffeta skirts around her. We were instantly surrounded by various swains who stood or smoothly pulled up chairs to sit or even knelt on the carpet at her feet. I looked in vain for Maceo, but he had not come into the house.

Ignoring the young men, Sofia turned to me. Lifting an ankle, she slid her skirt up so that full inches of her stockinged shin were visible to all.

"Look, Zenaida," she said, swiveling her foot from side to side. "What do you think of these cunning little shoes? They're from Paris."

She no longer wore her dainty leather boots. Instead, her feet were clad with a pair of black velvet slippers embroidered with gold fleur-de-lis.

"They're very nice, indeed," I said.

Only once she had slid her skirts back down again, turning to the young men as if no such revelation of flesh had occurred, did she appear to notice their existence. She began to express her grief and sorrow in a tone that can only be described as strangely vivacious for the occasion.

It impressed me that she'd thought to change from her boots, which had indeed—like everyone's—grown dusty at the cemetery, into something far more fashionable and well suited to the manners of the drawing room. It seemed a remarkable presence of mind for one bereaved.

After my father was shot down in the street, there were days when my mother forgot to wear shoes at all. There were days when I had to comb and braid her hair, when I had to wash her face, trying not to look into her listless eyes, to fall into the abyss they held. In the worst moments, I had to feed her, lifting the spoon to her lips.

I was then only a girl of thirteen, but I would not let her join him there, as she so clearly longed to do, in that unreachable realm of the dead.

It seemed to me that someone who could recall fashion in a moment of bereavement might not be quite as devastated by grief as Sofia kept repeating she was. The young men who surrounded us, however, seemed very moved to comfort her.

However, loss does strange things to people, and one must not judge too harshly. We must leave such things to God, my mother would say—if He exists, whether He is the strict God of the Hebrews or the Jesus of the Christians, kind and mild.

(Yet even Jesus threw the money-changers from the temple.)

ZENAIDA

On Friday night, Maceo invited me again to accompany him to the café, which had already grown raucous by the time we arrived. We settled at our usual table—we had a usual table!—and he ordered for us.

Julieta, the Robleses' servant, slipped in the door and beelined over to Líbano. Bending at his side, she whispered in his ear, and he nodded without lifting his eyes from the chessboard. She stood there for a moment, looking at him, but he did not look up. Crestfallen, she slipped along the wall and out the back way. I wondered what message from Señor Robles could be so urgent at so late an hour.

At the big round table, the lectors were arguing about words.

"Why must it always be called the fatherland?"

"Fatherland, motherland—always a parent."

"Why attach a person to it at all, and a sex?"

"Exactly! Not everyone had a good father, after all."

"Or even knew who his father was!"

People laughed.

"Some people have worthless fathers," said Feliciano, "and some fatherlands are worthless, too."

"No," I said, leaning toward them, interrupting the men against my better judgment. The unusual energy of coffee at night buzzed my shoulders, my belly. "I will not believe it. No human being is worthless, and no country, either," I said. "They might make mistakes, and even be selfish or cruel. But they can be put right."

"Ah!" said an old man. "She is her mother's daughter, to be sure."

Maceo gazed at me, his large eyes soft.

"But why not just 'our land'?" said one of the lectors. "Or 'homeland'? Always a father or a mother, as if the land weren't perfectly sufficient, all by itself, to love."

The arguing went on that way, and the violinist's fiddling grew louder, the laughter more intense. A woman in bright pink began to spin, her dress swirling out, her heels clacking the wooden floor. A man reached out and grabbed her hand, pulled her to his lap.

"I think of Cuba like a mother," said Feliciano. "The full green mountains, the lush blossoms, the sweet water—"

"To me, Cuba is Havana's dirty streets," said Líbano. Heads swung around to look at him. "Rats. Hunger. If she's a mother, she's the kind that loiters on corners."

"Your tongue is foul," Feliciano said. "But if parts of Cuba are as you say, it's only because Spain has starved and raped her all these years. We know from Victor Hugo why whores must ply their trade. If they had sufficient wealth, autonomy, and education, they'd no more work the streets than—than young Sofia Robles."

"Oh my!" cried the woman in pink ruffles, bursting into laughter and falling back into the arms of the man upon whose lap she sat, who seemed not at all displeased.

"It is the same with countries," Feliciano continued. "If Spain would take its boot off Cuba's neck, she would regain her dignity. Her people would not go hungry." He glanced at Líbano with compassion. "The people would be free, and the alleys would be clean."

Maceo scoffed. "You are a dreamer. Though Cuba's eventual victory is assured, for we fight on the side of liberty, Spain is still mightier by far. Go out on a battlefield and see how power works."

Feliciano swung around to him. "Then why are you not there, my friend?"

"What?"

"I've been wondering, Maceo. You're not wounded. Why are you here, arguing in cafés like a poet instead of fighting at the front?"

"I'm here to gather guns, to gather funds, to tell Key West what we need. When I return, I'll take gold and munitions for our cause."

"Fine," Feliciano said. "But why send a battle-hard soldier for a task any schoolmaster could achieve?"

Maceo's cheeks flushed. He glanced around. His voice dropped. "This is not the moment for such confidences."

Feliciano looked at him strangely. Then he nodded. "As you prefer." He turned back to the lectors and began talking about whether the United States should send its troops to help the Cubans fight.

I turned to Maceo. "Are you all right?"

"I wish he would not have asked me that so publicly."

I laid my fingertips softly on the back of his hand. "What is it, Maceo? What troubles you?"

"If you must know," he said, his voice quiet, "I've been sent. To gather funds and raise morale, yes. 'Look at the brave young soldier! Give him money and guns.' But not for only that."

"But what, then?"

"To gather intelligence. There are Spanish agents in your midst. I'm here to pretend innocence, to offer myself as a . . . What is the term?"

"What term? What do you mean?"

"A double agent."

"But why?"

"In the hopes that the Spaniards will trust me. Begin to use me. That they'll see me as a gullible youth, impressionable, and tell me of their plans. I'm to report to General Bonilla immediately upon my return."

"But, Maceo," I said, somewhat awed—and not a little frightened—"is this not a very dangerous game?"

"The only kind worth playing." He smiled, and I thought he had never seemed more dashing and attractive. "I was born for danger," he said, and I suddenly understood what novels meant when they spoke of women swooning.

The café doors banged open. In stalked Chaveta.

"Has anyone seen my stupid goat-fucker of a father?"

The fiddler paused his bow. Laughter rippled among the men—amusement, but nervousness, too. It was unseemly for any woman to speak so.

She wore her brown trousers, the sleeves of her white shirt rolled up. Her gaze swept the room like a lighthouse beam, and she rolled her eyes in disgust.

Her eyes caught me and swept over Maceo, our table, our coffee cups side by side. My pulse quickened. My breaths came faster, and I felt my lips part. I looked over at the lectors' table. Feliciano's eyes were tracking Chaveta's every move.

She put her fists on her hips, and her dark brows crashed ominously low on her forehead. Her hair had come loose from its customary braid. She was beautiful and furious.

"Try the docks!" someone yelled. He meant the bordellos.

"He needs to bring his damn money home. I'm too tired to be dragging him out of bars."

She meant bordellos, too, but no one would shame her mother by saying so aloud.

"Ay, Chaveta, you sure got a chip on your shoulder!" called a young worker.

"A chip?" She twisted her head as if to check. "Oh no, my friend. A chip is just a little thing." She held up her thumb and forefinger to illustrate, as if a thick pinch of salt were squeezed between them. "Inconsequential. A size very familiar to many of you."

The café had grown quiet. Everyone stared.

"Oh no, my friends." She glanced from her left shoulder to her right, the slim brown cords of her neck glimmering with sweat in the lamplight. "What I got here are bricks. One to build with"—she tapped her left shoulder—"and one to throw." She tapped the right. "And she's not only a brick. She's a parrot, and I'm her pirate. I tell her when and where to fly, and what to say."

"Speech! Speech!" cried one of the dolled-up women, laughing.

"We've heard enough," growled old Señor Gutierrez, his eyes tilting heavenward. "Someone find that girl a husband."

"A husband?" Chaveta laughed. "What would I do with one of those? I need a husband about as much as I need the Pope. Or the American president. Or the king of Spain." Her dark eyes flashed. "A husband is just another bastard telling you what to do."

"Chaveta, be wise," said one of the workers. "Watch what you say. You're sounding like an anarchist."

Chaveta laughed. "What do you think I am? Church, state, marriage—abolish them all. You think revolution is just about Spain?" She strode around the lectors' table. "Oh no, my brothers. I will bring down *any* man who calls himself a lion and dares to put his paw upon my head. You think revolution is just about colonial power? About abolishing slavery? No. It's against all power that is unjust. Revolution is about destroying and remaking." She patted each of her shoulders in turn. "You need bricks for that. Not chips."

I'd never seen Feliciano smile quite that way before. Was he simply amused by the spectacle of a girl speaking her mind in public, or was something more lighting his gaze?

"Revolution is about making," said Chaveta. She tossed back her head and laughed. "You think when real revolution comes, you're going to get to sit around jawing in cafés until midnight while your wives wash dishes and tend your children back home? Talk, talk, talk. Revolution is about action, boys, not chattering in cafés."

She crossed to a table where cigar workers were sitting. She picked up one man's full glass of whiskey, downed it in a gulp, and smacked it down on the table.

"Chip?" she said to the room at large. "Ha. I'll show you chip." She wiped her mouth on the back of her hand. "If you see my father, tell him to drag his dumb donkey-fucking ass on home."

She swept the room with a final withering glance, spun on her heel, and stalked out.

A burst of laughter attended her exit. The violinist resumed. Voices grew loud again. I felt very strange, tugged by a longing to leap up and run after Chaveta. Though sitting beside a handsome, rakish soldier (who was signaling young Valdés for more drinks), I felt a pang I couldn't name.

From the next table, Líbano studied me, his eyes dark with sympathy. He shrugged sadly.

"A body in motion stays in motion," he said.

SOFIA

One must be quite deft to fool all of the people all of the time, as the politicians say, and in fact I was. At first, I'd thought of burning the little cloth in the kitchen's cast-iron stove, but then I remembered what Zenaida had said about the smoke.

On Friday night, while my mother stitched in silence and the maids hurried about tidying up after all the visits we'd had from Key West's most illustrious families, I slipped out to the back garden alone in the dark, concealing in my skirts a silver spatula, the kind with a pointed end for serving cake.

When I was certain no one was looking, I dug a hole and buried the cloth beneath the poinciana tree.

ZENAIDA

On Saturday evening as a half moon lit the sky, I escorted my mother, as usual, to the San Carlos for bolita. As usual (when hunting had gone well), Chaveta was there, muttering with conspirators along the wall, as if she were a soldier destined for the battlefield and not just a girl my own age.

As usual, my mother chose the most propitious row for us to sit in, and we sat. She drew her bolita ticket from her reticule and unfolded it. Eighty-three, it said. She kissed it for luck and closed her eyes, and I knew she was praying to Yemayá for good fortune. I so longed for her to win.

Maceo joined the little knot of conspirators against the wall, and they all stood there talking and gesturing. I knew they spoke of the revolution. I longed to get up and go listen, but my mother preferred me at her side.

Señor Robles had returned to Tampa after the funeral, and Señor Salazar was away on business, so old Plutarco Alfaro mounted the stage and the whole ritual began. He chose eight young men to toss the bag and called Pura to the stage. She was shy and lovely in a fluttering white gown of cotton lawn and simple white slippers. Her movements seemed to combine awkwardness and grace in equal measure, if such a thing were possible, like a new foal taking its first steps in a barn.

My mother tensed as Pura held the winning ball aloft.

"Twenty-nine!" she cried. Beside me, my mother deflated. Around us, a few Cubans cheered and held up their winning tickets while most groaned or laughed. People began rising to their feet.

Against the wall, Chaveta whispered to Maceo, laying a bold hand on his arm.

I felt a sudden flare of jealous fear, like the scrape of a match.

70

ZENAIDA

After lunch on Sunday afternoon, while the boarders dispersed for siesta or leisure pursuits, my mother and I cleaned the kitchen and prepared the cold leftovers for the evening meal.

We were sitting at the corner of the long table sorting through a pile of black-eyed peas when Maceo came in.

When she saw him, my mother smiled. "Still hungry, my son?"

I kept my own eyes on the peas.

"No, ma'am." He remained standing, the broad strength of him heating the air beside me. "I'm wondering if you'd mind if I took your daughter for a ride."

Over the peas, my mother's hands went still. Her gaze swung to me.

"Mind, my son?" Her voice was warm. "I don't mind at all. But it's my daughter who will decide."

I looked at her eager and approving gaze. I knew quite well she wouldn't mind having a handsome freedom fighter for a son-in-law, especially one who was half-dark, half-light, like me.

I looked at Maceo, tall, firm-lipped, proud. I nodded. "Just let me finish helping my mother." My hands kept sorting.

"Nonsense, child. I don't need help. Go on." She waved the backs of her hands at me, as if shooing me away. "Go on."

I rose and untied the strings of my apron. "I'll meet you on the porch."

"I thank you both for this honor," Maceo said, and clicked his heels. He turned and strode out of the room. We heard the front door close.

"Don't say a word," I said.

My mother laughed silently into her hands.

I went outside, stepped up upon the mounting block, and took his hand. He swung me up sideways behind him, and we headed out onto Emma Street.

"Don't worry," he said. "I'll go slowly."

Without the stirrups of a sidesaddle to brace me, I had to hold him tightly to keep my balance.

"What do you call your horse?" We walked along.

"Her name is Sabotage," he said.

"Oh." I felt surprised. "That's very poetic. Heroic. I like it."

"You expected something simpler?" he said, his tone sharp. "Old Nell?"

"No." We rode on in silence. "Well, I suppose."

"Because I'm just a soldier."

"No. Because the horses' names I've heard are plainer. Babe, and that kind of thing."

The shops and houses thinned, and we soon reached the edge of town. He steered us left on United Street, a long, empty corridor of sand and crushed shells that ran nearly the length of the island.

"I like to read," he said.

"Oh," I said, surprised again. "So do I."

"I know. I've seen you reading that green book."

"Oh, that," I said, somewhat abashed. "They're poems. By Petrarch."

"Do you like them?"

"Yes," I said. "Very much. They're romantic." Then I felt embarrassed and fell silent.

His horse walked on. We passed through buttonwood groves. Ahead of us burbled the sound of frogs, and white herons glided overhead.

In time, I asked, "Are we going to the salt ponds?" Nothing else was out that way.

"Yes," he said. "Have you ever seen them?"

"Once," I said. "My father took us there for a picnic, my mother and me. He rented a carriage for the day."

"I see." His voice was quiet. Everyone on the island knew how my father had died. "Then you were still a child."

"Yes."

"Not anymore," he said.

His ribs under my hands felt suddenly electric, and all at once I became extremely conscious of the place where my left thigh rubbed against his hips.

We entered the mangroves, the dark thick green jungle of them impenetrable except where the road had been laid. Within the mangroves, everything felt shadowed and mysterious, like being inside a living green cave. Branches shifted softly in the wind. We rode on. I closed my eyes and let my cheek rest against Maceo's shoulder, imagining how it might feel to fall asleep against him that way, night after night after night.

"Here we are," he said. His horse stood still. My eyes opened. We were at the shore.

I had forgotten how beautiful the salt ponds were. In the blue shallows, hundreds of pink flamingos clustered, some standing on one leg like ballerinas, some slowly wading, their heads dropping underwater to feed. The tips of their long bent beaks were as black as if they'd been dipped in ink. Some stood as if asleep, their long curved necks bent S-like on their bodies, their faces nested on their own torsos, their small pale eyes closed. Some took flight and looped in leisurely ovals over the ponds before gliding back down to hit the shallow water at a full run and then slow. It was all a shifting pink flutter amidst splashes, scored by the chorus of their honking, and there was something ineffably comforting about the blended rhythms of their movement and stillness, their rising and looping and falling, the way their bright heads tilted toward us and then away.

I slid down from the mare's back, and Maceo dismounted, looping Sabotage's reins around a branch and knotting them.

The water glistened, rippling and viscous, and the leaves of the mangroves shifted darkly in the breeze.

Maceo came close and stood before me.

"Would you like to bathe?"

"Oh." I felt my face grow hot. I hadn't worn a bathing costume underneath my dress, and this wasn't at all like going to the sea in the evenings with my mother, when no one was about and we could strip down to our shifts. "I would," I said, "but—" I gestured across the pond, toward the drying sheds and warehouse.

Maceo followed my glance. "It's Sunday," he said. "No one's working."

"But—"

"And I won't look. I promise."

I did very much want to experience the thick buoyancy of which people spoke. Sometimes sickly women even came down from the North to float for hours in the salt ponds.

"Then turn your back," I said.

He did, sliding his shirt over his head and dropping it to the ground. He kicked off his boots and let his trousers fall. His muscles rippled, and his skin glistened in the heat. I couldn't stop looking. Over the years, I'd naturally glimpsed men in various states of undress in the hallways of my mother's boardinghouse as they scurried, embarrassed, to the privy or the washroom ("Excuse me, miss"), but never had I seen a man so beautiful. So smooth, so perfect, like the etching of a statue from the Renaissance.

"I'll go in first," he said. "I won't look back."

And he did, and he didn't, and when, bare myself, I came up behind him in the water and put my hand on his shoulder and he turned around, he kept his eyes closed.

At first.

Maceo kept his eyes closed at first, even when he turned to face me. With his eyes shut tight and his head thrown back, he looked like someone in church being touched by the Holy Spirit, but it was only my fleshly hands that stroked his chest, its firmness, only my mortal fingers that traced the muscles that rippled across his taut belly, so different from the sad furred paunches that sagged from most of the men in my mother's boardinghouse. I lifted my fingers to touch his face, the lovely broad cheekbones, the straight brow, the firm jaw—a face with which a person could fall entirely—

He jerked away, his eyes opening in irritation or pain. Then he recovered, his features smooth again, and smiled, but his smile was strange. He glanced down at my breasts, at my naked belly, and stood there motionless, staring at me, as if waiting for something to happen.

A dizziness swept over me. Why was he not taking me in his arms, covering me with kisses, and so on—the stuff in which romantic novels trafficked? I had waited so long for him, I had believed . . . Only the water's weird, thick pressure held me up.

"Maceo." My soft voice shook. "Do you not care for me?"

"I do." He sighed. "You're beautiful."

But his arms hung by his sides, his hands resting lightly on the water's thick skin, and he made no move to touch me. I crossed my arms over my breasts. "But what's wrong, then?" I asked, frightened. "What's wrong with you, Maceo?"

Pain flashed across his face, then anger. His whole countenance stiffened, and he turned without a word and walked to shore. He threw on his clothes, untied his mare, leapt up, and kicked her hard. She whinnied in protest and sprang into a gallop, bearing him away, her hoofbeats fast in the quiet afternoon.

I stood in the water, staring at the spot where he'd disappeared into the mangroves, my body stunned and rippling with shock, anger, fear, grief, and the confusion of leftover desire. Slowly, I began to cry, and then I sobbed, hard, and I kept sobbing, loud and hopeless as a child, until no more sobs would come.

Bending my knees, I sank down until the water met my throat. I lifted my feet from the sand and tilted back until I lay with my face to the blue sky, the thick salt buoying my body, the water cooling and soothing my scalp. I drifted, reseeing, refeeling the whole episode again and again, puzzling over it, trying to understand what had happened, how everything had shifted so abruptly. Why had his eyes looked angry—or pained—when I'd touched his face? And why hadn't he touched mine or looked lovingly into my eyes? Isn't that what lovers did? Salt water slid from my eyes down my cheeks and joined the pond. I lay there, letting the last tears leak away.

Spent, I righted myself and waded out. I put my shoes on my wet feet and carried my clothes in a bundle, walking down the white road of crushed coral. The warm afternoon wind dried my skin, and when I reached the edge of the sheltering mangroves, I dressed and then kept walking home.

It was dusk when I arrived at the boardinghouse. There was no light in the kitchen, which was unusual, so I climbed the stairs. The door to the bedroom I shared with my mother was closed, but a band of lamplight shone beneath it.

I pushed it open.

With her bare foot, my mother was shoving a coiled rope beneath her bed. The wooden chair stood askew against the wall.

71

ZENAIDA

On Monday afternoon when my chores were done, I walked to the shore to be alone. I didn't go to the cigar factory; I didn't want to hear Feliciano read about rich Russians. I felt sad because I felt alone, and I felt alone despite the fact that I shared a bedroom with my mother and the house with twenty boarders. I wanted to sit alone in a blue place of wind and sand and waves and feel sad where no one could see me, and not have to talk or listen to anyone talk. To sit alone on the sand and think words no one would ever hear, and neither censor myself nor posture.

The wind blew hard and kept changing directions, as confused as I was. The green fronds of the coconut palms shimmered, and their bare gray trunks curved and undulated, and the rush of the wind through the fronds made a sound that would ordinarily have been soothing. Occasionally, a white sailor from Fort Zachary Taylor walked by, or two white sailors, laughing, and I wondered if they were on their way to the docks to look for prostitutes.

The salt pond visit with Maceo had started as a dream and unraveled into something painful that I couldn't understand. I had dreamed of him, yearned for him—however innocently, however chastely—for many long months. An eternity in any girl's heart. He had seemed to love me, too.

I hadn't found the words to tell my mother what had happened. I'd had only the limited comfort of her embrace, and the price I'd paid for it had been steep.

When I'd found my mother shoving the rope beneath her bed, I'd stopped in my tracks. She straightened the chair against the wall, where it had always sat so benignly. Now it seemed suddenly an object of horror.

"What are you doing, Mamá?"

"Nothing, child. Not a thing. Just tidying up a bit."

She sat down on the edge of her bed and gazed at me. She took my hands in hers and pulled me down beside her.

"Did you have a good time with Maceo?"

"I did," I lied.

"That's good, my daughter," she said. "That's good."

I didn't understand. How could she not see the painful, confusing truth of my day at the salt ponds with Maceo all over me? She'd always read me like a book—her own book, that she herself had made. But she seemed far away, her mind preoccupied with other thoughts.

"Let me show you something," she said.

She eased her pillow out of its cotton case. Into the pillow was sewn a tiny pocket I'd never seen before, and I abruptly realized that never once, in all these years of housekeeping by her side, had I been allowed to change her bed linens.

She reached into the little pocket in her pillow and drew out a beautiful button made of horn. She turned it over in her fingers. Held it up to the light. It was a swirl of black and brown and cream.

Her eyes went distant, remembering. "I wasn't usually allowed in the main house," she said. "Missus didn't want me in there. But one day the woman who scrubbed the floors died, and Missus said the floors needed to be cleaned anyhow. So there I was for three days, on hands and knees, scrubbing all the wood in the upstairs rooms, all the tiles in the downstairs rooms. Had to move the rugs and furniture and scrub underneath. Another woman beat the rugs outside."

"Yes?" I said.

"I was alone in the music room, scrubbing," she said, "when I saw this button wedged down in a crack between two tiles." She turned it over and over in her fingers. "It was the strangest feeling," she said, "like my whole seeing and being shrank down to just this one small thing." Her eyes came back. She placed it in my hand. "So magical. So beautiful. So precious."

It rested so lightly on my palm that I could hardly feel it.

"I knew my duty was to hand it to Missus—that it had fallen off someone's dress or coat and had to be sewn back on."

I nodded.

"We weren't allowed to have pockets in our clothes, for fear of us thieving," she said. "But no one was in the room. My heart beat so hard I thought I would die. That button was the most beautiful thing I could ever hope to own."

It felt so small and light. So insignificant, even, resting there in the center of my palm. To tell the truth, it seemed—though pretty enough—like a perfectly ordinary button, a kind I saw all the time adorning ordinary clothes.

"There were no footsteps, no voices near," my mother said. "There on my hands and knees, I reached beneath my skirt and hid that button in the pocket a woman always wears." She shrugged. "Her husband was using it all the time anyway. Why shouldn't I? That night, I took the button back to the cabin and washed it and hid it." She sighed. "I would take it out and look at it by moonlight when the others were asleep."

She took it from my hand and held it up.

"Almost like the moon, isn't it? Like a whole tiny world."

I nodded. I wanted to cry, but I held myself still.

"When I ran, I took it with me, sewn into my clothes. And when I got to Havana, I worked and met your papa, and we moved here to the island. Then, when I had you, I never needed fancy things. Never had any longing for them. I always had just this one, and it was enough."

She put the button back in its pocket and took my face in her hands.

"Baby, I know it don't make sense to you. But the way I come up, this is how I am. Some folks spread their love out thin. Lots of friends, lots of nice things. Not me." She shook her head. "I loved your papa, and I love you. Narrow. Deep. Hard. And I know what losing your papa did to me. How it felt. How I stayed alive only because of you." She looked into my eyes, and I felt myself falling into their fathomless depths. "You're my button. You understand?"

I didn't, exactly, but I nodded.

"Someday, you've got to go. Go make your own life. And that's a good thing, baby." She smiled. "A real good thing." She nodded, as if it were herself she was convincing.

She gave me a hug and put me to bed. She tucked me in and kissed my brow, and both of us went to sleep.

Or pretended to. I lay there in the dark, thinking about the coiled rope, the chair askew, the wooden rafters that stretched above us.

Before that night, I'd often daydreamed about moving out one day—nothing elaborate like Sofia's many schemes, but just finding my own small room in a boardinghouse, a room with a window in it, curves and lots of sunlight and delicate furniture—or I thought about how I would redecorate the boardinghouse if my mother would ever let me. Everything in it was heavy and rough and dark and lightless, which was not a redundancy: vast slabs of wood stuck together at right angles, the long table, the heavy benches. My mother's creepy statue of Eleguá behind the door. His cowrie-shell eyes, blank but always watching.

It was my only home, yet I had never felt at home there.

But now, intuiting what I could about my mother's planned response to my departure, how could I ever leave?

On Wednesday evening, the boarders had mostly finished with their supper (my mother's delicious papas rellenas, picadillo, and sweet plátanos maduros, with her soft, creamy flan for dessert). Maceo acted as if I weren't there at all, as if I were some serving girl, a stranger to him.

"I've begun to speculate," said Feliciano, with a last lick of his spoon, "that The Thorn may be one of our African brothers." He drew a folded paper from his breast pocket and unfolded it. "Listen to this latest verse that adorns the walls of your town." He read:

The lion shakes his golden mane and roars.
Greed flashes from his glaring eyes.
Arrayed in glory, bathed in light,
He prowls the earth and growls his lies.

"Well? What do you think?" He looked around the crowded table.

"Your logic leaves me behind, brother," said Maceo. "That verse says nothing of Africa, much less slavery or a race war in Cuba."

Feliciano smiled. "Our poet friend is far too subtle for that. But look at the patterns of his images. The lion—which is imperial Spain, of course—is linked to images of light and gold. And now listen to the second verse." He read:

Beneath the ceiba's limbs, we lay our heads
like offerings, clad in night.
We lie in wait in darkness.
Obscured by dark's soft cloak, we strike.

"Do you hear it? All things truly good are associated with darkness. Darkness is what keeps the soldiers safe, what gives them cover. And though he's talking, of course, about those who must camp in the jungle, unless I am mistaken, that figurative altar at the roots of the ceiba tree also suggests the Bakongo religion."

"This is so," Maceo said. "You could be right."

The boarders began to debate the positions of the two most prominent Afro-Cuban intellectual rivals of the day: Martín Morúa Delgado, who was living in Key West at the time, and Juan Gualberto Gómez, a fierier soul who claimed that notions of racial superiority and inferiority were utter falsehoods designed to exploit and oppress us. He'd been imprisoned in Morocco and then exiled to Madrid.

My mother rose to clear away the empty plates. Her eyes were clouded. I knew she was thinking of my father.

I quickly busied myself with picking up dishes, avoiding her gaze, while the men leaned back in their chairs, settling in to argue.

"But why don't all Cubans speak against the Spaniards publicly?" said one old worker. "We are free men, but some are as cowardly as slaves."

My mother spun with a stack of plates in her hands, lifted them high, and then caught herself, lowering them to the table with a slowness more ominous than slamming.

Everyone fell silent. I stood still against the wall.

"Silence," she said, "does not make someone a coward." Her voice trembled. "What lucky men don't know is that enough pain and terror can rob you of your voice. And that's exactly what they want, the masters." She glanced around at everyone. "Just your body, its soft holes and hard labor. All body, no voice. No thoughts, no views, no soul with its own desires." She wiped her hands on her skirt. "Trust me: Enough pain can turn a strong man into a puppet, a strong woman into a doll. Mute and dependable as a machine, obedient, smiling on cue as if strings worked the muscles of his face. Same with some of the women down at the docks, dancing and slithering as if they really wanted what men do to them all day. Not all. Some like that work, and glory on their names. But some are broken puppets."

No one spoke. It was rare for my mother to say six words at once.

"When you see someone like that," she continued, "you cannot blame them. The shame is not theirs. You must remember—we must all remember—that the shame belongs to the ones who broke them. Those of us lucky enough to have any soul left—who escaped slavery with a thin ribbon of soul still inside us—you know what makes us different? Special?"

We all looked at her. I still held the dishes I'd been clearing.

"What?" said the old man quietly.

"Nothing," she said. Her voice was flat. "We are not different. We are not special. We just were lucky. We had not had all the soul broken out of us yet. That's all.

"It can be done to anyone," she continued. "You cannot always see it on the surface. Some learn to act like others, behave like others. They want to dwell among the living. But inside their hearts, they're dead. If they are still living under the yoke of slavery, they take on the master's desires as their own, as if they were mere extensions of his will. They don't even have to think *I want to survive, I want to escape more pain.* They honestly want what the master wants. They have become a tool.

"And if they escape slavery, they are lost until they find a new master. A general. A boss. A husband. They look for the strongest. And then they obey.

"It's the only way they can feel a little safe. Do not mock their brokenness as cowardice. The shame belongs to those who broke them, not to the broken ones.

"Obedience is written in their flesh," she said. She picked up the plates again. "This is the lesson of the lash."

72

FELICIANO

"When it comes to the question of slavery," I said from the tribuna, looking out over the crowd of five hundred workers rolling their cigars, "one thing for which the philosophers and politicians have not begun to account is the factor of pleasure."

I had finished reading Tolstoy for the day, and my throat was surely as tired as the workers' hands, but the words of Zenaida's mother had stirred my thoughts the previous evening, and I had ideas I wanted to try out upon an audience. I was thinking of writing a piece for *La Prensa*.

"Let me explain. I do not mean the pleasure of having one's fields worked or one's coffee brought in on a silver tray. In those countries where slavery is illegal, rich men pay for such labor and enjoy its fruits. But they must lure the worker with a wage."

"Amen," cried someone from the galley.

"With slavery, violence and fear make the slave into a tool, a thing—and how deeply good it feels to those who own them: that expanded self, as if one's realm had suddenly, exponentially increased."

This was the part Señora Baliño had not theorized. She had spoken of the psychology of the one enslaved, but not of the enslaver. I had my own ideas about what prompted men to enact such cruelty.

"In ordinary life, one can only move one's own arms and legs—can operate only one's own tongue and lips to form the words one wants to say aloud. But! But if you own slaves, all their arms and legs are yours, moving according to your will, and their tongues are dumb except for the sentiments you like to hear. Pain and more pain renders them docile, subservient, and though the newspapers prate only of economics and the good of the nation when they write of abolition, the truth is also, I believe, that some humans find exquisite pleasure in expanding their dominion such that their will flows through the limbs of others."

Murmurs arose from the cigar rollers. Some were looking skeptically up at me.

I raised my hands in entreaty. "No, let me continue," I said. "The master of others feels larger than an ordinary man. No longer is he limited to only his own body. It is a form of expansion—of transcendence, even: that thing about which the North Americans love to write their essays. Slavery enables the masters to transcend the limits of their individual powers. As such, it must be a godlike feeling. Heady. Seductive. How else could intelligent, rational men have framed a new country with documents that vaunted freedom—inspiring Bolívar, no less, who liberated half the world from Spain—and yet preserve the right to own another human soul? It was the seduction of slavery, more delicious than the honesty that would have ended it, that placed this paradox at the heart of the United States."

I drew a deep breath. This was uncharted territory. I'd written some scraps of thought in my notebook the night before but had not tried these new ideas aloud.

"At least a monarchy like Spain," I said, "has no deception, no hesitation to say, 'I am the king, and you are the subject, and if you disobey, I will kill you—or throw you in a dungeon to suffer until you wish I had.' Slavery, then, is congruent with monarchy. But the North Americans were liars. They lied to the world and to themselves."

A knife pounded wood, and then another, and another.

"But no one will admit the pleasure! They talk about the difficulty of growing cotton and the superior physical endurance of the Blacks. But sheer pleasure there must be, the pleasure of domination. What else explains why even poor men—who stand to add nothing to their pockets by the deed—beat their wives into submission? Because it must be a pleasure, a terrible and exquisite pleasure, to use force to render someone powerless, to have them cower and jump at your step and tend to your needs before you even utter them: your bed made, your floor scrubbed, your meals cooked, your clothes washed and mended, your nightly needs accommodated by a body that dare not protest. Like a slave.

"I have not felt these pleasures of domination, to be clear," I said, "but I have witnessed them all around me my whole life." A shiver ran through me. Never had I come so close to speaking of what I had suffered. "We must illuminate the similarities among these apparently quite different scenarios. We must connect these various dynamics, as the great Bakunin did when he called for the emancipation of daughters and wives along with that of workers."

Chaveta's knife knocked against the wood.

"It seems an obvious thing that there exists a sick pleasure in controlling another, and that this pleasure is widespread, and that no one will admit it, but they hide behind talk of economy or racial superiority or wifely submission." My voice rose to a crescendo, triumphant. "This is the other side of the equation," I said. "This is the lesson of the fist, of the rape. This is the lesson of the lash."

And as I said the words, I felt a sudden pang of guilt. My eyes sought the tall windows.

Outside, from beneath her yellow parasol, Zenaida's dark eyes condemned my theft.

73

ZENAIDA

At Sofia's house on Friday evening, Julieta set little white porcelain plates before each of us. In the center of the plates rested strange black tubes, like tiny snakes or the plucked-out bodies of snails, glistening with some golden sauce.

"Now, this fine delicacy is a specialty of Key West," said Señor Robles, "and Gastón has mastered it. The Caesars wrote of it in ancient Rome. You will love it, Galván. It is quite exquisite."

"What are they, sir?" Feliciano asked.

Señor Robles smiled and stroked the edge of his mustache into a fine point. "Just try it, my boy." He gestured to us all expansively, as if he himself were Nero. "Eat, eat!"

I cut a little tube in half and forked it into my mouth. It was fatty, thick, and firm, with a creamy texture and a rich, delicious taste, both salty and sweet, yet somehow disturbing, as if it were altogether too delicate and fine a thing to be eaten.

Everyone chewed and made appreciative sounds.

I swallowed. "Please do tell us, sir."

Sofia laughed with excitement and clapped her hands. "Flamingo tongues! Isn't it amazing?"

I pressed my napkin to my mouth. I felt wretched all through me.

Eating a beautiful creature's torn-out tongue . . . I imagined their pink bodies sprawled and lifeless, their bright round eyes glassy with death.

"Aren't you eating yours, Zenaida?" Sofia asked.

"You have them," I replied, pushing my plate her way. I turned to my host and hostess. "They are indeed a very fine delicacy, but I find I cannot continue, knowing their origin. I am too fond of flamingos."

"I understand entirely," said Sofia's mother, nodding. "I don't care for them myself." She waved Julieta over, and my plate was cleared away.

"Well, I hope you're not too fond of wild doves!" Señor Robles chortled. "Or venison. I didn't have Gastón cook all day for nothing."

"No, sir," I replied. "I do like both those dishes, and it's rare that we can have them at my mother's house."

"Well, there you go, then," he said. "A treat." His voice softened. "And you can take some home to your mother, if you like."

A glance passed between us. I dropped my eyes.

I sometimes wondered if Sofia's mother actually knew everything and just pretended not to see. She was far from stupid. Yet her mind was so caught up in books and dreams . . . Perhaps she preferred disappearing into stories to the sad truth.

74

SOFIA

Likely out of deference to Zenaida and her altogether too delicate sensibilities, Eduardo and Feliciano began to praise the exploits of Black soldiers in Cuba.

My father amiably agreed. "These Blacks can fight, all right," he said.

"Moncada's a fine fighter and an excellent commander," said Eduardo, "a noble man, utterly devoted to the cause of liberty."

"Let him fight for the cause, then," my father said. "Military power? Fine. But political power? Never. It's one thing to be free, but quite another altogether to be equal. I find it most troubling how fast these sons of Africa assume the latter. Damned impudent, in my book. Would you have us ruled by savages?"

"Even if what you imply is true," said Feliciano, "and our African brothers in Cuba do want another Haiti, would it be worse than the imperial savagery of Spain?"

"Come, come," said my father, waving his hand. "Call it imperial domination if you like. But savagery? Spain is a civilized nation! Ancient and cultured."

"And Ethiopia is not?" shot back Feliciano. "The ancient kingdoms of Benin, of Ethiopia—"

"And Egypt!" I said brightly.

Feliciano's eyes swung to me, alight.

"Just so," he said. "Heed your daughter, sir."

I knew I had plucked easy fruit. Everyone knew Egypt—and in truth, I neither knew much about the Dark Continent nor cared. Zenaida, who should have had something useful to say, was sitting motionless, her face a mask.

My father snorted. "Heed my daughter, indeed. You're a bit annoying, my boy, as far as I'm concerned, but you seem to amuse my wife— and precious little does. Very well, then." He laughed. "I'll put the question to the ladies." His wine-glazed smile swept us all. "Tell us, ladies. Would you like Guillermo Moncada to be the new governor of Cuba?"

"President," Feliciano said.

"Yes, all right. President. This Black who keeps a harem—"

"But those are only rumors," broke in Eduardo.

My father barely paused. "A harem full of white women, Black women, mulattas, all as his so-called wives to use as he pleases—and all of whom call him Lord, I'm told." He raised an eyebrow at the gentlemen and took a thick swallow of wine.

"Quite like a white plantation master, then."

All eyes swung to Zenaida.

"What's that?" my father sputtered. "What's that you say?"

"Quite like a white—"

"Monstrous!" he cried. "Completely monstrous."

"Yes, sir," she said. "I do agree."

248

They sat, eyes locked in a glare, as my father's fat red face grew fatter and redder than I'd ever seen it. No one moved. The clock ticked on the mantel. The maid stood in the doorway, hand against her mouth, eyes wide. I'd read about spontaneous combustion and wondered if we were about to witness it, and how rich I would immediately become.

Zenaida pushed her chair back, smoothed her skirts, and laid her napkin down.

"I have perhaps worn thin the welcome of my host."

"Perhaps?" my father blustered. "You come in my house, eat my fine food, drink my—"

"She only speaks the truth," said my mother. She flicked the gold rim of a porcelain plate with her pretty crimson nail. "Have we become so fragile at this table that we cannot bear to hear it?" She turned to Zenaida. "Stay, child. Drink my husband's wine and take your ease. You're welcome here."

My mother reached to pour more wine into Feliciano's goblet. The maid, who'd disappeared, materialized with coffee on a silver tray.

"Mamá," I said, "you're most congenial tonight."

75

ZENAIDA

After my run-in with Sofia's father, Feliciano changed the subject to his obsession: the intersection of poetry and politics, the question of whether or not poems could make anything happen in the real world. I was grateful, for my exchange with Sofia's father had left me trembling with anger.

"I don't know if art should be political," Sofia's mother was saying. "The realm of art is transcendent and eternal, floating above our mundane cares, while politics is all about fighting for position: who is the strongest, how much can they win—land, power, wealth . . ."

I took deep, slow breaths and pressed my palms together underneath the table, where no one could see, to help dispel the electricity that coursed through me. I did not feel polite.

"But cannot politics itself be an art?" asked Eduardo eagerly.

"Machiavelli thought so," said Feliciano. "As did Castiglione, and Sun Tzu. Many men across the ages have played politics as elegantly as chess."

"But chess is still a game," protested Sofia's mother. "It still takes place upon a board, which is just a peacetime version of a battlefield. There are always edges and corners, always a winner and a loser." She set her wineglass down with unusual force. I had never seen her so roused. "But art is free. And holy."

"Nonsense," said her husband. "Edges? Corners? Artists paint upon a canvas. Borders, my dear! They don't splash paint upon the street and claim it as a masterpiece. Anyone who did would be locked up as a madman." He stabbed his roast dove emphatically. "And the poetry you love so much—it's printed on a page, no? More edges, more corners. And when it's published, men argue about whether it's any good or not, so poets are winners and losers, too. And the same is true of paintings and sculpture. Men argue about the worth of art as loudly as they argue about baseball or bullfights."

"Even on the page," I observed, my heartbeat having slowed to its normal rate, "a poem does not run truly wild. The poet follows rules. The lines must rhyme and find some rhythmic pattern." Though often I wondered why it had to be that way.

"I agree with Feliciano that politics can be artful," said Sofia, glancing at him meaningfully (though it was Eduardo who had first claimed it), "but I must disagree with you, Mamá. I think that art can be political." She cast a little knowing smile around the table, preparing us for some bon mot she was about to drop. "*Bad* art." She tittered at her own remark. "Those poets who prate on about revolution and the like. Such doggerel! Romance and beauty are the poet's true métier, are they not?"

I looked down at my porcelain plate. Around its wide turquoise rim danced peacocks and gold pears.

"I must beg to differ with my young hostess," Feliciano said. "Romance may be one purview of the poet, yes, for we put in words the longings all men feel. But you paint with far too broad a brush— and one dipped in tar, no less—when you dismiss all poems of politics as weak. Some are heavy-handed, yes—they grate upon the soul—but then, so, too, do many poems of love."

He reached for his wineglass, but it was empty. Sofia's mother quickly filled it.

"It is not the subject matter that should render, a priori, the verdict on a poem's excellence," he continued, "but rather the poet's delicacy of feeling, his originality of expression, and the elegance of his verse." He raised a single finger, shook it meaningfully, and swept his gaze around the table like the beam from atop a lighthouse. "It takes a deft touch, to be sure, and a gifted mind—and even then, not every earnest attempt may succeed. But to dismiss out of hand all political art because of some clumsy specimens is surely to conflate the bathwater with the child. Why, even on the walls of your own town, I have seen some remarkable examples of political poetry. This writer who calls himself The Thorn—"

"Oh yes!" said Eduardo, smiling. "The Thorn again."

"He's a rabble-rouser, I'll say that much," said Señor Robles. "I'm no one to comment on the quality of poetry—I'll leave that to you ladies—but he certainly has stirred things up among my workers. All this talk of strikes and suffering. I can't say I care for the man."

"But why not?" Eduardo asked. "He is on the right side of history!"

"No, no. Listen to this. It's one thing to attack the Spaniards. All well and good." Señor Robles rummaged in the pocket of his jacket that hung upon his chair. "But now he's calling for a new uprising among the workers."

"What?" Worry flashed across Señora Robles's face. "We don't need any more violence here."

"We most certainly do not." Señor Robles pulled out a sheet of paper and unfolded it. "Especially when the workers win. Listen to this rubbish." He read:

Rich women live in luxury.
Rich men exploit us all.
But when their factories fail them,
The poor man takes the fall.

Despite his endless labor,
a poor man's always poor,
beset by bill collectors,
the rich wolf at the door . . .

He cannot feed his children.
His wife wears tattered clothes.
He bows and scrapes and feigns respect
To masters that he loathes.

I watched my mother struggle,
I heard my father groan—
Unless he joins a union
The poor man walks alone.

He shook his head in disgust. "This damnable Thorn! I'd like to get my hands on him. Incendiary, this nonsense!"

I felt a thrill, to hear such words shared aloud at a grand table like the Robleses'. To know they rattled a man like Sofia's father.

"Surely that's why he doesn't reveal himself," said Eduardo. "He fears reprisal, this masked man of the pen."

And so the evening wound on, from speculation about The Thorn's identity to Cuba's fight against Spain (where all conversational roads eventually led), as Julieta brought in platter after platter of food and took away our dirty plates. Forking up the small, sweet bites and listening to the talk, I couldn't help but think of the stacks of china she'd be washing alone long after we were all asleep.

Eventually it all wound down. We'd risen, and I was donning my shawl, when Eduardo most kindly offered to escort me home.

"No, my friend, let me," said Feliciano, "for I reside there anyway." My head inclined to thank him. "You are most kind," I said, "for I do not care to walk alone at night."

As I uttered the words, Feliciano's eyes locked upon mine most strangely, with a kind of warmth and pain, as if he were opening himself to me, and as if I were sinking into the blackness at their centers, and I were willingly falling in, and not minding. A strange heat filled me, and a confusion, and I felt intoxicated, yet it was not the wine.

We all moved slowly, chatting, as the Robles family ushered us through the door and then out onto their veranda.

"Ah! A very fine night," said Sofia's father, spreading his arms expansively.

And it was. Dark and warm and clear, with a full moon and all the constellations shining.

"The stars . . . ," I managed to say, having trouble catching my very breath.

"They are, indeed," said Feliciano, offering me his arm. As I laid my hand in the tender crook of his elbow, I saw Sofia staring at us. Her face bore a strange rigidity I'd never seen before.

I turned away to hide my smile.

76

SOFIA

I walked back into the dining room. My father stayed on the veranda to smoke with Eduardo Salazar. Slowly I began to lift the dishes from the table.

"My sweet dove!" my mother said, having followed me inside. "Leave those things. Julieta will do it." She approached me, took my face in her hands, inspecting my features. It was terrible, suffocating, having her hover so close. "What's come over you, my dear? Are you unwell?"

"I'm fine, Mamá."

I felt numb. Perhaps he had meant only to be courteous. But the gallant way he'd reached out, smiling, and the way she'd slipped her hand onto his sleeve—

"Don't be absurd," my mother said, taking the dishes from my hands. "Help her once, and she'll expect it always." She set the soiled things down and laid her palm against my forehead. "You're not warm," she said. "Still, you look pale. Go up to bed."

"I don't feel tired." Perhaps he'd smiled down at her in merely a brotherly way.

"Read for a while, then, sweet girl. But go. Go on up." She nodded her head firmly. "Go, my dear. You look as if you might faint."

I submitted my cheek to her moist, repellent kiss, and then made my way to the main hall and up the stairs and down the corridor and into my chamber with a thick, dead, heavy feeling, the way people walked at funerals, which I'd never understood. I'd always believed it only a performance, done out of respect for the dead. But now I felt that thick slowness in my own limbs.

Inside my room, I lit a candle, undid my dress, stepped out of it and laid it on the chaise, unlaced my corset, and slid my nightdress of thin voile over my head. I unpinned my hair, and it fell around my shoulders like a black silk cloak. I sat at my vanity, staring into the glass. Same face, same cherub mouth. Aristocrats from Spain, rich businessmen from New York, plantation owners from Cuba: all kinds of men had flattered and flirted with me at my father's table. Why would a lector prefer—

No, it was pity, surely, that prompted his courtesy to her. He was staying at her mother's boardinghouse, after all. It was simple politeness on his part, the way any gentleman would protect any woman, even if she were his inferior, or old and plain. I lifted my brush, held its cool silver weight in my hand, and began to brush my hair back from my face in long, slow sweeps. *One hundred, ninety-nine, ninety-eight . . .* Yes, most certainly, he'd acted from courtesy alone. And as for the walk home in the starry night, the warm temptations of that dark and private time . . . Well, Zenaida was dull—practically mute!—whereas he was a lively man, full of ideas. *Eighty-seven, eighty-six, eighty-five . . .* Her days were essentially the same as Julieta's, filled with stultifying housework. What could she possibly have to say that would pique an intellect like his? *Seventy-five, seventy-four, seventy-three . . .* My heart lifted. The terrible tension eased.

Yes, there was definitely nothing with which I should concern myself. Still, I would need to redouble my efforts. He was a clever man; I would be cleverer still. All his talk about democracy and equality . . . Perhaps that would be my entry. It was not that I wanted Feliciano Galván in any serious way, of course. He would never do. A rich patrón he may have had, but no truly respectable young man would live in a boardinghouse owned by a Black.

Nonetheless, I wanted his attention; I wanted to number him among my conquests. I wanted him to long for me and realize he could not have me, to write sonnets about my terrible beauty and his lonely dejection. What pleasure was there in being merciless, after all, if the swain was unaware?

77

FELICIANO

"You must forgive me," I said, in the strange hum of intimacy that had suddenly sprung to life between Zenaida and me. The full moon gilded her skin and lips with a silvery shimmer. "I should not have quoted your mother in the galley without giving credit to my source. It was wrong."

She gave a quiet laugh.

"What?"

The breeze blew the tendrils of her hair most fetchingly. Gazing at her as we walked along together, I realized she was, objectively speaking and by far, the most beautiful young woman on the island. Though I felt no amorous desire, for I knew almost nothing about her inner life, I felt strangely close to her.

"You're not the first," she said.

For a moment, I was startled, as if she'd read my thoughts. Then I remembered. "The first to steal your mother's ideas? But truly, it was beneath me. I am most embarrassed. I was simply caught up in the ferment of thought she had provoked in me. I was carried—"

"The first to use her concepts, but not include her name. I guess such things are common. My father did the same."

I stopped in the middle of the street and swung her around to face me. "Zenaida." I gripped her hands in mine. "Say that again."

She looked at me, her eyes confused. "I just said my father did that, too. He would rewrite her ideas in his own words and publish—"

"No, say it again, just as you said it before. In the same words."

She paused, trying to recall.

"I'll say it for you, then. You said, 'The first to use her concepts, but not include her name. I guess such things are common. My father did the same.' Zenaida, you spoke in rhyming iambic trimeter. As effortless as water."

Her eyes widened. "People rhyme all the time by accident," she protested. "We speak in iambic trimeter and tetrameter and even pentameter all the time without even noticing it. It's nothing. It doesn't mean a person is a poet."

"No, it's you," I said, blood pounding at my temples. "Those little remarks you make from time to time, the way you study everyone, so quiet yet so watchful—you have a poet's sensibility, and a political intelligence to match." I shook my head, all of the pieces tumbling together at once. "Do not deny it. You are The Thorn."

"I'm only a girl," she said.

The pulse throbbed in my ears; I could barely hear my own voice as I answered.

We arrived at the boardinghouse and circled around to the backyard. Moonlight spilled everywhere.

"You go ahead in," I said. "I will just walk for a while yet."

She tilted her head, her wide brown eyes studying me.

"You are angry," she said.

"Not at all."

"No, you are," she said. "I don't know why, but you are angry now."
"Not at all. Just in need of some exercise." I smiled and nodded toward the dark back door. "Go in. Sleep well. I'll see you tomorrow." Still watching me over her shoulder, she headed up the steps. I smiled again politely and watched her go inside.

I headed down Emma Street in the dark, drawn as if magnetized toward the well-lit business district, the back of my neck painfully taut and a strange, high ringing in my ears, the sound of the rushing ocean on my left, everything glistening with moonlight so unaccountably bright my eyes stung.

An uneducated girl: as good a poet as I.

Perhaps better.

It would take a while to sink in.

78

ZENAIDA

I had scarcely slipped in the back door when someone grabbed me in the dark. I cried out in fear.

"Shh!" My mother's eyes were wide and furious. "You come with me."

"Mamá, what—"

"You just come with me," she said, and pulled me by the arm through the dining room and parlor and up the front stairs. My mother's fits of rage were not uncommon. I had seen her angry before—when I had failed to clean a room properly or been what she called "too familiar" with one of the boarders, laughing too long at his jokes or letting him touch my braids—but never anything like this. She seemed furious enough to ignite.

"But, Mamá—" I said as she dragged me along the upstairs corridor.

"Hush," she hissed. "Don't you wake my boarders."

When she approached the attic door at the end of the hall, I knew. I sagged in her grip. She opened it and dragged me through.

Up the narrow stairs to the third floor we went as my mind sped through the catalog of everything I'd carefully remembered to do: wipe down the inking plate, the chase, the rollers; fold the little wiping cloth and hide it in the lowest drawer of the cabinet; take each small letter from the chase and place it back in the rack; cover the whole letterpress with the oilcloth again—

She yanked me over to the machine and tore the sheet aside.

"I knew it," she said, letting me go.

Moonlight streamed in through the little window, glinting on the forged iron of the flywheel and the inking plate. Long ago, I would help my father in the wee dark hours of the morning, my small foot pressing the pedal again and again to make the flywheel spin as he quickly laid each sheet of paper in and carefully removed it, getting the morning edition printed before dawn. I knew he didn't really need me; he let me help because I was always begging to spend time with him. As we worked, he'd talk about politics, the fighting, his dreams of a free Cuba. "The beauty of this particular press," he'd said, running his hands admiringly over its metal parts, "is that one man can work it alone." He'd smiled down at me. "That gives you freedom of thought, Zena. Independence. True freedom of the press. One man alone can write, can print—can change the world."

I'd looked up at him, thinking, *Could a girl?*

"I knew it," my mother repeated. "Sooner or later, I knew you'd be up here, tempting fate like your father."

And then I saw it, down between the iron bars, on the wooden boards of the floor: a single black drop of ink, still wet enough to shine. In my haste, I'd missed wiping it up.

I looked at the ink drop, wishing I could dive into it and disappear forever. I could not meet her eyes and the raw fear that filled them.

"You're that one they've all been talking about." She crossed her arms. "You."

It was not a question.

"And there's no stopping you, is there. Any more than there was him, no matter the danger."

Again, it was not a question. The breath slid slowly from me. I felt empty and scared and meaningless.

But I shook my head. "No, ma'am," I said. "There is not."

"Mm-hmm." She nodded. "Like I thought." Her face settled into a clear, determined mask.

She shook the sheet back over the press.

"Then you come with me," she said. She hustled me back down the narrow staircase, down the corridor, down the front stairs, through the parlor and dining room. In the kitchen, she lit a candle and then pulled me out the back door, down the steps, and across the yard to the shed.

For many years, my mother's cauldron had resided in a locked mahogany trunk inside the padlocked shed that nestled near the roots of the ceiba tree, the branches of which shaded the whole courtyard of our boardinghouse like a green canopy. I had seen this cauldron exactly twice before, when my mother had gone to the shed for other things and I had tagged silently behind her. I was forbidden to touch the cauldron, on pain of whipping.

The moon lit the black sky, and the shadows of the ceiba made the darkness deeper. A brisk wind snuffed the candle out. At the shed, my mother slid her sandals off and nodded, waiting until I did the same. She twisted the key, drew me inside the shed, and shut the door.

The packed earth felt cool beneath my feet. My mother squatted, relit the candle, and unlocked the trunk with the key that always hung between her breasts. She lifted out the cauldron, its round iron heavy in her hands, and set it on the ground. The candlelight flickered orange in all the cauldron's small declivities. She looked up at me, her eyebrow cocked, until I squatted, too. I had to lift my skirts; it felt unladylike.

The cauldron was lidded with oilcloth, which was bound tightly with a leather thong. She untied it, and when she laid the cloth to the side, a strange scent lifted from the pot: a clean, musky fragrance of damp earth and tangled vines, of wild green things mixed with the golden dust of amber. And under that, a deeper odor, ominous and powerful, like blood: the scent of strength, as definite as death. The smell of the iron itself.

She lifted out various sticks and pieces of metal, along with small packets wrapped in leather and tied with twine, and laid everything carefully aside on the smooth-packed soil. She did not look at me.

She drew out the final bundle, which was knotted in thick blue-and-white batik.

"Open your hands," she said.

I did.

She untied the fabric knot and peeled back the folded cloth. Five small white bones lay inside, thin like the bones of a bird.

In my open hands, she arranged them. The candle's flame shuddered and flared. My mother made a little pattern, and then I saw. The bones were a forefinger and thumb, pinched together as if gripping something small.

"If you are going to do this thing, you need a powerful protection," she said. "A father's protection."

I stared at her, but her eyes were hooded as she gazed down.

"He set type with his left hand," she said.

"So do I," I whispered.

She folded my hands around my father's bones and wrapped her own hands around mine. The heat of her palms seemed to sear my skin as she gripped me.

She shut her eyes and sang low words I'd never heard before, a melody that barely rippled up and down the scale. Her body rocked back and forth as she sang, and I began to sway in time with her. I closed my eyes, too, and let her voice fill me as the same words sounded again and again. A hot pulse beat in the heart of my hands as she held the three of us together. The scents of the cauldron grew stronger, overwhelming. The clean wildness and the power and the death. My thighs were trembling; I was not used to squatting for long periods. My head was nodding slowly up and down in time to the song she kept singing, and I felt it fill me, and then my lips were moving, too, and I disappeared.

Death was certain, Death was sure. Death owned me, one way or another. I felt Death befriending me.

My head began to buzz with a kind of intense pleasure that shot down through my belly and into the earth.

And suddenly I knew: This was the power. This was the protection. This was the freedom.

Not that Death would never find me.

But that it most definitely would.

And that therefore I could not let the fear of Death—and hence the fear of any human's wrath—keep me from anything I had to do.

That was the magic.

CHAVETA

On Sunday after supper, we sat on the porch for the breeze. With Papi's dominoes, the little ones built towers and knocked them down with a black clatter.

"I don't know about this new lector," said Papi. A cloud of cigar smoke clung around him. "The things you say he reads. Sheer anarchism."

"Nonsense." My mother held up the knee of my father's pants she was mending. "What in the name of God is wrong with you? Do you crawl around on your knees like a child? My God." She sighed and returned to stitching.

"Those trousers are old," my father said.

I said, "Galván tells it like it is."

Dominoes crashed to the wood. The little ones giggled.

"Maybe." My father puffed on his cigar. "But telling it like it is can bring danger. A lector's free to come and go. Take the next boat. Some of us are stuck here."

"Stuck?" My mother laughed. "Speak for yourself. What keeps us here? This leaky roof? Our possessions? We could pack in half an hour."

"All right, all right. That's not my point—"

Crash of dominoes. Burst of children's giggles. Horse's hooves clopping fast up the road.

Maceo trotted up on a brown mare and called a greeting to my parents. My mother rose to her feet and leaned against the rail. I stayed where I was, cross-legged on the top step.

Maceo halted his horse. "I'm wondering if you'd mind if I took your daughter for a ride."

My mother glanced at me, her eyes excited, her eyebrows raised in question. I shrugged. I'd been wanting a chance to be alone with him.

"Mind?" she said. "No, we don't mind."

My mother was so transparent. Maceo was a soldier, handsome and tall. He fought for Cuba. She wanted me married, and I was getting old.

"Go, my daughter," she said, excitement in her voice. "Go and have a happy time."

I got to my feet and dusted my behind. The sky still held a couple of hours of light. When Maceo offered his hand, it was easy to swing up behind him in my trousers. The little ones dropped their dominoes to watch from behind the porch railing, and I waved to them as he kicked his mare into a showy canter. After we rounded the corner onto Virginia Street, he let her drop back to a walk.

I wondered if he'd take me to the San Carlos for coffee or to the café next door. We could sit and watch the old men play checkers and backgammon and listen to the lectors debate.

Or maybe he'd take me to a tavern by the docks and buy me a short glass of rum, and we'd watch the sun set and sing rude songs with the sailors and whores. I knew the words—

But he steered his brown mare right on Edmonton. We passed more workers' cabins and left the edge of the settled town. The Catholic convent loomed a block away. We made a left on United and headed into the scrub trees and buttonwood groves where I liked to hunt.

It didn't matter. What mattered was the message I had.

"Let us speak of the revolution," I said.

He groaned. "Let's not."

I had learned from my mother that when a man says something you do not want to hear, ignore it. Keep talking.

"The leaders here want you to carry a message to General Bonilla in the field."

"Oh." In my arms, his body straightened. "General Bonilla?"

"Yes. We have crucial intelligence."

"What intelligence?"

"Urgent."

"Yes, but what is—"

"If you get it through to the general, it guarantees us a win, a win that could shift everything in our favor. It could end our struggle, give us victory, and set Cuba free at last."

"I will tell him," he said. "What is the message?"

"No," I said.

"Why not?"

"The leaders trust you, but they well know the methods Spaniards use. If you are caught, they'll torment it out of you."

He stiffened with pride. "Never."

"As you say."

Men. They all thought they were tough, but let them stub a toe, and they whine like babies for a week.

"Nonetheless," I said, "the leaders will take no risks. They will give you the message in writing, and you must deliver it."

"That makes no sense," he said. "What's to keep me from reading it—or the Spaniards, if they capture me?"

"Leave that to us," I said. "Are you willing?"

His mare veered too close to a buttonwood branch. We ducked.

"I am," he said. "Although I don't see why you need to be so mysterious."

"Will you be able to find the general?"

"Of course. I know his rough location now. Once I get to the area, I will find fighters who can direct me to him."

"It must be only you," I said. "The leaders trust you. This intelligence is decisive. You must put it in the general's own hand. You cannot pass the message to another soldier unless you are mortally wounded. You can trust no one else with it."

I didn't know what the intelligence was. I was just the go-between. But men respected you more when you pretended to know things.

"I will do it," he said. "I will carry out the mission." His voice was deep, his tone serious. Like always. Against his shoulder, I buried my smile.

We rode in silence for a while. I liked the rhythm of riding horseback with Maceo's ribs warm under my hands. My breasts jostled against his back.

"What's your horse's name?"

"Sabotage."

I laughed.

His face swung halfway back. "What?"

A proper girl would say nothing. "It's just funny. Exactly what a soldier in a novel would name his horse."

He shrugged, his body tense under my hands, and then kicked the mare into a gallop. I had to hang on tight to him and grip her hard with my legs. Luckily, this was not difficult.

After a minute or two of racing fast across the scrubland, he let her drop back to a trot and then a walk.

When we got to the salt ponds, the sun was turning orange. A thousand pink flamingos lounged in the shallows, like tourists from the North bathing at the shore.

The mare whickered. We slid down off her back, and Maceo flung her reins over a branch.

"Don't you need to tie her?"

"She stays where I tell her."

On the other side of the pond stood the salt warehouse and drying sheds, but no one worked on Sunday. A white heron sailed over us.

Maceo took my hand and led me to the shore. He took off his boots. Stripped off his shirt. Unbuckled his trousers and stepped out of them. He waded into the water and glanced back. "You coming?"

I followed suit and walked in. To my knees, to my waist. The underwater sand felt calm and cool beneath my feet. When I stood chest-deep, he came toward me, touched my shoulder with a single finger. Traced my collarbones.

"You're so beautiful." His eyes were dark and far away. "You've always been so beautiful."

I drew back. The blue water moved against me, thick as cream, dark as oil.

"I'm here to swim," I said.

Gently, slowly, his glance tentative, he reached down and grasped my wrist. He pulled my hand toward his groin.

I jerked away.

He froze. Frowned, his eyes worried.

I shrugged. "If you want a whore, go to the docks."

"I don't." His face had paled. He ran a hand through his wet hair. "I just want you to—" We turned to watch a cluster of flamingos bicker, then take flight. He looked back at me. "But I can give you money."

"No."

His frown deepened. "Do you have a man?"

I turned my back on him and waded to the shore. I didn't have a man. I had sixteen. In addition to Ramón, the butcher's son, I'd been jerking off men, ten cents per customer, three or four a week, for well over a year in the little abandoned storage shed behind Weatherford's

Saloon. It was an efficient operation. We sat together on a wooden crate. They knew what to expect, and often they were hard by the time they handed me a clean handkerchief and unbuttoned their trousers for the job. If not, I softened my voice and told them about the great cigar factory of Seville, built like a palace from stone and full of statues and fountains, where only women rolled cigars—on their laps, because the men of Europe liked to say they could taste the heat of women's thighs when they lit up.

"Just think of it," I would say. "Their quick and nimble fingers moving between their own legs, rolling."

Sofia had told me the story, and it worked every time if a man was slow to stiffen. Then my own nimble fingers would do their job: stroke, roll, tug, back and forth, quick and light, then firmer, jerking their stubby little sausages until the white stuff squirted, and then wiping up at the end, folding the handkerchief into a neat square, and tucking it into their pocket while they were still too sunk in happy stupor to move.

"Remember," I always warned, "say nothing. If the other men find out I do this for you, they'll want it, too. Then I'll have to charge you more. That's supply and demand. And if my parents find out, they'll lock me up at the convent, and then you'll be paying top dollar at the whorehouse, where they might infect your dick with sickness. You definitely won't get the hands of a virgin."

They'd nod, dumb with coming.

"Swear."

"I swear," they'd say.

"No, swear on the Holy Virgin of Charity of the Copper." Our patron saint of Cuba. And they'd swear on her. It always made me smile. I was the Unholy Virgin, and I pocketed their coppers.

Was it strange, how sinless I felt? It was just another kind of manual labor. Sometimes when I was rolling cigars at the workbench, I considered how the same basic skills were required: dexterity, sensitivity in the fingertips, efficiency, a high tolerance for boredom. Sometimes one of the men I jerked would walk by, his eyes glued to my hands as they patted and rolled that smooth tube into shape. I would pinch its tip, and he would wince. I thought of their squinched-up faces, the little worms of white that squirted out of them, how they collapsed afterward with smiles like sated babies. Some even drooled.

I liked Maceo, but only as a comrade, and I did not care to see him do those things.

"We're friends, Maceo. Let's stay that way."

"If you're my friend, then do this for me."

"No," I said. "I am Zenaida's friend first."

My skin was drying fast but filmed with salt. I pulled my clothes back on. Coming out of the water, he shook himself like a dog, his face furrowed with frustration. He dressed. His white shirt stuck to the muscles of his back.

"Maceo."

He shook his head and walked to his brown mare, pulling her reins from the branch. "What kind of girl are you, anyway?"

I shrugged and smiled. "Not that kind, I guess."

He stared at me.

"Look, Maceo. I'll be your friend, your comrade."

We stood there, staring at one another. Eventually the hurt drained from his eyes, and he nodded. He vaulted onto his horse's back and held out a hand, and I clambered up behind him and settled my hands on his waist. He gave Sabotage a soft kick, and we moved off, back toward town. The mare's slow rhythm rocked us.

What kind of girl.

I didn't know what kind of girl I was.

Wind blew against my face.

MACEO

I wasn't born disloyal. Sitting at the lectors' table at the café on Tuesday evening, I touched Feliciano's wrist, as if to emphasize my point about munitions, and there was no ill effect. He did not jerk away; he just nodded, smiling, and kept talking about the Haitian revolution. His fine hands gesticulated in the air as if a dancer had mapped their passage, and the bulge in his throat rose up and down as he spoke.

Suddenly he was turning to me again, his dark eyes bright.

"But what say you, Maceo? Spain's propaganda says our African brothers in Cuba want not just their freedom but to rule the island, and the wealthy white Cubans fear another Haiti. You've fought with the insurgents. What's your view?"

His full lips on the rim of his glass. I struggled to gather my thoughts.

"In the battlefield, we fight together," I said. "Men of all races, side by side as brothers. Do we fight imperial Spain? Yes. Do we also attack plantations? Yes, but for the cause of liberty for all men."

"Just so! Well said." He went on, his talk wending its way to Bakunin's writings about personal liberty. "The freedom to love whomever one will cannot be divided from the freedom from imperial tyranny," he said. "The desire of one for another is perhaps the most profoundly subversive force of all, for it challenges all the rules of sticking safely with one's own kind, of marrying a woman of one's age and color and class—or a little better, if possible."

Someone snickered.

"Yet secretly we crave that which is strange, that which challenges all we think we know."

His dark eyes found mine again, and I nodded, feeling myself stripped naked by his gaze. He turned back to the others.

"Perhaps the church and state set up so many prohibitions against free love precisely because its force so threatens the social order. The desires of the flesh can cut across Black and brown and white, rich and poor, married and single . . ." His voice trailed off.

The other lectors and the workers who hovered around us in a ring were quick to furnish ribald proofs of his claim. And so the evening went on.

When we all rose to go, I clapped him on the shoulder in a very manly way.

"Fine words," I said, my tone deeper than usual.

He clasped me to his chest and pounded my back.

"Brothers in arms!" he cried. He pulled back, both hands still on my shoulders, and smiled. "I am the pen, you are the sword." He clapped my shoulder and turned to join the others.

The golden flame in my belly leaped. Waves of heat ran all through me, like electricity through wires.

81

LÍBANO

Within the high iron fence that surrounded the Royal Tobacco Factory in the great city of Seville—made greater by the Spaniards' plundered riches from the New World (which was, of course, just as old as the old one)—there stood a workers' prison. To get to their cigar-rolling benches each day, all the women must file past it. Every evening they must pass it again. The cries of their jailed compatriots reminded them of the high price of trying to steal tobacco leaves by smuggling them out in their blouses or skirts.

I read this in a book. It had a reproduction of a lithograph of the prison. Women's hands reached out between the bars.

Here in Key West, the rules were very lax. There were no guards searching workers at the factory door as they left. The men were even given a weekly ration, to prevent temptation. This was the power of strikes. (Women received no rations, for it was assumed that no woman wished to smoke—though everyone knew a granny who could not live without her nightly cigar.)

I always looked down Chaveta's blouse as I poured her coffee: such an inviting landscape. But never before had I seen brown leaves tucked there, like today.

I felt surprised. Chaveta was no thief.

And why raw leaves, when she could more easily pocket a cigar?

82

CHAVETA

Night. Everyone slept. I sat alone at the kitchen table and worked in the pool of light from the kerosene lamp.

One leaf for strength. One for fragrance. Nothing for combustion. Instead: The note. The handwritten note for General Bonilla, penned in a code I didn't know, with a carefully drawn map of Cuban terrain I did not recognize: a river, small angles for mountains . . . Instructions that would turn the tide. And then the final line with which so many of our letters close, *Yours for the Revolution,* but with no signature.

Roll the two leaves into thin tubes. Roll the note into a tube. Roll all three of them together. Chop the ends with the chaveta. Roll them in two binder leaves, and then the wrapper. Smooth and seal it all together with tree resin. Shape it, press it down. Use the side of the chaveta to roll it smooth. Pinch the tip. Trim, trim, trim, smooth. And then wrap the band around it and seal it with a dot of resin.

I dipped my father's plume in ink and pressed a tiny black mark on the brown wrapper just next to the slender band.

Then I rolled three more cigars.

An elegant set, all four identical but for the small black dot on the one that held the note.

Just the thing to present to a general.

Just the thing to pass innocuously through any Spanish search.

83

SOFIA

At last—long last!—the pageant did arrive. I joined the other contestants on the wooden stage of the San Carlos—seventeen of the town's most marriageable girls, arrayed in a line, ranging in age from fifteen years old to a most pitiable twenty-two. My eyes scanned the line as I approached. Most of the town's best families were represented: the Salazars, the Herreras, the Mendozas, and the Orozcos; and then there were the poorer girls, like Celida Boza and Graciela Saenz—and Zenaida, tall and standing a little bit apart in a simple gown of yellow. Silk swirled around my ankles like thick cream, and my satin slippers slid across the boards.

Though Pura Salazar did look sweet in pale-pink taffeta—like a big rosy meringue—I had no true competition. The other girls each had an obvious failing: too plump, or weak chins, or no bosom, or dark. I sighed with pleasure.

My silk gown fit like water, and my maid had coiled my hair in elaborate twists and tucked two white hibiscus blooms in back. Zenaida stood at the end of the line, at the edge of the stage, closest to the steps.

Smiling, I stepped into place next to her. Very egalitarian and all. Her darkness and plain gown would throw my own fair beauty into greater relief.

Chaveta wasn't there, which would work in my favor, too. Rough she may be, but no one could deny Chaveta's beauty when her face was clean, and who knew what sort of dress her mother may have found and altered, and what it would do for her figure?

At the other end of the stage stood a long table draped with bunting: red, white, and blue, doing double duty for the future flag of Cuba and for the United States as well. Behind the table sat the three judges in their finest suits: Señor Casuso, Señor Lallanilla, and the handsome Feliciano Galván.

Below us, the auditorium was full, the audience chattering and rustling in their seats or craning to see us. Occasionally a man whistled and was slapped quiet by the nearest old woman's fan. I could see my parents in their usual row. What were we waiting for?

I fluttered my white fan in front of my mouth and whispered to Zenaida, "So Chaveta has defied her father after all?"

Her yellow fan flipped open. She inclined her head my way. "Perhaps so."

"If she doesn't come, her mother will kill her."

"No," said Zenaida. "Her mother will only complain and cry. It's her father who will kill her."

84

Maceo

I wasn't born disloyal. I wanted to love Zenaida. She glowed in gold there on the stage, beautiful and good and kind, with soft dark eyes and gentle hands. She cooked and sewed and cleaned. She could keep a neat home. Our children would be beautiful and healthy, and she would raise them well and teach them how to read and write. She would treat me gently, holding me in her long arms, soothing my brow when I was tired or sick.

My beloved. My brown dove. My dream. The one whose imagined angelic hand smoothed my forehead when nightmares woke me in the field. The one whose glow came with me everywhere, like the Virgen de la Caridad del Cobre, saving me from drowning in the undertow of my own mind.

But when you wanted everything, how could you speak a word? And when a woman wanted love from you, how could you say you were afraid to be touched, afraid you would not rise to the occasion? Zenaida, the girl I'd gladly have married. I'd thought her love, having healed me of my battle wound, could heal my deeper malady.

And nothing. A disaster. A girl like Zenaida was Martí's dream, not mine—or, yes: my dream, but a creature of dreams only, not of fleshly desire.

Fine. Many men didn't want their wives, as I knew from the laughing talk around campfires, smoking cigars on a half-full stomach and listening to the fighters. Some even preferred the fierce, electric mambisas who trailed behind us and sometimes fought at our sides to the softer, sweeter women who waited for them at home, heavy with babies and fear.

So then I tried to practice on Zenaida's friend, to find my nerve, to be cool and manly about it all, like soldiers at bordellos. It wasn't even Chaveta I wanted. I just thought, perhaps, if I could practice with her, I'd be able to do it right when I took Zenaida in my arms again.

But it didn't work. Chaveta, the little wild one, and her legendary skills—Chaveta, whose mere glance made men rise like magic wands, they said, and whose firm tug sent them to paradise. Still nothing.

And I had to listen to her talk about the revolution.

Nothing took. Nothing ever had. The whores down in Havana had only scared me, with their thick paint and loud smells. Their rough, leering talk, and the way they grabbed at me.

Perhaps it was because of my mother's suffering that I could not be with a woman?

The only way it worked was by myself, in the jungle, standing, my forearm braced against a tree, my forehead on my arm, my eyes clenched tight as unspeakable images flickered through my mind, my other hand—That worked.

But I well remembered the fire-lit face of a commander one night through the smoke, when he said loudly, "No real man uses his own hand."

Loud laughter roared.

And another soldier's quick rejoinder: "Real men use women."

A young fighter I didn't know scrambled to his feet, cheeks aflame. He kicked a log and ran into the trees. The mocking laughter of the company echoed through the night.

Never could I bear such shame.

85

Zenaida

Beside me, Sofia softly giggled, but my own mood—Chaveta's rebellious absence notwithstanding (Had she finally run away to sea, as she so often threatened?)—yes, my own mood was somber. Cool light from the half moon poured in through the open windows, as did the rushing wind. Standing there in a row with other girls to demonstrate our figures and fine posture, gazed upon by hundreds of eagerly chattering Cubans, I could not help thinking of the auction block.

Yet when I found my mother's face in the audience, her expression was as proud as I'd ever seen it. She smiled and nodded her encouragement. Guilt speared me. Each day, I saw how hard she worked. Fifteen dollars was a fortune, so I vowed to do my best. I quailed, though, knowing full well what Feliciano could reveal to the entire town if he wished. So far, I had denied it, and he had said nothing, as far as I knew. But he suspected. What if he planned to reveal my secret to the whole town at once? He might do it as a form of praise, innocently, but my mother would be terrified, remembering how my father had been slain, and I—I could never bear the heat of such attention.

Señor Lallanilla rose to his feet and turned toward the audience, raising his hands for silence.

"Ladies and gentlemen! Ladies and gentlemen." The crowd quieted. "Though not all of the registered participants have arrived, we must begin." He said some grand words about the flower of Cuban womanhood, et cetera, and then gave us our instructions.

Obedient to a fault, the girls began walking, one by one, to the judging table so everyone could observe the grace of their gait. Some girls curtseyed. Others, imitating the elegance of swans, extended a hand, which each of the judges kissed in turn. Then, as the contestant stood there, each judge gave a short speech, praising her modest demeanor, or loveliness, or lush curves, or abundant shining hair. The crowd was respectfully silent during these pronouncements. Each judge then made a great show of writing his score on a small card and folding it.

The irony did not escape me. Though Feliciano cut a fine enough figure, the other two . . . Portly and pasty, their heavy mustaches drooping, overwaxed for the occasion, their shiny scalps peeking through black strands of the hair they had left—the idea that these plump old men should sit in judgment upon us was entirely laughable.

I envisioned a reversal: the eighteen of us girls seated at a long table with pens and paper, the three men forced to parade before us in hopes of money, the whole town listening to our voices as we spoke of what we admired. Our speeches for two of them would be very short indeed. The speech for most men in town would be quite short, come to think of it—which was surely why such things never happened.

Maceo, though . . . Maceo would fare well. Sadness shot through me. His fine, bold shoulders, his handsome mouth, his large dark eyes . . .

My eyes roved the audience for him. Was he there? Was he looking my way? Did he regret what had passed between us? There seemed to be a million faces, though I well knew the hall held only some three hundred, even when they were standing, crushed against the walls.

But when my eyes finally located Maceo standing near the back, he was staring, like everyone else, at Feliciano, who was spouting some flowery business about Pura Salazar and the cheerful innocence of frangipani blossoms being not half so sweet as her enchanting smile.

Watching Maceo not watching me—and still struggling against the sway of my broken heart and blistered pride—I began to organize words in my mind.

So sweet, I must have looked like bait.
And you? A man dressed up as Fate.

Somehow, putting my feelings into form, into rhyming lines, eased the intensity of the pain. Instead of being helplessly at the mercy of the situation with Maceo—instead of feeling controlled by it—I could impose a kind of order upon the events that had confused and hurt me so.

I schooled myself to hope and wait.
Your words of love came far too late.

Expression, yes, but also a subtle kind of rearrangement: the exertion of my own will, my own views, upon the events. It was a kind of refuge.

I was the cake you had—
and ate.

The tight snap of closure satisfied me, the bitter reproach of it. It wasn't even true, though: Maceo had spoken no words of love.

But this was the power that poetry brought: one could rearrange things to be more flattering to oneself. I wondered how many men had done that, through the ages: reordered the world in words, to take its sting away. Reordered women in words, to rob us of our power to wound. I wondered how similar this process was to the exertion of force Feliciano had spoken of so eloquently from the tribuna—and I wondered who it silenced, as my mother described, and if I were doing a similar wickedness with my own verse.

Unlike Feliciano Galván, much less Homer or Dante or any number of the poets, I had no muse, it seemed, no masculine version of Beatrice to lure and lead me on to greater heights of beauty—if it was even possible for the muse to be a man. I'd never heard of such a thing, in a thousand years of poetry. No man but Maceo had ever magnetized my eye or hands, and even that was all over now. What's more, I had never felt moved to write a poem for him.

Perhaps one could say I was inspired by imagined men of long ago, like Hatuey—but even that verse felt bloodless, a rousing piece of propaganda.

My verses revealed nothing of my truest self, aside from my desire for everyone to be free. Hatuey was just a hero, sacrificed again to a cause—but this time by me.

I'd learned about another way of writing verse, different from the various sonnets and ballads I knew. It came from Japan and was a curious form: there was no rhyme. Only the number of syllables mattered. I read about it in a newspaper from Madrid that was lying in the San Carlos.

I had been trying it. It was all about counting the syllables in each line. It was odd and difficult, and I couldn't understand how a person could memorize and recite them; they were not musical.

However, they were short, which was a virtue—a virtue Feliciano could not fathom, apparently, for he was still waxing on about the beauties of various girls of Key West: "Yet there is only one young lady in town whose hand I would pursue—a bold and beautiful woman, to be sure."

Next to me, I felt Sofia's shoulders arch even farther back, though I did not think he meant her.

"But—because I am a stranger here and thus beholden to no man"—his gaze swept the other judges and returned to the audience—"I can freely speak my mind, so I can say that I would offend Aphrodite herself did I not choose the most strictly beautiful woman on this stage tonight—and you are fortunate, indeed, O you noble town of exiles, that this crowning blossom of young Cuban womanhood is not merely exquisite in the grace of her features and figure but also in the grace of her temperament."

I knew he had been spending a great deal of time at the Salazars' manor, even after he had begun lodging with us—dinners and so on—as well as at the Robleses'. Perhaps pale and lovely Pura, with her doe eyes and unfeigned innocence, had worked her magic on him unawares.

"Yes, my choice is a young woman with intelligence, depth, talent, and charm unmatched among my acquaintance in this city—"

He rambled on.

It occurred to me that perhaps I was not a natural Cuban woman at all—as the great Señor José Martí described the ideal woman in his essays: a beautiful blossom for men to admire, a maternal pillow on which their weary heads can rest, a caressing hand to soothe their troubled brows—

No. I could not locate anywhere within myself the fonts of romantic patience described in Martí's essays, much less in poetry and novels. Indeed, the antics of most men bored me (and, working in my mother's boardinghouse, I'd observed a great many men and witnessed a great many antics).

More confusingly still, the electricity I felt when Chaveta walked beside me, her arm linked in mine—the way the back of my neck seemed to quiver and my heart beat faster in my chest—was the same I felt when Maceo approached unannounced and stood behind me. I realized, standing there onstage wondering where Chaveta was, that I felt the same tenderness watching her from outside the Flores factory that I'd once felt watching Maceo sleep peacefully as his fever broke.

Moreover, and even more confoundingly, such strictly physical longings as I experienced—the ones that were supposed to make women swoon with love for a particular suitor—seemed to come rather from my own body, in waves, as if generated wholly from within me by some mysterious engine, and I needed no courtly lover, for I could solve them with my own hands.

I worried sometimes that I was as strange a conglomeration of parts and impulses as Dr. Frankenstein's creature.

Feliciano was still, astonishingly, talking. I fixed my gaze upon the wooden boards of the stage floor.

Haiku were supposed to reveal the time of day and the season of the year—but subtly, by alluding to nature: not mechanically, like *It's three o'clock in the afternoon on a winter's day*, but more like *A snowflake falls in the early dusk*. And then they were supposed to remark upon the transience of this earthly life. A tall order for a little verse.

When I tried to write some, though, they just ended up being about people. I wrote one about Maceo:

Hoof marks in the dust—
a horse's whinny echoes.
Thunder rumbles near.

Not very good. A lot of them ended up with food in them, too.

I peel ripe mangoes.
My mother cooks the skirt steak.
Workers gather near.

They seemed so simple and straightforward. I couldn't understand why a culture would prefer them to the flowery, ornate style most writers in Europe and Cuba produced.

For some reason, a number of them—the ones that flowed most easily—seemed to be about the Flores Cubanas factory. Of the lot I produced, they felt the most taut and meaningful, as if their compression somehow suited the modernity of the factory floor—paradoxically, for the haiku was an ancient form.

> A sepia hush
> falls. Gold dust motes sparkle
> in long, slanting shafts.

> The lector draws breath.
> Fragments of tobacco fall
> unmourned to the floor.

> Hands fly like sparrows,
> twirling brown straw into gold
> men will smoke to ash.

As I wrote, one set of hands in particular flew before my mind's eye, compelling my pen—and I noticed one day, reading over the labor of half an hour, that all of the little poems were in the present tense: *fall*, not *fell*. *Fly*, not *flew*—a thing I had not meant to do. But the form itself seemed to produce a feeling of immediacy, along with intensity: things stripped down to the bare minimum, to the simplest actions. Chaveta seemed best suited to the form.

I looked around the San Carlos; the crowd was rapt and eager, waiting for the final contestants to parade around. Sofia took her turn before the judges, and then I walked across the stage. I curtseyed and kept my distance; I did not relish the prospect of the hot, moist press of judges' lips against my skin. Sometimes men would use the opportunity to slip their tongue out and give a little lick. It was vulgar and disgusting. I turned and resumed my place at the edge of the stage. Sofia gave me a smile.

The judges conferred. Feliciano rose and began talking again: more flowery words—but now he kept gesturing toward me, looking at me. Something was happening that I didn't understand.

"Just as our homeland Cuba, as it's so often said, is the Pearl of the Caribbean—a gorgeous maiden: lush, beautiful, fecund, and perfectly situated at the mouth of the New World—and is fought over by many nations, so, too, would all men vie for the hands of her beautiful daughters."

He had come out from behind the judges' table and was walking directly my way, bearing the thin tiara. I shook my head, put my hands out in front of me as if to ward off peril.

In the audience, my mother's eyes were huge and glowing. Beside me, Sofia's expression was pure shock.

"Yet tonight it is my privilege to claim that no young woman here on this island is as exquisitely beautiful, as graceful, as innately poetical—"

A commotion erupted at the main door of the auditorium, all the way in the back. The crowd parted, murmuring.

"To put your metaphor to the test, sir," piped a pure, sweet, utterly familiar voice from the back of the auditorium, "do we not all fight for Cuba to be free?"

Hundreds of heads swiveled.

Chaveta shouldered her way forward through the crowd, her eyes furious and defiant, her curves draped in a blue gown.

Her dark hair was shorn short as a boy's.

86

FELICIANO

My heart came striding up the aisle.

"To put your metaphor to the test, sir," she said, "do we not all fight for Cuba to be free?"

Something within me lifted and began to soar.

"Indeed," I said, hardly able to contain the joyous laughter that welled within my soul. "Indeed, I declare as a gentleman, that is my poetic claim."

"Fair enough," called Chaveta, coming closer. "You wish to scale things up, from a beautiful woman to a beautiful land. But as a real-life, flesh-and-blood woman, I wish to scale them down."

On both sides of her, old ladies were crossing themselves as she passed, their eyes wide with shock at the sight of a girl with hair cropped close as a man's. I loved it. I wanted to grab her beautiful face and make love to her right then and there.

"If you are willing to kill and die for Cuba to be free"—she glanced around, sweeping the whole auditorium with her gaze—"then must you not also liberate every girl and woman in your midst? Must we not all be let alone, free and unmolested, to do as we will, and to choose whomever we want—or choose no one at all?"

She leapt up to the stage and turned to face the crowd, standing there like a human flame, like the pillar of fire from the Hebrew Bible, the one disowned by my ancestors so they would live through the Inquisition, so that I would, one day, get to exist.

"Yet how many of you see us only as playthings, or property, or pawns?"

Her pause grew pregnant. It stank of truth.

"Change your ways," she said. "If you would die for our homeland to be free, then free your wives. Free your daughters. Carlos Manuel de Céspedes struck the bone of truth when he freed his slaves before he issued the Cry of Yara. He knew he could not fight for his own freedom from Spain when he kept human beings in bondage."

She joined the girls where they stood arrayed, awkward, in their line, and took her stand between Sofia and Zenaida. She took their hands in hers.

"So, too, must you free the women in your midst if you wish your fight for Cuba to triumph," she yelled out over the crowd. "No fight can succeed if it's shot through with hypocrisy. As above, so below. I stand here in solidarity. I will not be judged worse or better than my sisters. Divide the fifteen dollars nineteen ways."

Nervous laughter swept the auditorium.

I quelled it with raised hands. Long practice as a lector stood me in good stead. I stepped to the center of the stage to join the girls.

"If we would have democracy," I said loudly, "then let us have a true one, in which any citizen may speak."

I smiled down at Chaveta, and then out at the sea of faces.

"And she has, indeed, spoken," I said, no longer able to contain my laughter. "I believe this pageant is adjourned."

The crowd exploded.

87

ZENAIDA

On Sunday afternoon, the sun shone bright and warm. I was squatting in my mother's garden, picking rosemary, contemplating the surprising events of the night before. One-nineteenth of the prize money jingled in the pocket of my dress. Perhaps I'd spend it on more foolscap . . . or buy my own drinks at the little café . . .

When Chaveta rode up on a brown horse, wearing her trousers, her shorn dark hair shining, I stood.

"Let's go, then," she said.

I took the handfuls of rosemary inside, untied my apron, and hung it on its hook.

I called to my mother, "I'm going with Chaveta for a while."

"Where?" she replied from somewhere in the boardinghouse.

"I have no idea."

Her laugh filtered through the air. "All right."

I went out to the back porch. The brown horse pawed the sand.

"Is this Sabotage?"

Chaveta smiled. "Get on."

"Does Maceo know?"

She steered the beast quite close to the edge of the porch.

I reached out for her, slid onto the mare's round back, and held Chaveta's ribs in my hands. She clucked and squeezed her legs, and we headed up Emma Street at an easy walk. A couple of neighbor ladies threw us the evil eye, but we soon left houses behind and headed up the quiet road of sand. To our right, pelicans glided low over the sea. At Division Street, we turned left and headed past the Catholic convent and across the island, toward the salt ponds.

We didn't speak. Wind gusted, but the air was warm. We headed through groves of buttonwood trees, and I closed my eyes. Red-gold light poured through me. It was enough to feel my breasts pressed against Chaveta's back, to breathe the scent of her hair—a fresh, wild smell of musk and soap and cigar smoke—and to feel the rhythm of the mare's steps softly rocking our bodies together. Her hooves clopped softly on the sandy dirt road, an easy beat. Wind rushed through the buttonwood leaves, a green sound. We rode on.

When I opened my eyes, we were weaving through the mangroves, the mare's hooves crunching the crushed white shells. An iguana, emerald bright on a branch, tracked our movements with its black eyes. We heard the honking of flamingos and saw them circling above, pink banners against the sky. When we got to the shore, Chaveta slid down and held out a hand. I grasped it and pushed off and landed, the shock running hard through my ankles and knees. She tied Sabotage's reins to a mangrove branch and walked to the water's edge. She turned to look at me.

She pulled her blouse over her head and dropped it on the sand. Then her thin camisole.

My fingers fumbled down the row of buttons at my back. I stepped out of my dress.

She unbuckled her belt, undid her trousers, and dropped them to the ground.

I pulled my chemise over my head.

We stood there, each in our little white pants, facing each other. She took hers off first, then spun and dived into the shallows. I followed.

All afternoon, we floated together in each other's arms just below the surface of the thickly salted blue water, my mouth finding hers again and again. Flamingos spun overhead and deer stalked by on the shore and Sabotage whickered softly as I did to Chaveta what I'd done to myself for so long, and she for me, until the sun faded and the wind grew brisk. We climbed out and stood on the sand, shivering and laughing with wonder, pulling on our clothes, her soft mouth finding mine again and again as Sabotage stamped an impatient hoof.

We rode back to town in the gathering dusk.

The familiar streets and buildings of Key West looked exactly the same.

Yet everything had changed.

88

FELICIANO

But Chaveta would not have me. She had rejected me time and again. After the pageant, I thought perhaps at last—but no.

Very well. I was a man, with a man's needs, and no good came from denying the dictates of nature.

In the little guesthouse at the back of the Robles estate, the soft lushness of flesh bloomed slowly under my mouth, soft like velvet perfumed with myrrh, her hair, unbound in a fall of black silk, fragranced with the oil of gardenias. She gave herself with abandon, and she took me as if I were her birthright. We went slowly some nights, fast on others, as if she'd tear the very clothes from my body, her gasped and whispered phrases sweeter than fragments of Petrarch.

Afterward, she lay there with her arms flung behind her head, her head thrown back, a sated smile playing over her lips: a voluptuary— and I her adoring addict, for she was wild and shameless as any denizen of the demimonde, sweet and sly as a virgin, succulent as the ripe fruits that drop from the branches of the Robleses' trees. The way she held me in her arms, enchanting me with her gaze—the way she laughed, innocent and delighted, at the heights to which our pleasure took her. "I never knew," she said again and again. "I just never knew it could be like this."

It was, all told, our seventh night together, and I lay, delirious and spent, with my head in her lap, my cheeks against her naked thighs as she stroked my hair, caressing me almost as tenderly as if I were a beloved child. It had been so many years since my mother stroked my hair. I closed my eyes, feeling it soak into my soul like a blessing and a benediction and a balm, like the stream of oil the rabbis poured on the brows of the anointed. I'd never had a lover like her, and all I wanted—with the mad folly of all poets—was to make it last, this lull of exorbitant pleasure, this idyll of sensual bliss.

We lay in each other's arms in the guesthouse's wide, soft bed, gazing out at the stars. She turned to me and took my face in her soft hands.

"My love," she said. Her eyes grew sad. "My husband returns again from Tampa tomorrow. He has concluded his business. We must cease."

"No," I said, pulling away and rising to an elbow. "No. We cannot stop. I must keep seeing you."

"It was a dream," she said. "A fever dream, an interlude of bliss— a bliss I did not know was possible on this earth. But now we must awaken."

"Come away with me." The idea strengthened within me even as I uttered it.

"What?" Her laugh was soft, rueful, half-confused.

"Yes, come away," I said. "You want to live in Spain? We'll catch the next ship east."

"Sweet boy," she said, "don't be absurd. How would we live?"

"I can read in any factory in Seville or Madrid. I can tutor or work as a journalist. Of course I cannot support you in such a fashion—" I waved my hand at the whole estate.

"But all this," she said, her hand echoing my own, "never mattered to me. It was my parents' avarice, not mine, that forged this marriage. I've grown accustomed to luxuries, it's true. But the price I was forced to pay for them has been far greater than their worth."

I shuddered inwardly at the vision her words called forth in my mind. "Then come with me."

"I cannot." She shook her head firmly. "You know I am a Catholic. I can sin and be forgiven. I can do penance for the rest of my life to be shriven for the sin of you—and gladly will I do so. But never can I divorce my husband."

"Very well, then." I shrugged. "Don't divorce, then. Just come away."

"Oh, never," she said. She sat up, clutching the sheet to her chest. "I cannot. You cannot understand the role of virtue in a woman's life. We are not built to be cavalier, like men, or to deceive. Even in some foreign country, I would never be able to pretend—day in, day out—that we were legally wed, pretend that you were my husband." She glanced at me. "Or my nephew." Her smile was fleeting. "I don't possess the constitution for deception. I do this now"—she gestured toward the bed—"only because I know my husband doesn't care, cannot imagine, will not ask."

Beneath the quiet flatness of her tone ran a stream of bitterness, and I realized she must have actually loved him once, felt the glow of his attentions, and felt betrayed when they waned. It came as a blow. I breathed slowly, accepting the truth. Only a foolish man would imagine a woman of her years had no past at all. I had been with many women. That she had once loved and longed for the husband whom she'd had no choice in marrying was a mark only of her innocence.

"But to run away with you and live in sin?" She shook her head. "I'd quickly be found out."

"It is no sin if we love one another," I said, thinking of Anna Karenina. "It is only society that says so."

"Only society." Her laughter was hollow. Wrapping the sheet around her, she rose and went to stand by the windows. I stood and followed. My hand settled softly on her naked shoulder.

"Please," I said. "We could be happy. I could make you so happy."

Together we looked out at the whole lush yard, gilded silver by the moon.

"No," she said, as if having come to some definite resolve. Her eyes were cast down, her whole face stilled by thought. She shook her head again, her beautiful jaw firmly set. "I can never leave my husband."

Within my chest, my heart plummeted from some internal cliff.

And then her brow cleared, and her face turned sweet, as if her mind had suddenly lit upon the solution, simple and blithe as a sparrow alighting on a cannon.

"But, Feliciano." Her eyes found mine, and she laid her hand on my arm as if startled by the movement of her own mind.

I gazed down at her tenderly. "Yes, my love?"

Her eyes were dark and strange and fathomless.

"If Narciso were to meet with some terrible misfortune," she said, "I would become a very wealthy widow."

ZENAIDA

As I washed dishes after supper, it suddenly struck me: I could write a poem that worked the way Chaveta moved: swift and sure. Unpredictable. A poem that spoke in her short, sharp, unrhyming lines. A modern poem, carefree and unstifled by the straitjacket of meter and rhyme, striding fast in men's trousers.

Its hands in its pockets, whistling.

FELICIANO

I walked toward Señora Baliño's boardinghouse through the smooth dark night, the stars obscured by clouds, the palm fronds tapping each other softly in the sea breeze, the scent of blossoms wafting on the air. I climbed the stairs to the second-floor side balcony and stood alone. Through the ceiba's branches, the thousand lamplights of the small city glittered.

Mere hours ago, I had been besotted, ready to throw away my new life in Key West for a woman I thought I knew. Now my heart lay cold and silent in my chest. I could never be the tool of violence she wanted. The idea repelled me—as did she, now, and the notion that I had ever lost myself within her arms. I had thought her different from her calculating daughter smoldering with greed. No. She was just as grasping. She was merely of an older generation, one that had been schooled to mask the impulses her daughter freely displayed.

She had not suddenly stumbled upon an idea as foul as murder. Of course not. She had plotted and schemed—and then smoothly played her role, assuming me the dupe. My mind began to compose the lines of a pitiless verse about the perfidy of women . . .

But perhaps not. I stared out at the flickering lights. She had been so tender, so yielding, her eyes so dark and true. Perhaps she didn't really mean that thing about eliminating her husband. Perhaps, like I myself had been, she was simply overcome with emotion, desperate to make a good thing last. Perhaps she spoke only from the heat of passion—

A hand fell on my shoulder, and I froze. I smelled the salt musk of a man, all cigar smoke and leather. Instantly, my body clenched, my heart began to race. A man's deep voice uttered my name, and I felt the soft, searching press of lips on my neck.

Rome, terror, the breath of boys, their laughter—

"What in God's—" I spun, my fists raised to defend myself.

There stood the handsome young soldier, his hands open.

"Maceo!" I cried, relieved, my heart still pounding fast, the panic rushing through my veins. "Maceo, my brother! What in God's name is wrong with you?"

Eyes wide, he stared back at me. Staggered backward. Turned, ran. His footsteps rushed down the wooden stairs.

"Maceo!" I called. "Maceo, my friend! Wait—"

Down below, he raced across the yard and flung open the door of the little barn. After a moment, I heard his mare's fierce whinny of protest. They emerged at a pelting gallop, and I listened to her hoofbeats fade as they melted into the night.

"Oh, Maceo," I said quietly.

I stood there, trying to quell my rapid breath, trying to slow the beat of my shocked and sorry heart.

91

SOFIA

We sat in the lamplit drawing room. Slowly I stroked the back of his hand with my finger. At least now my grandmother wasn't lurking somewhere to spy.

"If something were to happen to my father's factory, you see," I told him, "we would have to leave. To New York City, perhaps. I could open my tea shop. Or back to Cuba. I could ride in my carriage through the streets of Havana." I didn't mention Tampa.

The cafetero looked at me, saying nothing in his dumb devotion.

"And you see, I'd need a driver. Or a groom. I would make my father hire you." He did not move. "Don't you understand? You could come with me." I leaned closer, squeezing my arms just a bit against my sides, letting my décolletage gleam forth in all its glory. "We could see each other every day."

His eyes traveled down the crevice where all men's were wont to go.

"If something happened to my father's factory," I prompted. "Something destructive."

He looked up. "But he would be ruined."

I laughed. So funny, the difference in the meaning of *ruined* when applied to a woman rather than a man.

"My father would be fine," I said. "He has both my mother's plantation and his own. He owns stocks. Even the cigar factory is insured . . ." I laughed again.

In the doorway stood the damned girl. In a trice, I was on my feet. "What are you doing?" My slaps rained quick on her face. "Why must you always hover?" She deserved each blow, and worse.

"Miss, I just came to see if you needed—"

"Shut up! Shut your stupid mouth, you dumb Black bitch!"

In midair, the cafetero's hand caught my wrist. I turned to him, astonished. He shook his head.

He turned to her. "Go," he said. She fled.

"How dare you!" I shrieked. "How dare you try to stop me from striking my own—Get out, you fool! Leave!"

He did.

I stood in the drawing room shaking.

Hurling my teacup and saucer against the grate did little to ease my rage.

MACEO

He knows, he knows, he knows. It ticked like a deathly pocket watch next to my heart, the patient bomb of an anarchist. *What in God's name is wrong with me?* When I finally crept back to the boardinghouse and managed to fall into a fitful sleep, he haunted my dreams, mounting the steps of the tribuna, clearing his noble throat, sweeping the galera with his dark gaze, and declaring my sin to a hundred thousand cackling cigar rollers, who laughed hysterically, pounding their chavetas and calling for my blood.

Over and over I woke, gasping, heart hammering in my chest, sweat soaking my nightshirt.

He knows.

LÍBANO

The next night at dusk, I slipped into the Flores Cubanas factory, down on the ground floor, where all the bales of tobacco were stored, and where Señor Robles let me keep a few odds and ends—spare tin mugs for new rollers, an extra urn strap in case mine snapped, and things like that.

I left the door ajar so I could make a quick escape if someone came. I unpacked my things and laid them on the floor. I unrolled the cotton batting from Lowe's Dry Goods. I draped it over one of the tobacco bales.

"Líbano, no!"

Julieta grabbed my hands. She had followed me. Her quick glance took in the jug of kerosene and box of matches.

"No." She leaned close, her voice an urgent whisper. "You cannot."

Her face, so close to mine. Her softly parted lips, her dark eyes full of passion.

"Señor Robles may indeed be well insured," she said, "but this crime will lie forever on your soul."

I looked at her. I did not say my soul was a badly tarnished thing. I did not list the crimes I had committed in Havana simply to survive.

I just stood there, breathing the soft scent of her skin, feeling the warmth of her hands on mine.

"Líbano! Wake up! You're under her spell." She sounded desperate, as if she might cry. "You love her so much, you'll do anything she says." Such pained anger in her eyes, such anguish in her voice.

I shook my head, puzzled. "You are wrong," I said. "I hate Sofia." My voice sounded calm and faraway, though what I said was true. I tried to put more passion in my tone—to sound emotional, as others did—so Julieta would believe me. I tried to think of what the Count of Monte Cristo would say. "I mean it, Julieta. With all my soul, I mean it." It still sounded flat and vacant. I would never be a hero.

"Really?"

"I want Sofia gone. Forever. She's dangerous and cruel." I shrugged. "This seemed a logical plan. You deserve a kinder mistress."

Her brow wrinkled. "But if you do not love her, then why do you always come to the house? Always carrying messages? Her father can't need to know so much about coffee . . ."

I laughed. "Is it not clear?"

She stared at me.

"Can you really not know?" I smiled. "Then I will put it plain, Julieta. After she torments me awhile, where does your mistress always send me?"

Slowly, slowly, Julieta's sweet eyes filled with relief—and something more. "Oh," she said. "Oh." And then she was holding my face, and her hands were in my hair, and she was crying while laughing, the way books say women do when they are happy, and we were kissing.

Later, she helped me gather the incendiary things into my knapsack, and we left together in the dark.

94

ZENAIDA

After the dishes had been washed, I hung my apron on its hook.

"Chaveta invited me to a play at the San Carlos, Mamá," I said. "A satire. It's a theater troupe from Havana, a bufo troupe. They're said to be subversive."

"Is that so?" my mother said.

"Can I go?"

She broke green beans into a pot.

"Maceo didn't ask you?"

"Mamá."

"Well, did he?"

"I want to go with Chaveta."

She looked up at me for a long moment and then shrugged. "Why shouldn't you go? You girls have been friends for years."

"Thank you, Mamá."

"But take a shawl. The wind is high tonight."

"Yes, Mamá."

It was nothing for two girls to walk arm in arm down the street. Cubans did it all the time.

CHAVETA

The crowd crushed us, sweeping us out the door of the San Carlos and into the street.

Zenaida leaned against me, smiling. "The bufo troupe was good, no?"

I nodded, smiling back. I hadn't been drinking, but I felt drunk.

"Inflammatory in its critique," she continued, saying more words, her soft, pretty mouth opening and closing, but it was loud out on Duval.

I didn't want to take her home to her mother's boardinghouse. I didn't want this ever to end.

"Let's get a sherry."

She smiled. Our feet veered at the same time toward the café.

ZENAIDA

We sat at the same table where Maceo and I used to sit, and young Valdés brought sherry to Chaveta and me, round after round, as we gazed into each other's eyes and I kept saying things about the bufo troupe with soft little rushes of laughter, but the satire, fine as it had been, wasn't what I was thinking of at all—and neither was Chaveta, I could tell. Her hands played across the surface of the table, her lean fingers dandling this object and that, and I knew she wanted to take my hand and hold it, there in front of everyone.

For over an hour we sat like that, talking nonsense as Líbano played chess with old Señor Gutierrez and Sofia's maid, Julieta, sat on the bench against the wall watching the game, and Feliciano and Eduardo argued long and loud with the older lectors at the round table about the various merits of the satirical drama the whole town had just seen . . .

The clock passed midnight, and the crowd dwindled, but I couldn't rise to leave. Chaveta and I were held there as if by some strange power, some magnet. Neither of us wanted to go home, to reassume the mantle of daughter, to break the spell of being out together, almost as if we were—

Maceo shoved his chair backward from the round table. I hadn't seen him enter the café.

"Are you calling me a coward?" he yelled.

Feliciano, confused, set down his glass. "What are you saying, my brother? I said no such thing."

"Oh no?" Maceo's voice grew louder, as if drunk with rage. "Now you're calling me a liar?"

"My brother, you know I never claimed—"

"Would you attack my honor?" He stood. "Then draw! Draw your pistol!"

Feliciano spread his hands, helpless. "But you know I carry no weapon—"

"Draw, you coward!"

Things moved very fast then, but seemed to move so slowly. Seconds ticked in the silent interstices between each motion, and all the yells fell slowly through the hot, charged air. I felt paralyzed, glued to my chair.

Maceo pulled his own pistol from its sheath, cocked it, and aimed straight at Feliciano's mouth, that dark hole moving—

Chaveta's small body hurtled across the space and knocked him off his feet—

The pistol fired, the bullet flying wildly into the ceiling—

"Christ!" Feliciano ducked under a table.

"Chaveta, no!" I screamed.

Líbano threw himself at Maceo as well. They all tumbled to the floor, and the pistol fired again, knocking a chair into a half spin, before Líbano and Chaveta could wrest the gun from Maceo's grasp. In the corner, a lamp had somehow broken open. Kerosene and flames spread across the wooden floor. Smoke billowed around us.

"Help!" Julieta screamed. "Help!"

Maceo scrambled to his feet, glancing wildly around.

313

Rolling onto her back and sitting up halfway, Chaveta cocked the pistol and held it in both hands, aiming at his heart. He moved toward her.

"I'll shoot," she said. "You know I will."

He stopped. Step by step, he backed away, spun, and ran out into the night.

Feliciano scrambled to his feet, his eyes wide.

"Julieta?" cried Líbano. "Julieta!" She was nowhere to be seen.

Flames leapt. We helped Feliciano outside.

"Julieta?" Líbano's voice was frantic.

"Where's the cistern?" yelled Chaveta, grabbing a bucket.

97

ZENAIDA

Gravel rattling against my window woke me. Groggy, I stumbled from bed and looked out. The morning sun was already high. Through the ceiba's branches, I could see Chaveta down below. She threw another fistful. My mother's bed was neatly made. How long had I slept? I wrapped my dressing gown around me and hurried downstairs, my whole body aching with exhaustion.

All through the dark and early hours of Wednesday, we'd battled the fire, the whole town passing buckets from hand to hand, and then all day, choking with smoke. Only at dusk did we extinguish the final flames.

Then, wandering like zombies, covered in soot and ash, we took the measure of the damage. Our beloved San Carlos was gone. The city hall, gone. Eighteen cigar factories, utterly destroyed. Warehouses. Shops. The whole business district. Hundreds of houses burned to the ground.

My mother's boardinghouse, far from the center of town, was unharmed. Staggering with fatigue, I'd made it back home and barely managed to rinse my face and arms before falling into bed.

By the time I opened the front door, Chaveta was standing on the porch. She carried a small cardboard suitcase.

"Go pack," she said.

"What?"

"Come with me."

"What? Come where?"

"To Cuba. To fight. We'll join the mambisas. We'll follow the men and stay in a separate camp."

"What?" I almost laughed. "Oh, Chaveta, I can't fight."

"You can stay back in the camp. Heal the wounded, nurse the sick. You know the plants, how to tend injuries. You cook well. I'll fight. We'll be together."

"Chaveta, that's—"

"There's a Spanish ram docked at the pier, heading for Havana this afternoon. The *Jorge Juan*. The Spanish government is giving everyone free passage. Humanitarian aid, they're calling it." Her laugh was grim. "Half the city's leaving—either to Cuba or on a steamer to Tampa."

"To Tampa?"

"Salazar has a factory there, and Robles is opening a new one. Free passage on the steamer, free housing for a month."

"But who wants to move to Tampa?"

"A lot of people, I guess." She shrugged. "Let them. Go pack, Zena. Come to Cuba with me."

"Chaveta, I can't."

"You can." Her dark eyes shone. Her smile was serious and bright. "Go pack. Meet me at the dock."

Something lit within me. Could I? Could I leave everything behind and go? Could we live a life of bravery and danger? Could I share a tent with Chaveta, lying in her arms at night?

I couldn't breathe.

I nodded.

"Hurry," she said, and was gone.

98

CHAVETA

I paced the dock. Crowds milled. Gray faces streaked with tears.

The blast of the steamer's horn.

Workers and children trudged up the gangplank, heading for Tampa and the new factories. My sisters screamed my name from the railing. My parents held them back.

My chest ripped.

Feliciano climbed the gangplank, helping Sofia and her mother. Magdalena carried parcels, and Edmund heaved and shoved a trunk behind them. Other first-class passengers boarded.

My family, disappearing. The sisters and brothers I'd slept next to all my life.

The ship's white wake splitting the blue water.

Above, the blue sky.

Behind, the city, burnt black to the ground.

The *Jorge Juan* blasted its horn. People crowded aboard. Spaniards, insurgents . . . Maceo, keeping to himself, glancing at me as he boarded, tapping his breast pocket. A quick exchange of nods.

I paced the dock fast. It was time to board for Cuba. Zenaida was nowhere to be seen.

The horn sounded again.

99

MACEO

I wasn't born disloyal. Life made me what I am.

At eighteen, broken and bleeding, astonished that the brutes had left me my horse, I wrapped myself in a cloth from my saddle pack, like a Jesus loincloth, and limped bare-chested, bare-legged, leading my mare, until I heard the clanking and yells and hoofbeats of a regiment.

I went close. They were Spaniards.

My brain was just a shattered shell, my dream of the safe refuge of a palenque in the mountains discarded.

In this world, there was no escape from choosing sides.

I entered the Spaniards' camp and lied that I'd been taken from a coffee farm by the insurgents; that I'd served against my will for seven months, a captive; that they'd beaten me and left me for dead; that I'd rather be a slave to a good Spanish master.

They assigned me to a colonel. I brought his food, staked his tent, washed his clothes. Each day for months, I performed my perfect loyalty. Humility. Trustworthiness. Began to listen to him in the evenings. And then he wanted to listen to me. He asked about the insurgency, its movements, its tactics. About what I knew of Key West, the exile community. I spoke at length—but as if I'd learned all of it second-hand from the insurgent fighters rather than having lain, fevered, in the boardinghouse of Zenaida's mother, and having been nursed back to health by her brown angel of a girl.

"You're a fine young lad," said the colonel one night. "Observant. Sharp. We could make better use of you." He twisted the tip of his mustache. "We could make use of you in Key West."

My heart beat hard: Zenaida. Her dark and tender eyes—the first eyes that had looked at me that way since my mother's. Her gentle hands. Her kind smile. Her graceful, quiet ways.

Keeping the surface of my face perfectly still so as to betray no eagerness, I nodded only once, as if in mere obedience.

So began my career as a double agent.

Zenaida, if you had wanted me—if only I had functioned the way a man should—I would have stayed by your side in Key West. Willingly would I have joined whatever cause you wanted, just to serve you, just to see that soft glow light your face. You healed me once. Surely you could do so again.

Back in Cuba, a mile from Santiago, behind a stone hut, next to a ceiba tree, I'd buried three sacks of gold coins, Spaniards' payments, immune to rot. For love of you, Zenaida, I would have left them there, have let the roots of the ceiba sprawl over them and drag them down into good black earth.

But the salt pond. My fiasco at the salt pond.

My double fiasco at the salt pond.

And what the lector knew.

So here I was, southbound on the Spanish ram that had waited so conveniently at the pier the day after the fire, a ship filled with those desperate enough to head back to Havana. Four hundred or so. Silent, heads hanging. The ship pulled away from shore, and the burnt wreckage of Key West shrank behind us.

The salt wind brushed my forehead, my cheek, soft as a hand. Out before me stretched the bald horizon, bleak and simple as my future. Sea. Sky.

Choose. Always the mandate to choose.

Galván knew. He knew the depths of my depravity. And he could tell anyone, at any time. He could write a few words to his contacts in Havana. Word spread like wildfire from Key West to Cuba, Cuba to New York, New York to Key West. Nowhere would I be free.

I climbed to a quiet place on the deck, away from the others, who were far too wrapped in their own sorrows to notice me.

Down among the women, Chaveta's cropped hair shone. Her arms were folded on the railing, her shoulders flung back, her resolute face staring out to sea.

From my breast pocket I drew the leather pouch that held what she had given me, and I laid three of the cigars down on the deck for some other man to find. I drew out the fourth and inspected the small, deliberate fleck of black ink at its girth, just below the gold band.

I could not betray them, these earnest Key West utopians I loved, no matter what they thought of me. I could not deliver their note to my Spanish colonel and reveal the insurgents' plan—but neither did I have the slightest idea where General Bonilla and his troops might have been, nor did I wish to join them.

I was a sham, a hollow edifice of lies and sorrow, unworthy of my heroic name, unworthy of my mother's sacrifice and faith.

I clipped off the cigar's end and flicked it over the rail, watching it fall down into the blue Caribbean. I held my flame to its tip and sucked, puffed, puffed, until the brown leaf glowed orange and began to smoke.

The life of a man is a mysterious thing. We are given pains and lusts and grief no mortal could contain, then punished for our lack of strength.

I took out my small pouch of coins and laid it down beside the three cigars. I puffed and relaxed, closed my eyes against the sun's glare. Even a free Cuba could offer no refuge to someone like me, nor could the lion's power.

There's such a thing as too much for a man to bear.

I stood there reviewing the strange twists of my life in my mind's red eye. My mother's agony, which gained her nothing. All the suffering inflicted on my body, which then betrayed me. No, God had not been with me.

I sucked and puffed, incinerating the letter to General Bonilla with my own mouth.

I did believe a day would come, perhaps, when we who were deformed might shine. And in that way I, too, was a utopian, I supposed—but for a cause I could not utter. Not now, not yet. My only heroism: refusal, the gallantry of the damned.

Sometimes you sold your soul to the Devil because he was the only one who wanted it.

I dropped the burnt stub of my cigar into the sea.

And then I followed it.

1898

EPILOGUE

ZENAIDA

In the soft darkness of the boardinghouse, my mother and I sat quietly for some time, peering together at the old photograph of the pageant, unfolding the broadsides and rereading my lines of verse, speculating upon the whereabouts of various people who'd left after the Great Fire, and talking with a strange awe about the sudden thrill of this new American victory, after thirty long years of war.

"Your whole life," she said, as she had said so many times before. It had always been true. She took my hand. "Since before your birth, my daughter. War, your whole life."

"Yes."

"But now, a chance for something new."

I smiled. "At last."

She patted my hand and let it go. "I'm tired, my daughter."

"Yes, Mamá." I reached over and stroked the soft gray cloud of her hair back from her lined forehead, as she had smoothed my own hair back so many times.

I remembered how enchanted we all had been, back then, by Mr. Hugo's *Les Miserables*, with the saga of Jean Valjean. I thought about my favorite moment: how when Jean stole so much silver from the monsignor in his desperation and despair, the monsignor then gave him even more, the very last he had.

I had sworn to myself never to regret my decision to stay with my mother, that day I wavered and almost abandoned Key West with Chaveta.

I had stood in the bedroom, packing, trembling with excitement. Yes, the fire had been a devastation—but could we really start fresh, Chaveta and I, together, in the mythical land of which we'd heard so much? Could we fight for freedom with our best skills—she with a pistol and machete, me with my poultices and spells? Could we love one another in a camp full of women, living in a tent like nomads?

But standing there with my future in my hands, I'd been suddenly undone by the vision of my mother's dangling limp body, hanged in despair. I knew too clearly what she'd do if I left. I'd felt my knees dissolve, and I put my hands over my face.

Crying, I'd laid each folded piece of clothing back in its drawer. I'd stored my little suitcase—my father's, really—back upstairs in the attic, and then I'd gone to find her.

Like a ministering angel, my mother was carrying food and fresh drinking water to people whose homes had burned but who had decided to stay in Key West and rebuild. She glanced at me and gave a quick nod. I thought of Chaveta waiting at the docks—probably cursing. I saw her dark shining hair, her bright eyes, her soft lips uttering sailors' profanities. My heart trembled in my chest.

I picked up a bucket and began to work.

We made space for six families in our parlor and dining room, and we cooked for them all until they had places to live again. Within months, several of the cigar factories had reopened, and new workers from Cuba arrived every week. By 1890, Key West was producing over one hundred million cigars a year. I became a schoolteacher at the newly rebuilt San Carlos, the best thing an educated colored Cuban girl could hope to become. Somehow, my urge to write poems had died with the fire. My father's press had stood dormant in the attic all these years.

"Of course you're tired, Mamá," I said. "It's very late. We have worked hard."

She smiled. "But not too late."

"Mamá." I smiled back. "Enough, now. Go to bed."

She stood, kissed the crown of my head, and moved off. The stairs creaked as she made her way upstairs.

I sat alone in the room, feeling the silence swell around me, a kind of pressure no barometer could measure. I heard the echo of the Iyalorisha's long-ago words: *You will lose love and find it again.* Her promise, her prophecy: *You will die happy.* As if lifted by some force, I rose.

I took my new Waterman pen and a clean sheet of paper from the drawer. I added more oil to the lamp. The room filled with a brighter glow as I poured myself a glass of water and settled myself again at the table.

Sometimes you wrote a letter, not knowing where to send it, not knowing if it would ever arrive. You just knew it must be written.

I didn't know where she lived, or how to reach her, or even whether she was alive or dead.

I twisted the lid off the pen.

My dear Chaveta, I began.

1886

JULIETA

Revenge can be a very hidden thing.

Maceo's gun went off, and then went off again. I sidled toward the wall of the café. As they were all wrestling, I knocked a lamp onto its side. Glass shattered. Kerosene spilled out, and flames followed the liquid, flickering across the wooden floor.

"Help!" I screamed, as loudly as I could. "Help!"

And if it was the case that no one, in all of that commotion, saw me sweep my true love's knapsack up, slip out the kitchen door, and run down the dark street and into the Flores factory—

If no one saw me replace the cotton batting where it had originally lain, and pour the kerosene where it belonged, and strike a match or two or six—

And if I then returned to the grand mansion of that bitch and shook out all her fine French sheets on the floor of the well-stocked linen closet and poured kerosene upon them, too, and sparked them similarly alight—Well? What of it? My own Haiti. My conflagration. My night of fire.

Sometimes there are advantages to the swift efficiencies of service, to moving through the world unnoticed and unseen.

GRATITUDE

To the generations of my family—without whom this book could not exist—for their love of reading, writing, printing, wild tales, and revolution.

For most of my life—and I am fifty-four now—I knew nothing about the political history of Key West or its importance as a rebel base for the anticolonial insurgency in Cuba. It is a moment in US history that has been largely forgotten or erased—a utopian moment of hope for true racial and gender equality. Unfortunately, it was eclipsed by Key West's Great Fire and the events that followed.

My brother, Tony, and I found original copies of our great-grandfather Juan Pérez Rolo's *Mis Recuerdos*—which had been used as a primary source (quite wonderfully and unbeknownst to us) by scholars—among our father Libano Castro's effects after his sad, untimely death, but we had no context for it at the time, and neither of us is fluent in Spanish, because our parents' generation refused to speak Spanish in the home, lest we and our cousins be subjected to the racist prejudice and violence they had endured. I am immensely grateful to my son, Grey Castro, who was raised differently, for his translation into English of *Mis Recuerdos*, my great-grandfather's—his great-great-grandfather's—eyewitness memoir of late nineteenth-century Key West, where he moved from Havana as a nine-year-old boy in 1869 during the Ten Years' War and later became a printer and the editor of a small Spanish-language newspaper.

When I was growing up, this period of Caribbean/US history was not taught in public school or college. In my own lifetime, we were mostly poor and marginalized people; my father and older relatives never talked about the past. I thought—when I thought about it at all—that my family had simply moved from Cuba to Key West in the late 1800s as economic refugees.

Only in 2019, at the National Endowment for the Humanities seminar "José Martí and the Immigrant Communities of Florida in Cuban Independence and the Dawn of the American Century," did I learn the larger story, and I will be forever grateful to organizers James López and Denis Rey for designing and running that monthlong seminar at the University of Tampa, selecting the readings we discussed, and coordinating the visits of the scholars who shared their work with us in dozens of lectures and conversations. For me, it was a marathon of intensity, joy, and revelation.

I am grateful to Rhi Johnson, a wonderful scholar of Spanish literature whom it was my pleasure to meet there. The character Feliciano's poem to Sofia is my own adaptation of Rhi's unpublished translation of my Galician grandfather Feliciano Castro's poem "Quisiera . . . : To Elvira Salazar," a poem that was collected in his volume *Lágrimas y Flores*, published in Key West in 1918. I am very grateful to Rhi for her sensitive translation, her interest, her talent, and her enthusiasm for both Feliciano's poetry and this project.

I am grateful to the scholars whose work illuminated for me the larger context of the period, making this fiction possible: Anna-Marie Aldaz, editor of *An Anthology of Nineteenth-Century Women's Poetry from Spain*; Christopher J. Castañeda and Montse Feu, editors of *Writing Revolution: Hispanic Anarchism in the United States*; Phylis Cancilla Martinelli and Ana Varela-Lago, editors of *Hidden Out in the Open: Spanish Migration to the United States (1875–1930)*; Laurent Dubois for *Avengers of the New World: The Story of the Haitian Revolution*; the astonishingly brilliant Ada Ferrer for *Insurgent Cuba: Race, Nation, and Revolution, 1868–1898*, which was essential to this project, and for *Freedom's Mirror: Cuba and Haiti in the Age of Revolution* and her magisterial *Cuba: An American History*; Arlo Haskell for his book *The Jews of Key West: Smugglers, Cigar Makers, and Revolutionaries (1823–1969)*; Robert Kerstein for *Key West on the Edge: Inventing the Conch Republic* (and for the kind time he took to chat with me in Tampa); Lisandro Pérez for *Sugar, Cigars, and Revolution: The Making of Cuban New York*; Matthew Pettway for *Cuban Literature in the Age of Black Insurrection: Manzano, Plácido, and Afro-Latino Religion*; Gerald Poyo for *"With All, and for the Good of All": The Emergence of Popular Nationalism in the Cuban Communities of the United States, 1848–1898* and *Exile and Revolution: José D. Poyo, Key West, and Cuban Independence*; Teresa Prados-Torreira for *Mambisas: Rebel Women in Nineteenth-Century Cuba* and *The Power of Their Will: Slaveholding Women in Nineteenth-Century Cuba*; Consuelo E. Stebbins for *City of Intrigue, Nest of Revolution: A Documentary History of Key West in the Nineteenth Century*; and Araceli Tinajero for *El Lector: A History of the Cigar Factory Reader*.

I am particularly grateful to scholars Rhi Johnson and Gerald Poyo, both noted above, for their invaluable insights into early drafts of this manuscript, which helped me make it a better book, and to Luis Othoniel Rosa, whose reading strengthened it immeasurably. Their time, scholarly expertise, engagement, and generosity are true gifts to this text.

All mistakes are my own.

This book would not exist without the faith and insights of my editors Jodi Warshaw, Jenna Free, and Melissa Valentine, together with the production team at Lake Union, including Jen Bentham, Erin Cusick, Karen Parkin, and Abi Pollokoff; the advocacy of my wonderful agent, Steven Salpeter; and the quite extraordinary talents of my publicist,

Lauren Cerand. I am tremendously grateful to them all for their belief, support, generosity of spirit, and love of literature and justice.

My life is blessed by the love, enthusiasm, and constant support of my family—especially my son, Grey; my brother, Tony; my former foster daughter, Amara; my aunt Barb; and my remarkable husband, Marco Abel. For my wonderful family and all my dear friends, I am so grateful.

More than anything, I wish my father were here to read this. He was both the most joyful and the saddest man I have ever known. I can only imagine the happiness he would feel at seeing his history restored to the world.

This book is really for him.

ABOUT THE AUTHOR

Photo © Shae Sackman

Joy Castro is the award-winning author of *Flight Risk*, a finalist for a 2022 International Thriller Award; the post-Katrina New Orleans literary thrillers *Hell or High Water*, which received the Nebraska Book Award, and *Nearer Home*; the story collection *How Winter Began*; the memoir *The Truth Book*; and the essay collection *Island of Bones*, which received the International Latino Book Award. She is also the editor of the anthology *Family Trouble* and served as the guest judge of *CRAFT*'s first Creative Nonfiction Award. Her work has appeared in the *New York Times Magazine*, *Senses of Cinema*, *Ploughshares*, *Gulf Coast*, *Brevity*, and *Afro-Hispanic Review*; on *Salon*; and elsewhere. A former writer-in-residence at Vanderbilt University, she is currently the Willa Cather Professor of English and Ethnic Studies at the University of Nebraska–Lincoln, where she directs the Institute for Ethnic Studies. For more information visit www.joycastro.com.